DON'T SMELL LIKE SMOKE

DON'T SMELL LIKE SMOKE

A NOVEL BY
JEANINE A. ROGERS
FOREWORD BY ADRIENNE SAMUELS-GIBBS

Don't Smell Like Smoke
By Jeanine A. Rogers

Copyright © by Jeanine A. Rogers

ISBN: 9798543243527

To my mom, Cynthia,
my biggest encourager and supporter,
who stayed by my side through every fire...

To my daughter Raven, my bestie boo,
thank you for pushing me to finish!
I love you more

And finally,
To those who are in the fire or have been through the fire...

TABLE OF CONTENTS

Foreword

Prologue

Chapter 1 – Grace - Fire in Her Soul

Chapter 2 – Faith - House on Fire

Chapter 3 – Hope - Playing with Fire

Chapter 4 – Joy - Forged in the Fire

Epilogue

Acknowledgements

Don't Smell Like Smoke Workbook

About the Author

FOREWORD

Once upon a time, Jeanine Rogers and I were the scrawny little smart girls in French class. We were sassy, thought we were sexy, and for sure believed we knew all the ins and outs of school, men, and life - all at the grand old age of 14. Then? Reality hit. High school and college and our first decades of adulthood came and went. And we learned that what we thought we knew was only the beginning of a new lesson. Each lesson could have crumbled Jeanine, me, or any number of our small circle of girl-friends. But for some reason it didn't. We were sustained.

At first we thought it was because of our upbringing; we were "good" girls. But maturity teaches that so-called upbringing is only half the battle. A lot of Jeanine's success was due to her own grit - of which she has a ton - but also because of the prayers of her grandmother and her mother. The prayers of the community. The goodwill and good energy of good friends. And now we know the secret of the elders who stood in the gap: In their absence we must pray for ourselves, and for our children and for each other.

My birthday twin has been through it all. The ups and the downs. The joys and the sorrows. The births. The weddings. The divorce. The degrees. The promotion. The success. The illness. The deaths. But one thing that has been consistent with her is that she has always counted it all joy. And she's always come out on top. She knows her "why" and she embraces the reason and the season. With these stories my friend has delved deep into womanhood, motherhood, childhood and sisterhood. The workbook that follows offers a time and space to get present, to journal, and then to contemplate your own path through each 'hood she visits in her words. As you read, may you also find a version of yourself to celebrate, to see, and to pray for.

The only way to it is through it. This book pairs juicy storylines with juicy advice: Perhaps it's time to encourage yourself. May her words forever enlighten your journey.

ADRIENNE SAMUELS-GIBBS

DON'T SMELL LIKE SMOKE

PROLOGUE

Strangers

When you walk past someone on the street, you don't know all the roles they've played in their life. I often wonder if I am transparent when I pass others on the street and they stare. They stare at the tall, not-too-slim but just thick enough, brown sugar sister with long honey-blond hair, walking with purpose, heels click-clacking along the sidewalk that say, *I'm important and so is my business, so don't stop me unless you and yours are too.*

At first glance, the package is appealing, sometimes head turning, and oftentimes intriguing to look at, because there is not a hint of what is underneath.

Yet the stranger walking past doesn't see the roles I've played. He didn't see the perfect child growing up who always had to do right; the high school girl who's one encounter with church kept her a virgin 'til college; the Mary Jane girl who tried to become a wife, is a devoted single mother, a Christian, church goer, executive, former adulterer, liar, and thief. Walking past me, all he sees is my polished exterior, but what he fails to realize is that to live in my world requires the wearing and trading of many hats.

But I just say a pleasant hello with a half a smile that says, "You really don't know what you would be getting into, sir." He smiles back, and we continue on our way. I wonder would he be surprised to know where I've been, because I've been through the fire...but thank God, I don't smell like smoke...

CHAPTER 1

FIRE IN HER SOUL

GRACE

No Fairy Tales

I have always believed in happy endings. Like all young girls, I was told fairy tales of damsels in distress being rescued by a handsome prince and living happily ever after. The writers of these fairy tales should give a disclaimer at the beginning to the children:

"Warning—unrealistic tales of true love and happiness are unlikely to happen, so take caution to believe nothing you read in the upcoming story."

Perhaps, then, when a girl grows into a woman she won't expect a happily ever after but will rather be surprised when it occurs. The term "happy ending" insinuates a tumultuous beginning, which is how I could say my life as a young lady began. Just 36 short years ago, I, Grace Marie Johnson, was born into a union of untruths and deception according to my mother, Delia. Delia and Henry met at a smoky nightclub on a warm summer night. Henry bought Delia a drink and danced with her all night long, but when the clock struck 12 o'clock, Delia did not leave him behind. She was a nurse and he was a "businessman", so he claimed, and although he adored her, he always had some "business" to tend to. I can remember asking mama about my dad as I got older and she always told me, "Gracie Mae, where you meet a man is where he will always be." It seems to be quite true, because I've met a few in some places where I would like to leave them. But I digress...

Mama and Henry were together for three years when she found out she was pregnant. Henry was overjoyed but she knew it was just a matter of time before Henry was back out on "business" again. For a year or so, Henry was good to her, helping out, doting on Mama, and really being a good dad. Mama says he would hold me and look down into my eyes as if they were diamond mines and say, "You are my saving grace, my Grace." Then he'd leave back out for hours, nights, or even days at a time. Eventually Mama got fed up and confronted him.

Mama was always nervous about telling me this story because I know that she didn't want to scar my ideal hope that my "daddy" was this great guy who would come back one day. When I was about 15 years old, I made her sit down and tell me the story of why they actually broke up.

Mama warned me, "Gracie Mae, I don't want you to think differently about your father, but you're old enough to know the truth, so I'll tell it to ya."

I think she knew that knowing the truth would change my view of the world forever, like when you know all will work out well at the end of a story, but when the main character tragically dies or loses a loved one, it changes your entire perception of the story as a whole. It is shockingly piercing, like someone with their arms outstretched for a hug who receives a punch instead. It catches you off guard and your preconceived ideas about this person are forever skewed. That is what Mama's story did to me.

One afternoon, Henry came home from work or wherever he had been. Mama had been mulling over the decision for weeks, whether to leave Henry or talk to him about a separation, or just stay, in misery, for my sake. She knew leaving was like giving up, and she didn't want to do that without first trying to work it out, even though they hardly ever spoke or went out or even saw each other. Mama grew up in the time when couples stayed together no matter how miserable they were, but she couldn't leave, so her only choice was to have the talk about separation and see where it went. Knowing I would always put a smile on his face, she brought me to him first to make sure he was feeling good before she told him. But when she actually mentioned separation, she said his reaction was alarming. He went from looking lovingly at me, to a face full of rage, then disgust and violent anger. He ran out of the house ranting so loud the neighbors in the apartment next door peeped out to see if everything was alright. Henry flew down the stairs and outside to his car, and Mama said she could hear his screams through the open window in the living room, "Delia, you will never get rid of me! Ever!"

The terror in his voice chilled Mama to the bone, and as she told me the story, I could see the tension in her body and her hands began to shake as if she was reliving the experience. Henry ran back in the building and stormed up the stairs two at a time, reaching a locked door. Mama held me in her arms screaming, "Henry, calm down or I'm not letting you back in."

Henry's rage manifested into sonic booms on the door followed by outbursts. "Delia, you better open this damn door!"

Mama's fear was crippling but she knew he would not stop until she opened the door. After some time, she did open the door only to find Henry with a gun drawn pointed at her and myself. Mama sat frozen, the same as she said she was that day, and could not hold back tears as she described the scene. In Henry's eyes was sheer hatred for her, and she knew she had to talk to him or risk my safety or her own. After much coercion and pleading, Henry seemed to snap out of his trance, and utter heartache flooded his face upon the realization of his actions. Mama said he cried and begged her to please stay with him. Although she wanted to work it out, this chain of events had ended that possibility indefinitely. Mama went on to describe their decision to divorce, my grandpa's threats to kill Henry if he ever did that to her again, and Henry's disappearance. For months, he tried to make amends, but he finally gave up after about a year and decided it was easier to leave our lives forever.

I believe learning about Henry and my mom's relationship was my first glimpse into the reality of relationships. Until then, every fairy tale ending was real to me and there was no concept of misery, dysfunction, abuse, or anything else negative. However, when I saw my mom cry and I watched her shake at the memory of her ex-husband's violence, I knew that Henry could never be "daddy" again. Not to me. Henry moved on and became "daddy" for some other girl or boy while Mama became "daddy" for me. As a young woman, Henry had helped to shape my first hurdle in relationships—abandonment.

Growing up, I was a shy girl; a nerd, if you will. In school, I was the girl every teacher wanted to take home. "Grace is such a well-mannered child," the teachers would say.

My mother and grandparents wouldn't have had anything less. I ate, slept, and drank school, and I loved every minute of it. My mother delighted in seeing me experience the world, so she took me to museums, plays, concerts, and on trips. She always told me, "Gracie Mae, you can be whatever you want to be. Don't put any limits on your life."

My life became the rebirth of hers, and she poured into me every ounce of energy she had. I love my mama, and even though she had her moments when she was a little overprotective, she meant well. As an adult, I can appreciate the life that she gave me, and I realize that her response towards me was a direct result of her tumultuous relationship with Henry. Everyone responds to trauma and trials differently. Some cry, some get depressed, some abuse themselves or their bodies, some turn to others for comfort, and some pour everything they have into the work they have been assigned. That last one was Delia. She gave me her all without thinking twice about her life or what it could have been.

~

Runaway Love

When I was old enough to think about boys, my grandpa told me, "Your boyfriends are Reading, Math, Science, and Social Studies."

So much for that thought! But truly, I can say that I was not interested in the opposite sex until I met Ramon Hampton during my sophomore year in high school. Ramon transferred from the suburbs and all the girls loved him because he was the typical tall, light-skinned, pretty-eyes guy that was "in" at the time. Although I noticed him in class, Ramon and I rarely spoke until we both joined the swim team. We would see each other at practices and meets and we would always speak, but one day, although I can't remember when, we just became friends. Ramon would ride the bus home with me, and I would tease him because he always wore this worn out old blue A's hat. Every day I would try to take it from him, and he would try to take my book bag. It was the beginning of puppy love, and in those days, I didn't know what to do with the flood of butterflies in my stomach that began to come every time I would see him. Ramon would smile at me, and my heart would melt. But I could never tell him because I didn't want him to think that I was one of those girls who walked by him in the hall whispering, "He's so cute."

He always told me, "Those girls are shallow and desperate."

I agreed, but inside I would always wonder if that included me too. But I liked Ramon because of the way he made me feel when I was with him. Each moment was laughter and a comfort I had felt only with my closest of girlfriends. I wanted Ramon in the worst way, but something was stopping me.

That something was Henry. His absence had left me with a painful reminder of what could happen with a man and had scarred my emotional being. Perhaps if I had never seen or heard from Henry again after my parents' divorce, Ramon would have stood a chance. One fall day when returning home from shopping with my mom, Henry showed up unannounced. Seven years had passed since the last time he had seen me, so naturally I did not know who he was. When I asked my mother, she replied, "That's your father."

Now any girl who has ever been without a father and suddenly sees him is flooded with emotions – rage, bitterness, shock, happiness. But the only thing I felt was love. We embraced and I ran into Henry's arms screaming "Daddy" as if he'd just returned from war, unharmed. Our hug turned into conversation, as he boasted of his new job and home, and he was eager to set up dates to see me. At the time, Mama looked on with pure disgust and I couldn't understand her lack of joy at this Color Purple reunion. It wasn't until I ran into the house to call the number Henry had given me, just so I could hear his voice again, that I understood. "The number you have reached.....has been disconnected."

That day, my heart sunk lower than the Titanic. Thoughts flooded my mind as I wondered why he would lie to me, how he could do that. Mama tried to console me, but it was at that moment that I learned my first lesson in coping with men: Leave them before they can leave you. Unfortunately, nine years later Ramon was the first man to experience my tragically unearthed defense mechanism.

Unbeknownst to me, Ramon was quite interested in more than a friendship with me. It became apparent one day as we were riding the bus home together as usual, and we were standing up holding on to the handrail and talking. Only this day, there was something different about our conversation. Ramon seemed to be very in tune with me and every time the bus jerked we would bump into each other. I joked around, telling him, "You gotta lean on me now, huh?"

Ramon laughed but his gaze lingered, and it took me by surprise. Behind his smile was a look that said he wanted to do much more than lean on me. Instantly, my body stiffened as I grasped the reality of this attraction, but I didn't want to let on that I was aware of it. As we approached Ramon's stop, I knew he was leaving, so I said, "Bye, I'll see ya in the morning."

At that moment, Ramon leaned into all of my personal space, and he was so close I could smell the sweetness of his breath. But I was terrified at what would happen next. How would I react? What if my other high school friends saw this?

What would I do? At that moment, my wall went up, and as he leaned in to give me the kiss I had been dreaming about for a year, I turned my head and Ramon's lips gently brushed my cheek. He stood back, stunned at the rejection, and his eyes looked at me as if to say, "Isn't this what we were both feeling?" In that instant, I had blocked any connection we could have had, and his pride was hurt. He turned to exit the bus, and I watched him leave, inside wishing that time would rewind, and I could have another chance to show him that I felt the same way. But the moment had passed us by. To this day, I don't know if Ramon ever knew how much I wanted him at that moment, but our relationship changed forever. He never leaned into me again, and I realized that I was not ready to let anyone into my space because I was too afraid that they would hurt me like Henry did and leave.

Looking back on that day, and many days that followed, there were many "Ramons" that came and went, because I was unable to relinquish my inner self, for fear that my heart would be broken. It would not be until many years later that I would be able to open myself up and embrace the risk of love.

~

Real Love?

Love becomes foreign when the meaning of the relationship is lost. Lost in selfishness, lost in dishonesty, lost in harsh words, lost in time, lost in disregard – lost in guilt. It is at this point in my life, that I believe angels were sent to guide and guard me— human angels in the form of my aunts, Shirley and Sarah, and my cousin, Nichole. Aunt Sarah was the eldest sister, my mom's best friend of 35 years, and the no-nonsense auntie. She could listen to your problems and feed you, but then you had better get up and do something about it. You got no pity from Aunt Sarah. Sarah taught responsibility and hard work. I can appreciate these lessons. Although they were harsh to me as a teenager, they kept me grounded and focused in achieving my greatest potential.

Aunt Shirley was the baby sister, who always got her way and rarely had a moment when she did not pamper someone or comfort them, perhaps because that was all she had been used to growing up. Auntie Shirley was a talking and praying woman, the kind of woman who would get on the phone with you and say, "Girl, you know he is a fool!" then immediately start to speaking in tongues over your relationship! I admired her dedication to her faith, because every Friday night, without fail, she was at her prayer meeting, prophesying and laying hands on folks. Nichole and I were often her tag-a-longs and we would watch her from a distance with intrigue and curiosity. We wondered how a woman who was so hip, always in the newest clothes, hair done, and kept a man (sometimes more than one), was always so into praying. To me, church had always been fun, because I'd see family that Mama wouldn't often have time to let me see otherwise, and I got to sing in the choir. It never occurred to me that there was a deeper meaning to what I was being exposed to. It was more like a routine. When Aunt Shirley would talk to us, she'd speak over us, and I remember the day she told me, "Gracie Mae, you are gonna be somebody; somebody famous and important. I see you as a doctor or something." In hindsight, it just seemed like some more Aunt Shirley stuff, but it gave me something to look forward to and strive for. I've learned over the years that God can use anyone to speak into your life, from a random person on the street to the crackhead in your family. Aunt Shirley and Sarah's mom gave me my first bible when I was 14 and then Aunt Shirley took me to my first all-out church service. It was there, amongst the praying, speaking in tongues, tears, and people worshiping, that I felt at home. Mothers of the church said, "Do you want to be saved?"

All I could think was, *Yes, from this!* My flesh wanted out, but my soul wanted in. On that one Friday night, Nichole and I went to the altar and gave our lives to Jesus because it seemed like the right thing to do. Little did I know, then, that one Friday night would help me to begin to rebuild the lost love relationship with a father I had been missing.

Nichole was my ace boom coon, sista' friend, play-cousin, or BFF (as my daughter now says) for as long as I can remember. Aunt Sarah says that when we would get together it was always a competition. Who would sit in the front, push the elevator button, use the bathroom first, you name it...we argued over it. Call it sibling rivalry, but it never got serious. By the time we were following up behind Aunt Shirley, we were thick as thieves. Anything we needed to talk about we shared, from first kisses, to our first periods, and even to Nichole's first encounter with her future husband, EJ.

EJ was an around the way boy, thugged out, kinda cute, but always too cool to really speak; he would just nod at us. I remember the day I came to visit Nichole at the house, and she was clearly upset. Head down, no smile, I couldn't figure it out. "What's wrong with you, cuz," I said, slapping her thigh.

"Ooh, don't do that," Nichole winced through her teeth.

"Why? What's wrong with you?" As I tapped her a second time, she grabbed her leg and began to rub it.

"Grace, I got a bruise there...quit," this time with agitation in her voice and embarrassment on her face, Nichole dropped her head.

Given our relationship, I knew we could talk about anything and we had seen each other, as cousins do, getting dressed and swapping clothes, so I said, "Let me see."

Nichole slowly rolled up her shorts to show me a purplish-blue bruise the size of her fist on her leg.

"How the heck did that get there?" I screamed with disbelief.

"Well, if I tell you, you'll get mad at me," Nichole lowered her head a second time.

"Look at me Nichole," I lifted her chin, "You didn't do that yourself, so tell me who did it. I won't get mad at you."

The next two letters sounded like the bell at a heavyweight fight that cued me to step into the ring. "EJ."

"That sick fat bastard put his hands on you, Nic? Oh... where is he? He is about to get told!" Before I knew it, I was standing over her pacing and ranting at the same time. "What in the world made him put his hands on you? And why are you so calm? Wait till I see him!"

"No, Grace," Nic grabbed my arm. "You can't say anything, he'll get mad."

"Seems to me he has had enough of getting mad and taking it out on you! I'm saying something and I promise you, he won't hit you again! Let's go, we are walking down the street to his house now!"

Halfway out the door, I saw EJ walking down the street. You know the way a kid walks in the room grinning after they've eaten a cookie, thinking you don't know what he did, but there are crumbs on his mouth? That's the way EJ walked. Cocky, yet knowing I knew, because my eyes read fire and were shooting daggers at him the entire walk down the street. As he opened the gate, I stepped off the porch and Nic slunk out the front door onto the porch behind me.

"What's up, Grace," said the menace. For a second, I looked up and realized my opponent was much larger than I had imagined. Standing about three inches over me at 6'0" tall, he was about twice my width and could probably knock me over with one breath. But the anger flowing through my veins erased all that fear away.

"Don't what's up me, EJ. What's up with you putting your hands on my cousin?"

EJ snickered, which sent my blood to its boiling point. "What you talking about, Grace?"

Two steps closer. I could smell the Frito's he had eaten for lunch and feel Nic's eyes on my back, as she was probably shaking behind me. I couldn't back down now, even though in the pit of my belly a voice screamed, "Walk away!"

"Don't play stupid, EJ. I saw my cousin's leg. Let me tell you something, what happens between you and her is your business. But as soon as you put your hands on her, it becomes MY business. Consider this your warning. Next time you wanna lay a hand on her, you gotta go through me first, and I ain't scared of you."

By now EJ had stopped snickering and I couldn't figure out if he was gonna hit me or walk away. I prayed for the latter. However, a fool rarely knows when his time is up. He tried to push past me. "Did you understand me? You ain't talking to her today without me being there. So, if you got something to say, say it through me."

Maybe it was the wild look in my eye, or maybe it was the fact that Nic seemed to have gained enough courage to stand tall behind me or the broad daylight that stopped him from wanting to make a scene, but EJ listened. He backed up and asked, "Can I talk to her, Grace? I ain't come to argue." Nic nodded, and I said okay, but I sat there the entire conversation, a silent guard.

Unfortunately, I couldn't shield Nic from EJ forever. But our relationship became closer that day. We depended on each other, I depended on her for encouragement, and she needed my strength. When I was tired and wanted to give up in school, it was Nic that pushed me to keep going. And as we got older, and she and EJ went back and forth, it was my shoulder she leaned on for support and my hand that dried many of her tears but could never totally ease the pain from the scars he left. It's amazing how situations and people can leave imprints on your heart and your soul. For me, it was Henry who had left immovable scars that were forever losing their scabs in new situations, and for Nic it was EJ who left his mark on her for most of her natural life.

~

A Different World

Whoever said high school was the best years of your life lied. College definitely trumped any experiences I had in high school. Seventeen and free, I looked at college as a new beginning; starting fresh; a place where no one knew my name, my background, or my Henry hang-ups. College was my opportunity to become the woman I wanted to be, and not be a product of my inner-city circumstances. Mama always made sure my grades were on point, so we weren't surprised when I got a full academic scholarship. But I was so grateful because my other choice was the university an hour from Mama with most of my high school class: the stuck-up girls I passed in the hall daily as they snickered and exchanged gossip, the guys I had liked, or not liked, along with the quiet people I wished I had known better. Although Mama could have afforded to send me away to school, she allowed me the freedom to make my own decisions.

My best girlfriend, Leah, and I went on a college tour together with our moms, and I immediately found the right school. We walked onto the wide-open campus filled with 99 miles of bike trails, with grounds covered with every type of tree or shrubbery found in the Midwest, the sparkling river that ran through campus, and friendly faces who walked by and said hello, unlike city folks; we knew we were home. At least I did. I had told Mama that day that I had made my decision, and after much persuasion and despite her reluctance, Leah decided to go too. The scholarship was a Godsend because otherwise I would have stayed in state with Mama. Instead, it was time for Gracie Mae to become Grace.

Going away to school presented many challenges for me, but thankfully Delia raised an independent young lady. She had sat me down and given me the "don't drink anything you haven't seen poured" talk and "don't be focused on them boys" talk, and the "you better keep them grades up" talk about a thousand times before I actually left home. My mind was clouded with visions of new friends and new faces, as well as coming into my own and deciding my life path, so much so that I barely listened to her warnings. But I didn't forget them. And I wasn't allowed to. You know how your Mama tells one family member, then they all give you the speech, well that was Delia. Granny, Auntie, Uncle, Cousin, God-mommy, you name it; I heard it all over again from them.

At the time, it seemed so irrelevant, because I had already had my share of experiences with alcohol in high school. A few parties here and there, without Delia's knowledge, had left me with a keen sense of the morning after syndrome – dim lights, aspirin, and no loud noise. Thankfully, I had seen enough friends get into man trouble that I didn't need to have my own, I could live vicariously through their drama. In hindsight, I realized Aunt Shirley taking me to Friday night bible study was probably the main thing that kept me pure until college. I always felt I should save my precious pearl for someone who truly deserved it. I didn't know what that someone would look like or what he would say to deserve it, but I knew I hadn't met him in high school. The only person who even came close was Ramon, and that had become a faded fantasy. I did have one opportunity with Ramon in senior year, but by then my wall was so far up to shield me from hurt that I wasn't even interested anymore.

So, the only real worry I had going into college was my grades. Being an overachiever was my role in the family. Nic had left EJ senior year and got engaged to another guy, then ended up pregnant. The last time we talked before I left for school she told me, "Grace, you go on to college. You always have been the smart one. I'm gonna stay home and get married and start working. But I want you to make something of your life."

I reassured her of my commitment to not drop out and I told her, "You know after you have the baby, you can go to school too, Nic."

But the look in her eyes said more than her mouth could say. Her eyes spoke the broken dreams, her mother's disappointments, her own guilt, and shame. It didn't matter what I said, Nic had already accepted her life for nothing more than what it currently was, and now it was up to me to be successful. Even though I knew Nic would love me if I was a bum on the street, her words of encouragement were motivation for me to do well, along with the family's watchful eye. There was no room for error for Grace. And grace was what I needed –supernatural help to make it through and meet all their expectations. Just like high school, I was to graduate with honors, in four years, of course, top of the class, make a name for myself, and make them proud. Their aspirations for my life weighed on my shoulders like a mountain, and I knew that the slightest trip and all their disappointment would come crumbling down on me. And as if that wasn't enough, I had to keep a B average to maintain my scholarship. Growth was inevitable for me, whether I embraced it or not.

Initially, I did not embrace growth. I shrank from its grasp, cowering under the protective shield of Delia's nightly conversations and Leah's familiar friendship. Life was great just the way it had been, comfortable and familiar, where I knew the formula for success, knew the bumps in the road and how to deal with them. Every night, for the first two months, I would call Mama, "You think I made a mistake coming this far, Ma? I miss you, I miss Granny. It's so boring here and I don't know anyone but Leah. I want to come home."

Mama would reassure me, "Gracie Mae, this is where you're supposed to be. I was scared when I left home too, and I was just an hour away. But we will come see you soon. And don't worry, soon you won't even miss home anymore."

Slowly, I opened my eyes to my new life and began to crawl out of my shell. If I was going to make the best of college, I decided I'd better start living the life. So, Leah and I began to venture out together to meet people. Leah and I had been best friends since seventh grade, and we were inseparable; we knew each other inside and out; we finished each other's sentences; she knew my sounds and I knew her looks. Yet as much as we were excited to be free and together away from home, we felt somewhat isolated. Leah and I were the only Black girls on our floor, and we had to answer the "what's a perm" questions and "are all Black people in gangs" questions all too often. Our floor mates were fun, corn-fed, country-raised girls, whose only experiences with Blacks were watching them on the 10 o'clock news. Needless to say, we were desperate to make some connections with some people who had shared some of our experiences. Through the cafeteria, also known as the official meeting place, we met some other Black students who told us of the first party of the year. Finally, a chance to see what college life was like for real.

"Girl, what you gonna wear?" Leah bellowed over the Old Dirty Bastard song that blared on the radio. As I sorted through my few options in my closet, my head and shoulders had already begun to loosen up as I bobbed my head to the music. The thought of actually going out and not having to report in at midnight was exhilarating. "I have no clue," I said. "I should have gone to the mall to buy something, but I don't' really have money to blow like that. I don't care, as long as I'm there! I'm so excited!"

I turned around and Leah was in the mirror singing and curling her hair, and at that moment she looked up and we both sang along, "Ooh baby I like it raw!" and busted out laughing.

"I can't believe it, we are actually in college, away from our parents! No more sneaking in the house or trying to sneak out. We can do what we like!"

"Until Delia calls and checks in on us," reminded Leah. "You know she will want a full run-down afterwards."

"Well I'll just tell her we had a good time. Cause we are gonna have a good time! Now let's get ready to go. I don't want to be late for my first party!"

Two bus rides and a not so short walk later, we arrived at the parking lot of the party. The spot was an old abandoned department store, with half of the name scrubbed off. If it had been daytime, we would have passed it thinking it was condemned. Leah and I looked at each other questioningly but decided to keep going. Cars were beginning to pull up and it was clear by the end of the night the parking lot would be full of men leaning on their cars, hoping to get some girl's phone number and ladies walking by smiling at every guy who whistled. No doubt, this was exactly where we wanted to be.

Inside the party everything was different than home. From the attire to the music, we felt like we had stepped into a twilight zone, only it wasn't scary, just exhilarating. Walking in, we looked around and Leah looked at me as if to say, "You feeling this?"

I just nodded and kept moving. The baseline was pumping through my ears, I was starting to feel the beat, and even though I didn't know not one of the dances they were doing, I was ready to learn. So, we jumped on in, doing our own thing, dancing to the beat of a different drum. Freshmen were usually spotted right away, and we got our share of looks, but that didn't stop our groove. Leah was approached by a tall, dark, and very awkwardly dancing guy, and we looked at each other and laughed as his shorter sidekick began to dance with me. At first I paid no attention to this cute little guy in front of me, but as the reggae started to come on and I felt the vibe, his body moved with mine. I went left, he followed, he rocked his hips and I watched his moves and smiled. He was kinda cute…so what he was a couple inches shorter than me? One dance turned into an hour, and by the time we stopped, we were dripping sweat. Leah managed to fake exhaustion and get away from "Big Baby" and had moved to the wall. "Hey girl! Whew, you having a good time?"

"Sure…looks like you were," Leah teased, "What's up with him?"

"I don't know, he's kinda short, but he's cute and he's got hella moves," I yelled over the speakers that were vibrating the entire room. "He gave me his number and said to call him, so we'll see. What happened to the big guy?"

"Girl, I had to inch away from him, he was too gross!" Leah laughed and we both bent over holding our stomachs and feigned his spastic dance moves. "We definitely had a good time tonight!"

"Yes, we did," I smiled as I glanced at my new friend, "this could be the start of a good thing."

~

Next Level

"Feels like heaven when I think about you, sparking that love, oh yeah, within my soul. And when I touch you yeah, I can't describe it, sending chills yeah, down to my bones. Just like an angel watching over me, you protect me from my fears. I was once was blind, but now I see, ever since the day you appeared, I just want

to say I want you in my life till the day I die baby...I just wanna
tell ya that I love ya..."

-D'ANGELO, HIGHER (1994, BROWN SUGAR)

It's amazing how the lyrics to a song, the melodies in your ears, can tell the story of your life's seasons. It was a good time in the world: Bill Clinton was the coolest president the U.S. had seen in at least 12 years, the economy was great, crime was down, and it was the best of times, especially for me; for in the midst of the lush, greenery of the state campus amongst the winding river to the smooth sidewalks along the main street, I found a cause to let my walls down. Its name, or shall I say his name, was Brandon Dowell, but everyone called him DB, cause on the dance floor he was always found doing some moves no one else would dare to do – just dirty Brandon. I wish I could say that was what attracted me to him, but honestly that wasn't it. That night we danced, I actually went home and lost his number. But fate brought us together again at a Black student rally where Dick Gregory spoke on the state of Blacks in the nation.

Months had passed since those nightly phone calls with mom, and I had become used to the freedom of this new world. Classes kicked my butt first semester, and I was very close to a B average, but not quite there, so my focus shifted from having fun to hitting the books. In an effort to broaden our intellectual abilities and meet some other like-minded Black students, considering there were only a couple thousand of us, Leah and I decided to go to the rally. It was pretty routine; a large auditorium with a podium down front that made the speaker feel light years away from the audience, much like being in lecture halls. Only difference was the auditorium was filled with all 350 of the Black students who were concerned about our current predicament, and Brandon was one of them. As we were leaving the auditorium, someone walked up and tapped my shoulder. Knowing Leah was in front of me, I turned around expecting to see one of my classmates or one of the few down-to-earth girls I had met as of late. Instead, I wheeled around to see a not-so-short, quite handsome Brandon. He was dressed for the sharp cold of mid-winter in the midwest; a long sleeve thermal which hugged every curve of every muscle in his arms, layered with a hip vest that gave him some girth and a little bit of height. To top off his outfit, his pants were loose and sat atop his freshly cleaned Timberlands. *Hmm,* I thought. *He looks better than I remember.*

"What's up, stranger?" DB said with a slight, sexy grin that said stranger was not the way he wanted to remain.

"Hey Brandon, how you doing?" I replied courteously, hiding my pleasant surprise. "Good to see you, did you enjoy the rally?" I asked, trying to continue in light, non-threatening conversation.

"I did, but I'm enjoying it much more now." Brandon's accent came through as he spoke and I could tell that he was from some island, not Jamaica, but who cared…it was sexy. I couldn't help blushing at his comment. We continued walking as I caught up to Leah and saw she had run into Big Baby again. I cracked up as I walked toward her with DB and saw her give me the eye over Big Baby's shoulder to run interference. I obliged.

"What's up, y'all? See you found my girl, Leah." She breathed a sigh of relief as if we had showed up just in time.

"Man, how you doing? It's good to see you too. I was just telling Leah we should all kick it." Leah seemed to be trying to read my expression while I was simultaneously trying to read hers. Initially, she seemed against it, but she looked questionable.

"What you all doing later?" DB asked us while looking at me. "I'm not ready to call it a night, are you Grace?"

I was intrigued by DB and contemplated chilling with them, but I didn't want to leave Leah in an uncomfortable position. I could hear Delia's voice saying, "Don't go to any strange men's houses, that's how girls get raped." I had a good feeling about DB, but truthfully, I didn't know him and I didn't want to be in a situation I couldn't get out of later. "Let me talk to Leah, and I'll let you know in a minute," I said as I nudged her to walk to the side of the room. "What you wanna do Leah? I could just tell him forget it. You didn't look like you were enjoying Big Baby's conversation."

Leah laughed. "Girl, I just didn't want to be stuck over there talking to him by myself. He is actually pretty funny, and I wouldn't mind hanging out with them, and it seems like DB is digging you, big time. You gotta promise me, no awkward moments, and we stay together if we do go."

"Deal! Girl, you know I ain't getting down like that. I don't even know him, but I got a good feeling 'bout him. We can just chill for a few hours. I hope it's close though, because it's too cold to walk!" Leah and I high fived as we walked over to the guys.

"So, what y'all decide?" DB asked.

"We're up for hanging out. Got any ideas?"

"I stay in the campus apartments…we can chill there and watch some movies. I parked out front, so I can take you all home afterwards." I gave Leah the "it's a go" look, and she gave me the gas face. What now?

"And how can we trust you? We don't even know you," Leah looked skeptically at DB.

"Don't worry, it ain't like that. We can go to Denny's or something if you want instead," DB offered. "I just was thinking of where we could go for free. We are college students!"

We all shook our heads in agreement and mumbled, "Yeah, you right."

"That's cool with me, if it's okay with you, Leah," I said questioningly. Leah and I looked at each other and she shook her head yes. We would go. The guys seemed harmless and my gut was telling me that all was well. I now know that was the Holy Spirit looking out for me. Thank God, because we could have easily become statistics; two beautiful freshman girls were raped and murdered by undercover criminals. Thankfully, much to the contrary, what began was the start of a new lifelong friendship and the beginning of the decline of an old one.

I often look back and wonder how DB got in. What did

he do that let him get inside my closed interior? Many had tried over our first few months at school, and I even got a little serious about one guy, until I found an open condom wrapper by his bed one night after a party. It was clear to me that he was not worthy of my time or consideration since I wasn't giving him none. I came to this new world declaring that I would not just agree to give up the goods just because I had survived all of high school. The same standards and rules applied; a man had to earn my trust and love before I would even consider it.

Maybe it was the way DB and I just clicked immediately, or the genuineness of his words, but that first night we all hung out, I knew that he could be *the* one. Watching movies, we all sat around and laughed and talked until Big Baby and Leah got tired and DB and I got closer on the couch. Big Baby agreed to take Leah to the dorm, and because it was so late, and she was extra tired, she didn't resist the offer. She made me agree to call her first thing in the morning, and I made her agree to call me as soon as she got in the dorm. The door closed and there I sat on the couch with DB. He had gotten comfortable, taken off his vest, and settled in next to me; not too close, but close enough that our legs would brush past each other as we talked or our hands may gently touch as he reached for the remote. I knew what he was doing, yet I didn't stop it. I had such a comfy feeling with DB, and we talked for hours. One o'clock turned to 3 a.m., and DB and I both ended up sleep on the couch cuddled up together. I rested my head on his stomach as he lay out across the couch with his arm resting on my back. Each time I moved, I felt his hands rubbing me, and through my sleepiness I began to lose myself to his touch. His fingers gently moved to the nape of my neck and up into my hair and he caressed my cheek ever so gently. I almost thought I was dreaming until his lips touched mine and I jolted awake. Every electrical sensation in my being sparked and I found myself wrapped up in his embrace. I didn't pull back, I didn't stop it, I just let myself go in his arms.

"DB, we gotta stop this," I whispered as I came up for air and looked in his eyes. There was so much chemistry between us, and I was trapped by his sensuous stare. But we both knew we had crossed into an area that was on a road to something that felt right but that I knew was against everything I had stood for up until this moment. "I gotta tell you something, DB." I sat up and ran my fingers through my hair, attempting to regain my composure. "I really like you and I have enjoyed this night with you, but I don't want to do this here, like this. That's not the kind of girl I am."

To my surprise, DB stretched his hand out and grabbed mine, "Baby, we don't have to do anything you don't want to do. I'm patient and I will wait as long as you want. I don't want to mess this up."

"You mean that, Brandon? You won't be upset, will you?" I asked to be sure. As if a woman needs to ask a man if he is okay with her decision. Young women too often do that, and I have learned that if it is your decision, who cares if he likes it. Stick with it, and if he's worth keeping, he'll respect it. And respect it he did.

"I told you, as long as you want. Now it's late, lay down and get some rest. We'll go to breakfast in the morning."

Our lips touched and behind the kiss was understanding, mixed with bridled passion that would soon grow into love. I fell asleep in his arms that night, and I felt security that I had never received from Henry. I trusted DB's words, and I felt like I had met a man who would truly respect me and my feelings, no matter what it took. On a cold, winter night in January, I realized it was DB who would take me to the next level in love.

~

"Hey everybody, I want to introduce you to my girlfriend, Grace."

The sea of movement and conversation in the room paused as everyone politely said, "Hi, Grace." I was the new kid on the block of DB's friends who seemed as if they'd known each other since grammar school.

It was spring now, and DB and I had been an item for a couple of months. Every day with DB got better. We spent much of our time together at his campus apartment because there were no restrictions, no signing in, and no roommate. Although Leah and I were best friends, I recognized that it would be uncomfortable if there were three of us in our minute dorm room with two twin beds. So, I opted to be with DB more, and he wanted me to get to know his friends, so we went to a potluck dinner one of his friends was hosting. Walking in the door, I had butterflies, and I told DB I was nervous that they wouldn't like me. He was four years older than me, and I thought they'd look at me as a young, dumb freshman even though DB didn't see me as such.

Much to my surprise, they welcomed me with open arms. The first person who welcomed me was Big Baby, and his hearty embrace immediately eased some of my fears.

"What's up, G!" he said. Big Baby was the only one who could affectionately call me G, and it was so genuine it didn't really matter to me.

"Hey B, what's up? I'm nervous I don't know anybody," I whispered to him.

"Girl please, we are not that kind of group. You will be just fine, and I'll introduce you to everyone," Big Baby put his arm around me and started leading me into the kitchen where a large group of ladies were talking. "Hey y'all, this is DB's new girl, Grace. This is Sharon, Nina, Deborah, and Allison."

All the ladies smiled and said hi. They were welcoming and told me to come on in and join the club. Nina immediately took a liking to me and said, "Girl, you are a cutie. DB, you did good!" giving him a head nod. "Come on out to the porch with us and talk, girl. You know the boys will be doing man talk anyway."

That day, I met the "fam." Sharon was the chef, and she would always be found cooking at any of the functions. Folks around campus lined up at her door on Sundays because they knew she'd be throwing down on some good home-cooked soul food dinners. Nina was the diva of the group, level-headed and smart, but extremely prissy. Everyone knew Nina was not getting her hands dirty, but she was down to earth and kept it real. Deborah was the eccentric one. Always sporting a new hairstyle and a funky outfit. She had a major no one had ever heard of, urban affairs, and would go out of her way to help any human in need. Allison was a little mix of them all. She was like a mama who would love you up then tell you about yourself, but she would never leave you to fend for yourself without having your back. These women took me under their wings, and in that one sitting told me how to keep DB in order and that I was welcome to come around, even if he wasn't there. Suddenly, Delia and home seemed farther than ever, and I was the most comfortable I had been all of freshman year. Even more comfortable than I had been with Leah.

I noticed that as DB and I got closer, Leah and I grew further apart. Despite my many invitations to go out, hang out, or introduce her to people, Leah refused to be social. Her reasons were always that she didn't feel she belonged. I felt bad for leaving her. But I couldn't force her to come out, and I didn't want to punish myself by staying in. I wanted to embrace this new world and all it had to offer, whether it was education, relationships, friendships, or new experiences. Mama always told me to go out and make the best of life, and that's what I was doing. Only I couldn't make Leah do it with me.

There came a day when Delia called, as she normally did, and Leah answered the phone. Usually when I was with DB, Leah would tell Mama I was in the shower or out, then call me and tell me to call Mama back. Although DB and I were not intimate, I didn't need Mama lecturing me about being at his house and giving me the Spanish inquisition about what I was doing there. But on this particular day, Leah didn't give Mama a message; she gave Mama DB's number.

Now DB and I usually spent the weekend together and being that it was a Saturday morning around 8 a.m., we were still in bed cuddled up when the phone rang. DB answered it and immediately sat up. I knew something was wrong. "Hi, yes, how are you?" he spoke in cryptic code, so I wondered if it was a woman.

Then he said, "Yes, she's right here," and handed me the phone.

I looked at him and asked, "Is it Leah?" He just shook his head and mouthed, "Your mom." My mouth dropped and there was no hiding at that point.

So, I spoke. "Hello." It told all my business – I'm in bed, half sleep, next to this man, in his apartment on Saturday morning, so I spent the night.

"You are right next to him?" screamed Delia into my ear. But I was too tired to argue.

"Yes mom, we were sleep," I admitted and sighed. I braced myself for what was coming next. I guess DB could sense it, and he got up and went in the living room.

"You slept in the same bed? I thought you said you slept on the couch at his house?" Delia's voice was coated with anger and disbelief, with good reason. She was not aware that I stayed there regularly when I did I told her we slept separately. So much for that story.

"Look mom, I was tired, and I got in the bed. Nothing happened." I could have told her the sky was red at that moment and it would have sounded just as truthful as that statement. I knew there was no way of me proving that to her, because she would never understand how a man would agree to not sleep with a woman because she wasn't ready. That wasn't normal. But DB wasn't normal. I just had to figure out a way to make Delia understand that.

"Hell, Grace Marie Johnson, how long do you think that man is gonna have you come to his house and sleep in his bed before he wants something more from you?" Mama was mad now, and DB could see my face and tell that this was not a good conversation.

"Look Ma, I told you nothing happened. Okay? You have DB's number so if you need to reach me and I'm not in the room, I'm probably here. Can I call you later?"

"Yeah, when are you going home?"

"Ma, it's Saturday, I don't know but sometime today," I said, trying to exert my independence, what little I felt I had.

"Fine, goodbye," Mama hung up before I could respond. I was not looking forward to that conversation later. What Delia didn't understand was that everything DB was doing to wait for me and get to know me as a person made me want to be with him so much more. This was no game to us, it was real. Mama's continued grip on me pushed me closer to DB and farther away from my innocence.

DB's birthday was coming up and I wanted it to be special. In the months leading up to it, we had discussed what he wanted to do. DB always responded with "it doesn't matter" or "I don't care as long as I'm with you." Although he was incredibly easy to please, I wanted our first time celebrating his birthday together to be special. I settled on taking DB out to dinner at one of his favorite restaurants, then coming back to the apartment and having a quiet night alone. Candles, soft music, and me. I had decided that this would be the day I had waited 18 years for. Everything in my body told me that DB would take care of me, comfort me, be gentle with me, and love me, whether I wanted to go forward or not. Because of his unconditional love, I was ready to allow him to love all of me. No other man had loved me as much in a romantic way. I knew that he had my best interests at heart, and I would not regret this decision.

Dinner was superb. The waiter waited until just the right moment to bring the birthday cake surprise and sing to DB. During the meal we talked and laughed, and I told him that he meant so much to me and I was enjoying every moment with him. We were so in love with each other, it just seemed like the night would naturally lead to making love. When we got home, I lit candles, turned on the soft music, and as we got ready for bed, DB stopped me and grabbed my hand. "I know what you're doing," he said, with a sympathetic look in his eyes. "You don't have to do this for me now. I told you when you're ready."

As if I didn't have confirmation, this was it. Here I was, a young woman thinking that the best gift I could give DB was myself, all of my femininity, and all he could think about was how I felt. He wasn't concerned with having me in that way. He loved me and told me that if he had to wait till his next birthday, it was fine. I think we were so in tune that he could sense my nervousness. I had been scurrying around all night, and although I was trying to stay calm, my conversation had been a little spastic, not to mention, my constant talking, even when there was nothing really to say. I sighed with relief, yet disappointment.

"But DB, I want to do this. It's not because it's your birthday, it's because I want to give myself to you." DB smiled and kissed me softly, holding me close as if he was protecting me.

"I thank you, baby, and I love you for that. But let's wait. It will happen when it should." That night as we slept, my ear to his heart, I heard the beats of love that I had longed to hear from Henry so long ago. I was safe in DB's arms. And the next night, we shared our love. It was everything I hoped for, and everything I thought I needed. For a while...

~

DB and I became closer than ever, and by the end of freshman year, Leah and I had grown into two different people. She had never found her niche at school and decided to go home. Although I hated to see her go, and it reminded me that I was truly on my own, I looked forward to the opportunity to prove my independence. Delia had raised me to not depend on anyone, and I knew how to survive. I had DB and I had the new friends I had made, but most of all I had my faith.

In the midst of all that was happening, God had placed some angels in my life to keep me grounded. One of the greatest influences on me that first year was my freshman advisor. Shari was a heavy-set, dark-skinned woman, who was kinda homey and kept to herself. She lived on our floor and helped make up the 2% of African-American women in our wing. When I was really feeling down, Shari would call me into her room, and we'd watch some comedy or listen to some gospel music. Shari loved to laugh and what most people didn't know about Shari was that she was a great listener. She had the gift of laughter and encouragement. In her "upperclassmen apartment" I always felt comfy unwinding and leaving all the stresses on my mind outside the door. In her room I didn't have to think about the 3.0 GPA I was just 0.6 away from, Leah not wanting to hang out with me because of DB, or the fact that I missed Chicago so much. In Shari's room she would tell me funny stories of being a preacher's kid and how her sound upbringing kept her grounded through grad school. Shari and I would share our church experiences. I told her about getting saved with Nic and how I had managed to stay pure throughout high school because of my faith foundation. Shari always listened without judging, yet, encouraged me to stay true to my ideals. She would say, "Maybe you don't have everything you want, but God knows exactly what you need and makes sure you have it."

So, at night in the dorm or at DB's, I always made sure to read my bible that Aunt Sarah's mom gave me. Psalm 1 was my favorite. Aunt Sarah told me to put my name in wherever I saw "he" so that I would personalize that message. It is still true today, and I remember reading that word kept me from breaking down when times were hard and prepared me for the storms that were forthcoming.

"Blessed is Grace that walketh not in the path of the scornful, nor sitteth in the seat of the unrighteous, but my delight is in the law of the Lord and in His law doth I meditate day and night." - Psalm 1

~

Flowers Wither

A seed that is planted and takes root only continues to grow if it is consistently cared for. My grandmother always used to say, "If you want your plants to grow, you have to talk to them, give them some attention."

She would gently touch their leaves, water them with the utmost care, and always reassure them that she would be taking care of them. I thought it was rather ridiculous to watch someone have a full conversation with a plant that would never satisfy her with a verbal response. Yet, as crazy as it seemed, it never failed that the plants Gran devoted the most time to blossomed into strong, sturdy plants that she boasted of each time I would visit. As I got older, I came to understand that Gran's plant convos were actually "garden relationship counseling." Much like a plant, if a relationship is to grow, the two must talk and give each other attention. Everyone wants to know that their significant other can be trusted to take care of them and be gentle, making sure to water their dreams, goals, and aspirations. The worst part of visiting Gran was when a plant died. She would mull over it for hours saying, "I don't know what happened." Then remembering, "I didn't give this one as much water. I should have done more. It could have bounced back if I had caught it sooner."

My relationship with DB had been growing. DB loved me, and I opened up my heart to love him. Our mornings, if not together, were spent talking on the phone or meeting in between classes for lunch. Afternoons and evenings DB would pick me up or I'd walk to the building where he was working on his architecture drafting classes and then wait for him so we could go home together. Every possible moment we could spend together, we did. He gave me all the attention Henry never did and I supported him through every tough decision, test, or difficult class he had. The times we separated were when we had to study, or I needed to go back to my dorm to get clothes or a free meal during the day. For the most part, we were inseparable. DB's friends had totally welcomed me, and Nina and I had even gone out a few times with DB and his boy she was dating. Sharon was always inviting me over for dinner and even reminding me that I was always welcome, even if I got rid of DB. Of course, I reassured her that wouldn't happen, but the kindness I felt affirmed my feelings that I was in the right place.

A few months after freshman year ended, DB's parents

came to visit. DB was from a Southern family with soulful roots and stonewall traditions. In DB's family, women could cook, they were the praying women who raised the children and stood by their men. DB's mom was the epitome of a strong southern woman; the first time I met her she said, "Oh she's beautiful, Brandon."

We went to dinner, and his dad told funny stories of how DB was awkward as a child and not the sexy, self-assured man I met. DB's mom, Gladys, even invited me to their house in North Carolina, which we drove to a month later. As I said, she was a praying woman, so every decision had to be prayed about. Whether it was small, like DB having a test or our journey to Raleigh, she would always pray first. Oftentimes, if she would call DB's apartment and catch me, she would ask to pray with me and give me scriptures to read that dealt with whatever situations we were facing. His parents' acceptance of our relationship allowed me to release myself to DB even more, and I fell in love not only with him, but his family as well.

Everything around our relationship pointed towards a seriousness that I had never felt before. I had never felt comfortable with a man romantically, intellectually, spiritually, and emotionally as I did with DB. I even brought him home to Chicago to meet Delia. Her reaction was polite, yet humorous, because she never believed I'd fall for the southern gentlemen type. But she liked him, or at least she pretended to while we were there. Back at school, we had a few conversations about our future and the "M" word had already come up. We decided if it were to happen, we would wait till we both graduated before making that move. DB even gave me a promise ring to solidify our decision, but we would not share that with our parents until we were absolutely sure. Delia was concerned about me falling head over heels for the first guy I "gave myself to" and I was determined to show her that I was not making an impulse decision about DB. So, I went out of my way to make it work with DB to prove that I could be successful at a relationship with a man, despite my circumstances. It worked for a while, but then something began to change.

What started out as a whirlwind romance had slowed to a merry-go-round of awkward moments. Instead of DB and I meeting after class for lunch, he'd call and say he'd see me at home later. Some days, I'd decide to just stay in the dorm. I attributed it to me needing some personal space and not wanting to smother DB. But the signs of less attention were becoming more apparent. Rather than stay up all night talking, laughing, and making love, we would now sit and watch a movie in silence, fall asleep, and maybe hold each other in the bed. Our school schedules became hectic; DB was concerned with passing his architecture classes as he only had one year to graduation, so most of his spare time was spent in study groups or in the drafting lab. Likewise, I was nervous about losing my scholarship, so I buckled down into my studies as well, causing me to devote less time to our relationship. On the days we did get together, we were both recovering from the week, and although we still enjoyed each other, the brightness of our union was fading fast. Like a flower without sun and water, we were beginning to wilt into a couple who rarely spoke or showed any affection. Whenever I brought it up, DB got very testy, reminding me he wanted to make sure to stay on track to finish school, and I would continue to remind him that I needed some love and attention too. He made some effort to spend time together, but it was evident that things were not the same.

Four months of lack of attention climaxed on a cold November day. I was in my single dorm room sitting on my twin-sized bed relaxing and watching TV. It was a short break in between studying, and I was hoping to talk to DB. My phone rang, and I stretched out on my bed and smiled as I heard DB's voice. "What's up, G," he said. DB's voice didn't sound excited to hear from me, yet not disappointed either; just there.

"Hey, baby, I was just thinking about you. How you doing?" I replied, trying to lighten up the mood.

"I'm good, just got done talking to Big Baby. He's going

through some stuff with his moms and I was trying to help him out."

"Oh, that's sweet of you. Is everything okay?" I asked.

"Yeah, for the most part – we started talking about all this other stuff, like friendships and being loyal. I was telling him that I was so glad him and I had been cool for so long. I talked about you too."

"Oh really?" I was intrigued now, because it had been a long time since I had heard DB talk about me to his boys. I was hoping to get some insight into what was going on with us, without continuing to pry and ask questions. "So, what's on your mind?"

"I was just telling Big Baby I was glad to have friends. You know, people don't get many. And you are my buddy, G," DB said with assurance.

My eyebrow rose at this remark and I sat up on the bed. How was I to take this? "Your buddy, DB? What you mean?" I was now looking at the phone as if to say, "Don't mess up or I'll have to go against my first mind and let you have it."

"I mean, like you my buddy, Grace…my dog."

"Your buddy?" I stood up and all the softness left my voice, "Your buddy? I'm your dog? That's it, that's all I am to you now?"

"Grace, I mean, that's kind of what we've become lately," he attempted to apologetically say.

"Oh yeah, alright then, buddy. Goodnight!" I slammed the phone down and paced my room frantically. His buddy? Did he just call me his damn buddy?! After all we'd been through, granted we'd been up and down lately, but this was your idea of me? Tears began to stream down my cheeks as I recounted DB's words. They resonated in my ear like sirens. My buddy. I didn't give my virginity away to a buddy. I didn't open up my heart and let you into a place that no other man has ever been allowed to enter, except Henry, as my buddy! If I wanted a buddy, I'd go home to my dog!

The phone rang again. I looked at it, but I was too furious

to answer. My heart felt like it had been crushed in two. For months I had seen our beautiful and blossoming relationship begin to wilt, but this felt like someone had just ripped the stem out of the ground. The room became blurry as the tears clouded my vision. I wiped my eyes, yet the flow seemed unstoppable. The phone rang again.

"I hope he doesn't think I'm answering, I'm just your buddy!" I screamed at the receiver. Immediately, I began to gather all of DB's belongings. I got his old sweatshirt that I would curl up in at night and smell when we were apart, just so that I could have his scent near me, the cards he had given me for my birthday last month, our picture on the nightstand, miscellaneous clothes and things I had brought from his apartment. The garbage bag was almost full by the time I stuffed everything into it. His buddy! I was so pissed at the thought that he could not say anything more than that. He couldn't say, "Grace I been meaning to tell you I think we should just be friends" or ask, "What's happening to us?" Just, "You're my buddy."

Well, I was determined to let him know that if a buddy was all that I was, he had no need to take up residence in my heart any longer. As I got ready to tie the bag and put it at the door, I noticed the promise ring on my finger and sank onto my bed. The t-shirt I had on was now stained with tear drops as I looked down at the ring DB had given me just six months ago. It was nothing special really; a gold thin band with two rows of small diamonds (probably CZs knowing DB's budget) going in two different diagonals. It was minor, but it symbolized something so major. Promises. DB had promised me he would wait for me in the beginning; he had promised to take care of me, love me, and together we had promised that someday he would marry me. "Broken promises," I managed to say through the tears. I slowly slid DB's ring off of my finger, went into my dresser drawer, and grabbed the small golden box it came in. I placed the ring back into the box and dropped it into the bag. "You can have it all back, buddy!" I said and dropped the bag by the door.

I was gathering up the pieces of my broken heart and stuffing them into the garbage bag, but as soon as I sat down, my phone rang again. Since I had calmed down, I decided to answer it, expecting that it was DB calling for an explanation. I was prepared for the worst. "Yeah," I said as dryly as I could.

"Hey Grace, how you doing?" I heard Sharon say cautiously but with concern.

I couldn't hold it any longer. I just broke down. "He said I was his f*@!ing buddy, Sharon! His buddy! After a year and a half of my life, all that we've been through, I gave everything to him and I'm his buddy now! I can't believe this. It feels like somebody just stabbed me in the heart, Sharon. Why would he do this?" By now, I was sobbing and gasping for air. My chest felt like a Sumo wrestler was sitting on it and my stomach.

"Calm down, Gracie. I just talked to him. He is upset too. He said he wants to talk to you, cause it didn't come out right, and he wants to have a chance to explain."

"What's to explain, Sharon? I don't know a right way to say that I'm his buddy. I'm his woman. I love him, but he thinks of me as his buddy. I don't know what to think right now. I packed up all his stuff and he can come get it!" My voice had become raspy from all the crying.

"I understand Gracie. Why don't you just listen to him? You can give him his stuff, and you don't have to change your mind, but at least hear what he has to say."

"I don't even want to look at him right now," I said with disgust.

"Well, he asked if I'd come too, so I'll come and you can just look at me while he's talking, okay?" Sharon pleaded.

"Fine. But I'm not changing my mind."

I had decided that I would take the bag down to him and listen to what he had to say, but no matter what, there was no way he could take back those words. They resonated in my mind the entire time I waited for him, and I was not going to be a fool who allowed a man to hurt me more than once. I slowly felt my walls creeping back up around me and DB being pushed out.

When they arrived, it took me 10 minutes from the time Sharon called to say that they were here for me to get it together. I glanced in the mirror and was shocked at the sight. My eyes were bloodshot from an hour of nonstop crying, my nose was red and puffy, and I looked like I'd been hit in the eyes by Rocky. There was no hiding that, so I just threw on my coat, sweats, and gym shoes and walked downstairs. I opened the door and there stood Sharon, Big Baby, and my new buddy, DB. Not the least bit of compassion swept through my head as I looked at his dejected face. He had obviously been crying too, but I could only tell because he wouldn't look me in the eye. He held his head down the entire time.

"Hey Grace," Sharon broke the ice and gave me a hug. I couldn't help but sniffle as the tears welled up in my eyes again. But I was not going to break down in front of DB.

"Hi Sharon, thanks for coming." There was an awkward silence. Big Baby just stood there because he didn't know what to say or do. DB was still standing with his head down. I looked at Sharon as if to say, now what?

"Well, DB, go ahead," Sharon broke the silence.

"G baby, I didn't mean for it to come out like that. I didn't think before I spoke, but it's something that we've both known for a while. Things haven't been right between us, and I can't hide the fact that it seems like we are more like friends now than boyfriend and girlfriend." DB finally looked up at me and I looked down as the tears began to flow freely. "You know I love you G," he reached out to grab my hand, "but this isn't what I want for us. I am confused and I don't know how to fix this. I've been trying to focus on my studies and improve my grades, but then I feel like I'm neglecting you. I don't want to give you part of me, G, you deserve 100%."

"Who said you had to figure this out on your own? Why couldn't you just talk to me, DB? I understand what you are going through, and I told you I would stick with you through it all. I'm not trying to take you away from your education, I want you to study and graduate. You don't have to feel like you have to do everything for me, I'll be here, DB, you know that." Sharon and Big Baby quietly retreated to the car as the conversation began to get more intense.

"G, I appreciate everything you are saying, but it's not working for me. I'm so focused on school, I haven't thought about anything else. Haven't you noticed I've been less affectionate lately?"

"Yes, I thought it was just cause we were busy," I sat down on the stairs in the front of the dorm, because I began to feel nauseous at the thought of where this conversation could lead.

"No, Grace, it's because I am not sure I can be all you need me to be. I don't want to give you 50%. I'm a 100% guy, all or nothing. And if I can't give you all of me...," DB paused.

"Then what? That's it? So, you don't want to work this out? We said we wanted to be together and it won't always be perfect DB. We will have to work at it. But you just want to give up? You don't think we could work this out?" I pleaded in disbelief and anger. How could he just have decided all this without me? Did my feelings even matter?

"Right now, Grace, I think we should just be friends." He could have just taken a knife and rammed it into my chest, and it would have hurt less. My emotions welled up in me and busted out into a loud shrill cry that I couldn't hold back. Face in my hands, my back began to seize up and down as the reality of DB's words hit me. I could hear his voice from far away saying, "I'm sorry, G", but I couldn't bear to look at him. By this time, Big Baby came and took DB back to the car and Sharon came and sat next to me. I felt her arm around me, and I just leaned into her shoulder and sobbed. I cried because I had allowed myself to be totally vulnerable with a man, something that took 18 years, and the result was this, another man leaving me. Just like Henry. Where was his will to fight? It was all about him, just like Henry. The more I thought about the lonely nights that would follow, the harder I cried. Then, when the ocean of tears ceased, when my throat became so tight that I could hardly swallow, and the scene around me finally began to come back into focus, something shifted in me. I had felt it before, but I didn't recognize it immediately. It wouldn't be until the next day that I would recall this new state of mind.

It's 7:30 a.m. Who in the world is calling me? All I could think was this had better not be Delia because after the night I had just had, I was not in the mood to chat. "Yeah?" I answered, letting the person on the other end know their call was not welcome at this hour.

"Hey G, I just called to say good morning and see how you were doing?" Did I just hear DB's voice? I sat straight up in bed and a wave of rage swept over me. He must have lost his sanity to think he could pick up his phone and dial my seven digits like he hadn't just annihilated my heart less than 12 hours ago.

"What?" I was groggy, but the attitude came through very clearly. "You called to see how I was doing? How do you think I'm doing?"

"Look G, I still care about you. Can't I call and check on you, as a friend?" DB sounded so oblivious to the fact of our new reality. That's when I remembered the shift I felt the night before. It had been almost 13 years since I felt it, but it was the same shift I felt after I called Henry and got the operator's voice - a 360-degree turn, from love to hate. Where softness in my heart once was, there was only stone. Red hot lava could not have melted the barrier that had just gone up, and DB needed to know it.

"Just 24 hours ago I was your woman. Then you woke up and decided we were just friends. Last night you broke my heart and I cried myself to sleep. And you say you care? You cannot care for me; you didn't care last night, and I am definitely not ready to be your 'friend'. No, you cannot call and check on me. Matter of fact, I don't even know when I'll be ready to speak to you again. Until I call you, don't call me!" I slammed the phone down. If I was going to get past this, I could not handle hearing his voice every morning like I used to.

From that day on I began to heal, grieve, and grow. It was DB's pain that pushed me into progress. Sharon and Nina and the rest of the fam became closer to me now than ever and reassured me that we would remain friends. I was grateful for their consistent friendship, despite their history with DB. Some days I would sit in my room and just cry. Other days I'd go out and explore the campus, places I'd never gone, or always wanted to go. I threw myself into my studies and managed to get a 3.0 average by the end of the 3rd semester.

At parties, I would see DB. The first time I saw him, his eyes had a glimmer of hope in them; hope that I might speak. But to me DB had become invisible. If I was going to survive being on campus, I had to forget he existed. So, I walked on by and said nothing. There were awkward times when the family was all together laughing, and when DB and I would pass each other, we'd simply look the other way. There was no regret behind our eyes either. Just sheer disgust, anger, and hate. I hated him for what he did, and I wanted him to think I was fine without him. Inside, the hate ate away at my joy.

Eventually, I began to examine myself and I realized that I allowed DB to be my everything, something I thought I'd never let a man be. I put my all into him, but I forgot that DB was just a man, and a man can never be all I need. Man is not God, and only God can supply all of my needs. On the days when the anger subsided, I began to understand that DB was doing his best and it just wasn't enough for me. It maybe wasn't the best way to break up, but he was doing all he could do. The fault belonged to us both, and it was unfair for me to put it all on him. I began to forgive him in my heart, but I needed to tell him face to face. I needed to know what I did to make it go wrong. I needed to let go of the hold that was gripping my heart so that I would be able to love again.

The day came as a surprise, but I woke up on a June afternoon, almost six months had passed from the breakup, with DB on my mind. It was time. Time to move forward. Time to let go of the anger and hurt, and time to remember what it was like to love again. Not a man, but myself. Every day I held onto the hurt of my past, I held up my future. So, I decided I would call and arrange a meeting.

"Hello," Brandon answered. The sound of his voice sent me through a world of emotions. Anger, disappointment, longing, love. I had to remember to remain focused.

"Hi DB, its Grace," I said politely.

"Hey G, what's up. How are you?" DB sounded genuinely happy to hear from me. I had to admit, in the past few months I had seen him a few times and said hello and even thought about this moment. But now that it was actually here, I was speechless. How do you pick up where you left off after almost half a year? It felt like we were two strangers at first, and I wondered if we would be able to actually get past this awkwardness.

"I'm good, DB. It's good to hear your voice. I wanted to check on you and see how you had been doing. You have been on my mind, lately."

"Wow, that's a surprise," DB said sarcastically. "It's good to hear your voice too. I've just been busy with class and working. Trying to finish up this degree next year."

"You know you can do it, DB," I reassured him. I wanted to say more, but I was afraid of falling back into the girlfriend role, and I didn't want to stir up any feelings that had not already surfaced. "Well, I wanted to know if you wanted to get together one day to talk. Maybe have breakfast?"

"Sure, G, I'm off this weekend, how's that?" DB replied.

"Cool, I'm free Saturday…let's hook up then. Meet at the pancake house?" I asked.

"For sure. I'll see you there around 10."

"K, bye DB," I said.

"Bye, G." That was one of the hardest conversations I had ever had, but I was excited about the possibilities. In my months of thinking, I realized it was probably better for me and DB to be apart because we were just going through the motions and eventually it would have happened anyway. But I wanted us to end on a good note. There was no sense in us harboring any anger or ill will toward one another. I wanted the best for DB, and I wanted to move on.

Since DB and I had broken up, I felt free, in every area of my life. I was free to change my physical appearance, free to think what I wanted, go when I wanted, do what I wanted. So, when I met with DB, my freedom was evident. When I walked in, his eyes bucked, and a smile slid across his lips. The long hair he used to run his fingers through was now a short, well-manicured bob and I walked with a new confidence. It's amazing how a devastating situation will force you to come face to face with yourself, even if it is not a pleasant reflection staring back at you. My time alone had caused me to really reflect on what I needed or wanted from a man, and I regained my inner confidence as I realized that no man could do more for me than God. So, as I sat down with DB, my entire new attitude resonated in me.

"Wow, G, you look great. I like your new haircut."

I was glad he noticed, but a part of me wanted to say "Ha, your loss." Instead, I heard my voice of reason say, "Thanks, DB. You too." And he did look good. Almost good enough to...

"I'm glad you called me because I wanted to talk to you. I've wanted to talk to you for a while," DB began, "I am so sorry I hurt you Grace." DB reached his hand across the table and grabbed mine. I jumped at his touch, yet I was comforted by the feel of his hand. But I didn't want him to see it. "You mean the world to me, and you always will G. I didn't think through anything I said to you that night, and in hindsight, I probably just should have sat down with you as a man. I think I was scared of hurting you, and I ended up doing it anyway. I understand why you didn't want to talk to me, even though it really hurt me for us to not talk. But I wanted to say I'm sorry, and I still want to be your friend." DB's eyes were sincere and his hand never wavered from mine.

Sitting across from him listening to these words almost melted my heart, and I wanted to say, "let's just start over", but I knew we couldn't. Although there was hope in his words, there was also finality. "I appreciate your honesty, DB. I was very hurt, and I couldn't bear to talk to you or even look at you for a while. I just needed some time to get my head together and accept the situation. I understand that it was the best for us, although I don't understand why we couldn't have worked it out. I would have been patient with you. We didn't have to break up, I was in it for the long haul. When you love someone that's what you do." My voice was beginning to expose my underlying hurt that had been buried for months.

"But G, you know you deserve the best, and I couldn't be happy with myself just doing half. It just wasn't sitting right with me. But I still loved you, and I still love you."

How do three words have so much power? Instantly, I forgot all about the anger, and I just wanted to hold DB. I wanted to go back to our fun times in his apartment, cleaning up, singing, watching TV, and holding each other, making love. I wanted him all over again, and my heart ached. Tears welled up in my eyes. "I never stopped loving you, DB."

We sat in silence for a few minutes, both of us realizing that our bond had not been destroyed, just shattered. With each glance, our eyes searched, and our hearts wondered if we'd done too much damage to put the pieces back together again. The waitress broke our silence and we managed to order food and carry on a light conversation. Deep in my heart I wanted to give it another try. I wanted to have that feeling of love again. It was okay if I didn't have a perfect relationship. I was willing to work it out as long as I knew I'd be able to have DB's love and share mine.

Breakfast turned into lunch, then an afternoon. DB and I agreed that we were at a point where we could be friends again, and I was hopeful for the possibilities that were ahead. Maybe we would rekindle something, or maybe not, but I was happy to have him around again.

As weeks passed, the family started to get together again. It seemed as if the family was forced to separate when we broke up, but since we had decided to be friends again, family gatherings and BBQs became more frequent, and the more we were around each other, the more we fell back into step. However, DB was not happy with some of the habits I had picked up, and he let me know it. Hanging out with Nina I had started smoking cigarettes to blow off steam from the breakup. It wasn't all the time, but with my new freedom, I had no problems smoking in front of DB. He hated it and would remind me of that each time we talked. I would try and stop when I was around him, or wait till he wasn't around to smoke, but it was hard. In the empty space he left, I replaced it with something that I thought would take my mind off of everything. Hanging out more, I began to drink more and just let loose at every opportunity. DB made every effort to stop me or he would make a comment about my actions. So, I slowed down, and I decided I'd quit smoking, at least as long as DB was around. His concern, coupled with my weakened emotional state one night, led us back down a road we traveled before.

After one of the many family gatherings, I agreed to go to DB's house to hang out. Perhaps it was all the time we had been spending together or just a case of the loneliest, but DB and I didn't last five minutes alone. Before I knew it, I was waking up next to DB in his arms, smiling yet confused. I didn't know what to think of this new development and I didn't want to put any pressure on him or jeopardize our new friendship. My mind knew it was just something that happened, but inside I wanted to be with him more than ever. Unfortunately, the separation had separated our hearts. DB still loved me, but he had also grown accustomed to his freedom. He made it clear after we woke up and he took me home. "I had a good time G, maybe we can do that again one day."

I felt cheap; it felt polite and there was no feeling behind his words. It was an awkward morning after, and I decided that was one mistake I didn't have to let happen again. As I got out of DB's car and turned to say goodbye, I looked at DB and I knew it was the final goodbye. Goodbye to first love, goodbye to hurt, goodbye to settling for less. As much as I wanted to be loved and feel the love from a man, love that Henry never gave, I didn't want it at the expense of real emotion. On that summer day, I learned the value of waiting for great instead of settling for something to do. Walking away from DB I left behind the naivety of Gracie Mae and was introduced to a new Grace.

CHAPTER 2

HOUSE ON FIRE

FAITH

Imitation Of Love

I wish that I could start all over again. In my mind, this same thought repeated itself every day, but I could never say it aloud. It would be coming face to face with my reality, and that was too hard. "Whew," I said as I looked into the bathroom mirror with the show time lights shining on every crow's foot, line, and shopping bag around my eyes. "You look tired, Faith," I heard myself say. Probably being up late with him again did it, I thought.

I'll make it a point to be sleep when he gets home today. Or maybe I'll take a nap when Haley goes to sleep. No, I need to clean the house, and he said it had better be clean today or he's gonna start throwing all my stuff out. I know I've been letting it slip too. It's just been so hard with Haley being sick and me trying to keep up with school. My thoughts were racing from yesterday, to today, to once upon a time. "I don't know what you're gonna do about all this right now, Miss, but you better get in the shower and get your day started before you ain't done a thing," I said to my reflection with a faint hint of sarcasm.

As my lips curled up to a slight pout, I saw a flash of my dimple. When was the last time I had smiled? I used to love to smile so much but lately it was so rare. "Busy being a mother and a wife, you have lots to smile about." I knew the words were lies as they came out of my mouth.

With a limp hand, I turned on the faucet and attempted to smile as I let the water run; it was such a foreign feeling—happiness. But I was happy once, a long, long time ago. Stepping into the hot shower felt so wonderful on my hazelnut skin. I leaned my head back and let the water pour down all over me. This was one of the few places I could find peace. No one would knock on the door or ask me what's wrong; even Lucas allowed me my few moments alone in the shower. So, I cherished this time; it was where I was able to let my teardrops mix with the cleansing drops from above and only I knew that one drop was full of pain. In here I prayed to God that my marriage would be better; that I could convince Lucas to be happy with me, love me, and be the husband I wanted him to be. It was here that I prayed that God would make me into a good wife and mother, help me to be patient with Haley, and bring joy to my house. And it was here that I cried when I felt none of my prayers were being answered. I often felt that God heard me, but this was just the hand I was dealt, and I should quit complaining and find ways to be happy. So, as I opened up my favorite Bath and Body scent, I felt a smile coming back as I inhaled it and memories of college and good friends returned.

What if I could start all over again? I had this thought at least once a week lately, anything to escape from my listless reality. Maybe I would have married Jacob, even though we never seemed to have our timing right. Or maybe I'd be single and just enjoying myself. "No use dreaming about that, you didn't," I regretfully remarked. *But it's cool*, I thought. *I have a beautiful house, a gorgeous daughter, I'm married, and now going back to school. We have a roof over our heads and food on our table. I have a lot to be grateful for.* As I replayed this in my head, like a mantra, I was hoping that it would start to sink in, and I might believe it one day.

I turned the water off and stepped off, just as I heard the whimper of Haley in the next room. My time is over—back to mommy time. "Be right there, Haley…Mommy's coming," I called out to her in the sweetest voice.

Haley really was the only joy in my life. Every time I looked into her eyes, I fell in love all over again. It was amazing to think that just 24 short months ago she had been just a seed in my belly, but now, at one year old, she was a walking, talking reflection of me and Lucas. The amazing thing is I never really wanted children. I still remember the day that I found out I was pregnant. It was like someone had dropped a bomb on me.

Lucas and I had been dating for about a year and had just started sleeping together about a month earlier. I had done everything right; got on the pill and made him use protection. But when I missed a period and I started having all these gastric problems, I decided to get it checked out. I figured I had developed an ulcer or some strange stomach ailment that was causing me to have gas and bloating, but to my surprise the nurse came in and exclaimed, "Baby you are 200% pregnant! Congratulations!" I froze. *It must be a mistake*, I thought.

"I'm on the pill, and we used protection," I said as if to tell her she must have the wrong results.

"Well, dear, all it takes is one slip up and sometimes it just doesn't work. How long had you been on the pill?"

"About a month," I said, trying to remember if there had been a slip up. I was sure there hadn't been.

"All I can say is that maybe it wasn't totally in your system yet, but you are pregnant, baby. I'll send the doctor in to talk to you. It will be alright," she said as she patted my shoulder. No, it was not alright. Tears began to well up in my eyes and my throat got tight. I am too young; I don't want to be a statistic. I want to finish school; I'm supposed to graduate and be a successful journalist. This is not happening! By this time, I was sobbing, and I couldn't help but be mad at myself and Lucas for putting me in this position. What would I tell my mother? Oh my God...and my grandmother? There was no way I could be going through this! Thoughts raced through my mind, and I had visions of how my life was now completely ruined. I had done this all wrong. I was supposed to be married first. I could have an abortion, but that's against God. What was I to do?

What seemed like hours in the doctor's office were actually just minutes. By the end of my visit, I had decided I would tell Lucas, and we would discuss our options. As the doctor said, "There are always options." That's the nice way of saying, "You can get rid of it," without actually saying it.

This was way too hard of a decision for me to make alone at the age of 21. So, I called my girls and we had an emergency meeting first. My closest girls Grace, Leah, Jen, and Melody were there.

"Girl, you know I just went through this exact thing, and I kept it, and look what happened. So, I don't know what I can say except don't marry him just cause of this," said Melody who had just lost her child in a miscarriage a few months prior. She had married her boyfriend because of that, and now she was "stuck".

"I know I wouldn't have married him otherwise."

"I know, girl, but my mother is so traditional. I don't know what she'd say if I don't marry him," I said.

Jen chimed in. "Well, you know my thoughts, I'll drive you home from the clinic. I believe we all have choices, and the choice is ours. I survived it, and I am happy because I wasn't ready then."

"Uh…we know you are the pro-life advocate, Jen," Melody added sarcastically. "You should be the poster child for abortions!" We all laughed, because it was no secret that Jen had had a couple and had no shame in saying it was the way to go.

"I mean, it wasn't easy, y'all, but it's what was best for me. Bottom line, you gotta do what's best for you."

Leah added, "Faith, talk to Lucas and see what he says. A lot of men say they will support you, but when it comes time to buy diapers and take care of the baby, they bail. So, whatever he says, just understand that this is still YOUR baby. Do what you want to do." Leah was often the voice of reason in the group. I respected her opinion.

"That's true, Leah, I mean, I am capable, but it would mean putting off my career and he doesn't have a good job right now or anything. We were talking about moving in or getting married in the future, but now it's like staring me smack in the face. It's like I've been forced to grow up at warp speed."

"You know life will do that to you sometimes, Faith," said Grace. "We think we have it all figured out and life throws us a curve ball. I'd say talk to Lucas, do some soul searching before you do, and decide what you wanna do. And, of course, pray on it!"

"I am. I wish I could have a cocktail to calm my nerves. Guess that's why I haven't wanted a cigarette in a while either."

"Well girl, if we go the clinic, I will buy you a pack and a drink! You just let me know!" Jen said. We all burst out laughing!

"Girl, Jen, you are a mess!" Melody said in between laughs. "But I love your crazy self!"

"I love all y'all and thank you so much! I'll keep you posted."

~

Here I am, almost three years later, mother of one Miss Haley Lucille Simmons. When the responsibilities of motherhood, being a student, and a wife overwhelm me, I find peace in Haley's eyes. It's amazing how having a mini version of you can completely change your perspective on life. There are days that I just sit and enjoy Haley's laugh, or dance with her to some silly kid's show, and I feel like I've never been better. I'm able to last another day in my unrelenting situation.

"Hey, Hales," I coo at her as I pick her up and hold her close. Her whimpering becomes a silent whimper as our heartbeats meet. The doctor said a child knows her mother's heartbeat because they are in the womb listening for 9 months. Sometimes just having her close to me will calm us both.

"You must be hungry, sweetie. Let's make some lunch." Haley and I walk down the hallway and into the spacious kitchen. There are only two places I feel at home—in the kitchen and sitting with a pen and pad, writing. Cooking and writing, the Olympic workout of skillet, fork, and pen are to thank for my recently added 20 pounds. Haley is a little old for me to call it baby fat still.

Spread out on the dining room table is a sea of papers.

I glance over at the waves of unfinished papers, articles that have been started and left undone, and my laptop open on the table. "I used to be so organized, Hales!" Will I ever be again, I wondered. My life has become a mosaic of unfinished projects. I am determined to finish this class I'm taking now, though, no matter what. I never used to understand when people would say children completely change your life, but now I do. I love Haley, but I find myself so into making sure she is taken care of that I don't have nearly enough time to accomplish a quarter of the things on my to-do list. Hence, my to-do list has dwindled tremendously over the last year or so. Lucas seems to be inconvenienced by my lightened load, as he feels that being a student and mom couldn't compare to his long hours of work. Ha! Little does he know I work too, but I can't remind him of that anymore. Last time I did...I suddenly had a flash of that day when I tried to tell him about how much work I do. It was the last time I said something like that.

Haley had just turned three months and it was my 90th day of no sleep. My eyes were yo-yos as images bounced up and down, back and forth, almost in a drunken stupor. I was warming Haley's bottle as she practiced clearing her lungs for the fourth time in 15 minutes. Slumped over the counter as the water warmed the milk in the pot, I tried to hold back the tears. Hands shaking from exhaustion, I picked up her bottle to check it and the sound of the phone ringing was like an alarm clock blaring in my head. I scooted my house shoes across the kitchen floor to the phone. "Hello," my mouth managed to say through the sandpaper dryness that had set in from exhaustion. The phone receiver felt like a barbell pressed against my head, and all I wanted to do was hang up. But it was Lucas; so much for that thought.

"Hey, I gotta stay late tonight, so I won't be home till 7:30 or so."

"Uh huh," I said over Haley's cries that seemed to have raised an octave. Maybe she was screaming for her father to come home and rescue her. Or rescue me. "Coming, Hales," I tried to yell, but I realized she probably couldn't hear me over her cry song.

"What's wrong with Haley?" Lucas asked. "Why is she crying like that?"

Cause she's a damn baby, I wanted to say. But I couldn't refer to her like that. "Cause she's hungry," I snapped back.

"Why didn't you feed her, Faith?"

"Uh, I'm not starving her, I'm waiting on the bottle. She just woke up and I didn't have one ready." I guess my exhaustion had transferred through the phone into an attitude because Lucas quickly got one.

"What's your problem? You know I don't understand how you didn't have it ready. That's all you have to do…get the bottle ready. I don't want my baby crying like that anymore, Faith. You gotta do better than this."

"Wait a minute!" Suddenly I had enough energy to speak up. My stomach boiled with anger as he attacked me and I wasn't going to take that, or so I thought. "I have to get up with her every night, stay up to feed her, take care of her all day. I'm tired and I'm doing as much as I can! It's not like you're much help! You just come home and sit on the couch. I am doing the best I can, Lucas!" I was now screaming, and my tears mixed with Haley's as my volcano of exhaustion erupted into his ear.

"You know what, I work hard every day, 12 hours, and I don't have to put up with this kind of talk, Faith! All you have to do is be at home with our daughter. I'm tired of you saying you're tired. You ain't doing nothing! I'll be home at 7:30 and make sure you leave my dinner out."

"I'm not cooking, pick something up, Lucas." That was the final straw.

"You better cook woman. You better get your big, lazy butt up and cook me some food. All the money I spent on those groceries and I'm supposed to eat out. You better have some food on the table, or you can forget about me paying for that class you want to take. Oh yeah, and the car you wanted to get so you can get to school, oh well. You need to walk anyway to walk off some of that baby weight. Feed my daughter and I will see you with dinner later."

I tucked my head down and looked at my body. Lucas was right. I had gotten a lot bigger—65 pounds heavier since having Haley. It had just been so hard to get rid of the weight without me breastfeeding. And I really wanted to go to school again. "You're right Lucas, I'm just being lazy and complaining. You know I want to go to school really bad since I couldn't finish because of Haley. You said you would pay for it," I pleaded.

"Well you need to get it together, Faith, or it's not gonna happen."

"I said I would, Lucas. See you later. Have a good rest of your day," I said softly.

"Yeah, I will. Love you."

"Love you, too." He did love me, even if it was tough love. It was good that he kept me motivated to do better. *He could have said it nicer*, I thought. But that was just Lucas. I grabbed the bottle and went to get Haley and feed her so I could get to cooking dinner.

~

Tip Toeing to My Dreams

Almost two years later, I did get into school. Lucas paid, but of course, I have to hear about it all the time. I never mentioned how much work I do again, though. I didn't want to upset him and make him change his mind. Life has taken many different turns for me. The great thing is I am back in school, and I am back writing; not much is finished, but I can see the light at the end of the tunnel. I have so much in my belly that I want to write. Each time I pick up the newspaper, I imagine my name in the byline. I was lined up to get an internship at the Chicago Sun-Times until I got pregnant. I couldn't accept the position because Lucas said I had to work to save some money because he wasn't gonna just support me while I was off. It made sense that I save some cash for our necessities, especially because we wanted to get a new place too. Now that we're here, I want to finish school so I

JEANINE A ROGERS

can look into getting back on the market. Haley will have to go to daycare, but I think she can handle it. She's a toddler and we've spent the majority of her first two years side by side. It will be an adjustment, but I think I will enjoy the time out of the house. I just hope Lucas will be okay with it. He's been under a lot of stress at work, hours being cut and talks of layoffs. I want to tell him, but I don't know how. "What do you think Haley? Wanna watch mommy cook Daddy's favorite dinner?"

Haley laughed and said "Da-Da," as she clapped her hands. Just the mention of his name made her smile.

"I hope he smiles like that when I tell him this, Hales." Smiles don't happen often with Lu, usually after a few drinks or during a game, but otherwise it was rare. Lately, the stress of work was draining him; I usually ended up waking him out of intoxication in the middle of the night to get in the bed. Sometimes it was the happy drunk; sometimes the mean one. Never knew which one I'd meet, but I'd learned to deal with both. As long as I didn't make him mad when I woke him, it was usually okay. The happy Lu wanted sex. Intimacy was a foreign word in our house. Sex was a requested act, during which I usually thought of the many things on my to-do list and how soon I could get back to them. Hopefully, tonight I'll be able to get Lucas happy, so we could talk about school.

The table is set so beautifully, I think even Martha Stewart would be in awe of it. I put on the new yellow and white checkered tablecloth, pulled out the wine glasses, and good dishes. "No paper plates tonight, Hales."

She just smiled and kept on banging on the pots and pans as if she was creating her chef's masterpiece. I was determined to have everything set up before Lu got home. I spent all day making all of Lu's favorites – fried pork chops and his mama's homemade mashed potatoes with sautéed green beans. Once he's full he's happy and easy to talk to. I fed Haley early so once he gets home she'll already be sleep. My idea is to discuss the paid internship I got offered, and how the finances would help us and take the load off of him. Then I'll hit him with daycare for

Haley. I am also planning to look especially sexy in my just snug enough jeans and my low-cut, V-neck top, two items that show off my best assets. He may need just a little extra persuasion.

"Hey, guess who picked up some extra hours?" Lu says as he walks in and plants a soft kiss onto my lips and playfully hits me on the bottom. That's his way of showing affection; I've never liked it; it always feels cheap to me, like some grimy old drunk's way of showing love. But I've learned to let it go, especially tonight, because I need him happy. The aroma of his favorite meal makes him take a deep inhale.

"That's great, Lu. Why don't you have a seat—dinner's ready," I motioned for the dining room. He's cheerful; that is definitely to my advantage.

Setting the table, my hands rattle the dishes from the anxiety I am feeling inside. "Why you shaking, Faith?" Lu asked as he grabs my wrist.

I try to stay calm, but my voice quivers, "I'm good, just tired I guess. I'll be fine," I manage to say.

Lu's eyes soften. "Take a break and sit down." I slide into my seat timidly and unexpectedly sigh. Well, here goes. "So, what is the occasion for this special dinner?" Lu asks.

I wonder how to begin, but before I can think it through it just comes bursting forth. "I got an offer for an internship – $1,500 a semester. I was thinking this could help us out and possibly be my door to getting my journalism career started. It starts in two weeks and the hours are 8-4 so I'd have to put Haley in daycare. But Ms. Robinson said we could work out a price that suits us. What you think?" I jump up with my head down, trying to look busy bringing food to the table. Lu is sitting there eerily quiet, and I can't tell what he's thinking. Heaping piles of mashed potatoes on our plates, I try to lighten things up a bit since he isn't responding at the moment. "These are from your mama's recipe, baby. I hope you're hungry."

I glance up to see Lu's face and he is not smiling at all. How can I describe the look on his face? Amusement. Sarcasm. Disbelief. My body tenses as I brace myself for his reaction.

"Please don't let him hit me, God," I pray silently. Finally, the ice begins to give way and Lu's voice pierces the silence.

"So, this is what you been doing all this time huh, Faith? I'm at work all day, thinking of ways to provide for you and Haley. Working six days a week for you to be able to live the life you want and go to school. Bought you a car, but now you wanna work? And leave the baby with a stranger?" Lu's voice is bold, laced with anger as he goes on. Now leaning on the table, he towers over me.

Slowly, I stand up and begin to walk towards the kitchen to get the steak. I need some distance from him. "Ms. Robinson isn't a stranger, Lu. I've known her for 15 years. She's like a second mother and I trust her with Haley. Plus, I can pick her up right after my internship. I thought the money would take some weight off of you, babe."

Lu's breath is a wave of hot air on my neck as I attempt to control my fear. I turn around and smile, rubbing his arm, hoping it will ease his mood. "I'm not the one the weight needs to come off of!" Lu laughs and pinches one of my many love handles. "I'd love to have some more money coming in here; we could use it. Then I could cut my hours and have some time to relax. How much is Ms. Robinson gonna charge?"

Thank you, God...he laughed; he didn't hit me. "Bout $80 per week – that would leave me a couple hundred to play with and put on bills and the car."

"Ain't no such thing as play money, Faith. I got too many bills for you to have play money. You will have to write up a budget for me to approve and make sure you include gas money and insurance since you are the one who wanted a car."

"No problem, babe." I kiss him gently. "Now let's enjoy our dinner." I breathe a sigh of relief. At least he listened. Granted, we need to discuss it some more, but that is one victory for me. I can sleep soundly tonight.

After much coercion, a wonderfully cooked meal, and a very late night of performing acts I dare not recall (don't need to relive an already unbearable experience), Lucas agreed to my offer. First on my agenda is to square away my intern/job start date, since I told my future boss I'd have to find out how soon daycare could start. Ms. Robinson already agreed and is actually going to have a trial run today with Haley while I meet with the boss.

I woke up so thrilled to be starting this phase of my life again. To me it was a renewed lease on life. A chance to show my mama, my family, Lucas, and most importantly, myself, that I could be successful and not a statistic. I have met so many housewives and soccer moms at playgrounds and parks with Haley. The conversations are always the same: "What activity is your child in?" "What are your day care dilemmas?" "Growing pains?" "Toddler triumphs and tragedies?" Yet, behind each of these, "I'm so happy to be a stay at home mom" convos lurks the ghost of a dream deferred. Perhaps, these women, and even myself, have justified tossing our life's goals out the window to be housewives. Hats off to us for having the courage to do what many don't have the opportunity to do. We subliminally pat ourselves on the back and award trophies for how many accomplishments our children have made before three years old. But I just wonder do we ever look back at the dreams we placed on the shelf? Does the idea of that business deserve to be dusted off? Or the corporate job we put on hold? I have enjoyed every second of Haley's two and a half years, but I still want to explore my goals. At 24 I don't believe my aspirations must live eternally on the shelf.

I don't lack concern. Haley's adjustment to the outside world is important to me. How will another know how to comfort her when she cries? Will Ms. Robinson be firm enough if she has a bout of terrible twos? Will she be too tough? Will Haley want to be with me less? I am going through these questions as Haley toddles into my room. She is the brightest light in my life. Her mile-wide smile can always lift my spirits and ease my fears.

"Mama," she utters and lifts her arms up towards me.

"Yes, irresistible little sweetie." I kiss her cheek as I scoop her up into my arms. "Today we're going to see Ms. Robinson, remember?"

Haley just laughs, unknowingly, as I put her down; she's so happy and carefree. I pray every day that she will keep that freedom. No pain, no worries, just love. If only I could shelter her from life's disparities. She'd never have a broken heart, unfulfilled desires, or regrets. But we live in reality, so I must prepare her for it. Hence, today's launch into a new season. For Haley, she will take her first baby step away from me and towards her independence. For me, I take my first step towards the life of a working mother and taking my dream of journalism off of deferment.

"Hey, Ms. Robinson," I smiled as she opened the door.

"Hey sweetie, come on in." Ms. Robinson was the sweetest woman ever. Everyone she met got a name – honey, sugar, baby, pumpkin pie, or some other dessert. Ms. Robinson was the neighborhood grandma who everyone loved. Standing at a majestic 5'6", Ms. R could always be seen with her hair tied up in a colorful scarf, wearing her duster with house shoes to match. In fact, when people on the block saw her outside dressed in street clothes, they were always shocked. Some almost didn't recognize her. Her greetings were warm receptions of love. She made you feel like being with your mama and everything would be okay.

When I was a teenager, we moved onto Ms. Robinson's block and she took me under her wing. When Mama was working, Ms. Robinson would teach me how to cook and talk to me about being a young lady. What I liked about her the most was the way she always listened. Sure, she probably had something else to do, but she never told you that when she knew you needed her. Next to Mama, Ms. Robinson was the second most important woman in my life.

Now Haley would have the chance to get to know Ms. Robinson herself. "Child, this girl is as cute as can be! And growing fast! Seem like just yesterday she was in diapers. "Ms. Robinson picked Haley up and held her close. "Sweetie we are gonna have a great time," she said smiling.

Haley giggled and melted in her arms as all babies did. I don't know why I was ever nervous—this was the best place for her.

"Well, she ate some cereal before we left the house, and there are two changes of clothes and her shoes..."

"Now Faith," she sounded just like Mama, "You know I been taking care of children since before you were born. Ain't nothing different about Ms. Haley. You go on to that internship so you can get start doing something for yourself. We'll be here when you get back, right sugar plum?"

"You're right. I guess I am just nervous because it's our first real time being apart." I hugged Ms. Robinson close. "Thank you, again. I love you."

"Love you too, pumpkin. Now go, before you are late." She smiled and nudged me towards the door. I kissed Haley and headed out the door towards the car.

"Alright, Faith," I exhaled, "Let's do this!" I would have kicked my heels, but my feet don't jump off the ground anymore. Instead I turned up my radio, hit the highway, and headed to my first day of work.

~

Leap of Faith

"Good morning, welcome to Chicago Sun-Times, how can I help you?" the receptionist inquired cheerfully.

"Hello, I'm Faith Simmons. I have an 8:30 appointment with Ms. Morien."

"Ah, yes, she's expecting you. Have a seat and help yourself to coffee if you'd like. I'll let her know you're here." She gestured towards a comfortable seating area, with a table full of coffee pots and condiments.

"Thank you." I smiled and turned towards the seating area. Entering the lobby had been intimidating. It had been eons since I had been in the workforce and I felt as if I was the outlier in this set of professionals. Everywhere I turned there were men and women with purpose, on their cell phones exchanging business deals and gathering information for their day. Shoes clamored down the lobby, the click clack of heels of the women, and men's trench coats danced with every step on their primary mission—getting to the elevator. There was a sense of urgency that permeated the place and created a spark inside of me. I felt the energy in the room, and I wanted in. The most energy I'd felt was from Haley running around the house or crying for attention. But at that moment, when I entered this atmosphere, I wanted to fall in line. My soul was thirsty for this excitement, and I had buried my desires for so long that I think it was shocking when I felt it.

I looked down as I reached for the coffee cup and smiled at another woman in the waiting area. Wonder if she's here for the same position. Normally I would make conversation, but there were too many thoughts floating around in my head. My fear of rambling on nonstop about my insecurities and uncertainties halted me from even making further eye contact, which would in turn strike up a polite conversation with a woman who could be interviewing for the same position.

I had gathered together my portfolio from college and a few pieces I had written recently once I found out I would be re-entering the journalism world. My girlfriend, Grace, had helped me update my resume. She had encouraged me to go back to work immediately after I had Haley, but I wasn't ready yet. Now was my time, and I needed all the help I could get. Grace had also loaned me her Kenneth Cole portfolio case to complete my professional look. "You can't go in there with this old raggedy folder, Faith! They will laugh at you and turn you around!" Grace had said.

I had to laugh at that thought. I was so far removed that I didn't even realize what the norm was anymore. So, I held my dress coat over my arm, my portfolio, and my coffee cup, and I took a seat on the couch away from the other woman. I smoothed my blue jacket and crossed my ankles. I had chosen the traditional navy suit, with a baby blue blouse underneath, and navy pumps. I had toned down the formal look with a silver bangle bracelet, a silver chain, and left my hair down and in layers. Professional, but not uptight. Fashionable, not eccentric. Down to earth and real, that was my MO.

As I began to thumb through today's paper, I saw Jonathan Reynolds's column. He was the pulse of the paper. What he wrote, people talked about. Whether it was the new political candidate, the recent financial crisis, school funding, or who will win the Super Bowl; Jonathan Reynolds had something to say about it, and people listened. I could only imagine working at the same company as him and have far off dreams of ever actually meeting him. Just as I was imagining what I would say if I saw him, a tall, thin, stately woman came towards me. "Faith Simmons, I'm Kathleen Morien," her outstretched hand extended towards me and I stood quickly, careful not to waste the coffee or drop the paper, or both. What an impression that would be!

"Pleased to meet you, Ms. Morien," I shook her well-manicured hand firmly and smiled. She was firm, no nonsense, and at first glance, she looked like she'd never smiled in her life. Her hair was short and trendy, with dusty blond and streaks of golden blond on top. She was well put together in a tailored gray suit to fit her perfectly and three-inch heels that could have clearly cost more than my entire outfit.

"Let's go talk," she spoke and turned on her heels, without awaiting my response. There would be no easy ins here.

I watched her walk stealthily down the hallway with the stride of a gazelle. Graceful, yet strong, she was respected. Each cubicle we passed housed a writer who paused in the midst of their column, email, or tweet, to say, "Good morning, Ms. Morien," followed by a glance in my direction, and a smile or nod, and then back to work. Our long walk ended in an office of glass floor to ceiling soundproof walls. As I walked in I saw framed photos of major front-page stories, degrees, and cases of books. I quickly sat and reached into my briefcase and retrieved my portfolio.

"So, I read your resume, Ms. Simmons, is it? What took you away from journalism for so long?

I had been rehearsing in the mirror for a week how I'd wow her with my writing abilities. But the first thing she asked was about my personal life, the one part of my life I was escaping from by returning to work. However, this was neither the time nor the place to have a pity party, so I squared my shoulders and began wowing.

"In 2004, I was awarded an internship here for a semester. One week later I found out I was pregnant, and in turn got married and started a family. My Haley is two now, and I've found purpose and solace from the busy schedule of a family woman in journalism. I decided it was time to get back on track. I know I may have to start at the intern level again, but I am willing to go through whatever it takes to move up to writer." I sat a little straighter, and I felt confident I had answered well, or so I hoped.

Ms. Morien's eyes were sizing me up as I could tell she was comparing the real Faith to the "resume" Faith. It was hard to get a read on her; she had an excellent poker face. She spoke skeptically. "I sense healthy ambition from you. It's an admirable cause, you returning to work, with a child. But this will not be an afternoon, cup-of-tea writing job. I've read your work and you have a knack for integrating feeling with facts and that's something I look for. How long, on average, does it take you to churn out a piece?"

Somewhere inside of me relaxed a bit – she was interested. But I had to prove that I was worthy. Faith kicked into full wow gear, "On average a day or two, but if I am on a roll, I can have a finished piece in a couple of hours," I replied.

"News happens here, and it happens fast, so we work in hours, sometimes minutes, but rarely days. You'll have to work on that. I think your style is similar to Jonathan Reynolds', so I'll have you interning with him for the next three weeks. If you can keep up with him, then you're worth taking a second look at. He'll report your progress to me. If it is working we'll go from there," she said matter-of-factly.

"I am so grateful for this opportunity. I have always admired his writing," I was beaming with awe and excitement.

Ms. Morien stood and warned, "Well, let go of that wide-eyed look. This isn't a job yet. Anyone I consider must be able to keep up with him. You are his shadow and depending on how much you can learn and retain, we'll see if you have what it takes."

"Oh…I have what it takes, Ms. Morien," I said as I gathered my portfolio because it seemed my five minutes were just about up.

"Great. Report to his office at 8 a.m. tomorrow. He's the third door down on the right." She pointed towards the hallway we'd just come from but in the opposite direction. I nodded, although I couldn't see where it was, I'd figure it out. I dare not ask questions; she didn't seem like the question type. I rose and shook her hand firmly and gathered my belongings. As I turned to walk out, I said thank you again, and she waved passively as she was already on to another call and the business of the day.

Thank you God for favor, I thought. Three weeks to prove my worth. I would do it—I would prove to myself I still have it. I was already looking forward to going home and preparing to meet Mr. Reynolds, looking up some of his own articles and getting some rest so I'd be ready for this new journey.

~

Day 1

My stomach was a sanctuary of butterflies chasing bats through a never-ending maze, fluttering, flapping, and causing shifts in the air's stability. "I've been writing for 10 years so why now?" This was my morning pep talk—minus the pep and extra extreme anxiety. Ever since I was old enough to know an S was an S and could put s-u-n together and make sun, I'd been reading the articles and columns of this prestigious newspaper. Now, here I was, walking into the building once again, on my way to meet one of the most famous writers this side of the Mississippi. I opted for the gray pants and black turtleneck sweater with 2" black heel boots. Professional, yet comfy, my outfit appeared to say "take me serious, yet you can be laid back." I wore a thin silver necklace with a string of small circles on it that was discreet. I debated for a while, but decided my other necklaces were too fancy.

As I hesitantly strode towards the elevator, I reached for the button and was met by another woman. She smiled and I quickly jerked my hand back, allowing her to press the button. It's funny how it's an unspoken rule of etiquette to be courteous to the elevator button leader. Like when I was a kid, I remember racing to the button to press it first. I smiled at her and she spoke, "Good morning." I responded, in the same manner, and we stepped onto the elevator as it chimed, "Going up."

Riding the elevator, I noticed, in her hand, a folder labeled – Cover Story – McNair. At that moment, I realized who she was – Jennifer McNair, one of the leading reporters for the Sun. I'd been reading and analyzing her techniques for years, modeling my samples after hers, using nuances of humor infused with deliberate exposure just as she had. At that moment it hit me— I would be working alongside some of the most notable writers in Chicago. Immediately, I was humbled, and for the first time since college, I realized I was beginning to get back on track with my life.

My brain was attempting to formulate an intelligent, yet not star-struck way to say hello, and just then the elevator woman said, "Floor 4" and it was time for me to get off. "Excuse me, have a great day," I managed to utter as I smiled and exited. *So much for being outgoing*, I thought. But there was no time to dwell on that moment, for instantly I was catapulted into a world of ringing phones, open laptops, and the hustle and bustle of breaking news and investigative reporters.

Walking purposefully, yet humbly, down the corridor, I became a profound observer. In one corner was a man, obviously a business reporter, standing with flailing arms staring at the TV while the latest figures flashed by; he was uttering every synonym of imbecile he could find into the mouth of his headset. Two rows over behind a cubicle of glass was the lead sports reporter, John Mellan, watching ESPN.com and laughing with what appeared to be the sports groupies of the floor. As I continued off the open floor of various cubicles and desks, I rounded the corner to my right and ran smack into a fork in the road. To my left was a set of EXIT stairs (FOR EMERGENCY USE ONLY) and to the right was the cherry wood door of Mr. Jonathan Reynolds, my new boss. For a split second, I contemplated the consequences of going left. I could say I tripped and hit the door, or perhaps, 1,000 butterflies in my stomach could serve as a need for an emergency exit. Absurd! "Deep breath, Faith," I said and smoothed my clothes, readjusted the hold on my portfolio, and raised my hand to knock. Immediately the door flung open and a man who seemed to have just received the brow beating of his life, trampled me. "Oh, uh, excuse me," he muttered and continued past me with his head down, whispering his own scolding under his breath.

I started to say no problem, but he was gone; the door was closing, and I didn't want to risk it not opening again. I caught the door and stepped into a colossal room with floor to ceiling windows on one side and a set of chairs and couches on the other. Seated on the desk with his back towards me, obviously in deep thought, was Mr. Reynolds. From the back I could see the rolled-up sleeves of his button-up, no tie, but a well-tailored shirt. Though his head was down, I could see the clean lines of his haircut and the curve of his muscles through his back. *Humph*, I thought, *I didn't know he was so...*
But that daydream was interrupted abruptly.

"Are you going to just stand there staring or state your business? It is customary to knock before barging into someone's office," he said, clearly agitated at my presence.

"Uh, uh, I apologize, I was knocking but that man left the door open and I just..."

"Your name and business please?"

"Sorry sir, Faith Simmons, your new intern. I was told to report here at 8 by Ms. Morien," I managed to say and extended my hand. He looked at it like I was a leper. So much for friendliness.

"Humph, she did mention something like that yesterday. Have a chair, I have some business to tend to and then we'll talk." He motioned to the sitting area and walked out, and the cherry wood door closed loudly behind him.

"My God, this will be rough! He didn't even shake my hand," I said aloud in amazement. Maybe he had a rough morning with that man. I'm sure it'll get better; I hoped so anyway.

Glancing around, there were few decorations in this vast office. A degree or two on the wall, a slightly cluttered desk, a copy of the morning's paper on the table, and a small refrigerator. I picked up the paper and began reading the front page story, which coincidentally, Mr. Reynolds had written. I wondered would my name ever be on that byline. About 10 minutes later, Mr. Reynolds reemerged, a little less tense, yet still short.

"Sorry for running out." He approached the chair as I stood, "You can sit, Faith. We may as well be on a first name basis since we'll be working together these next few weeks. I'm Jonathan," he said and stretched out his hand. *So, he does have manners*, I thought. His handshake was warm, yet firm.

"I have three requirements from every intern...show up, shut up, and keep up. I expect you to show up every day on time and on location when needed. When I'm investigating, you listen. I've built a rapport with almost everyone in this town and I don't need some green intern saying the wrong thing and blowing a story. Keep up with deadlines, facts, me, etc. I won't ask you to get my laundry or coffee, but if you have an inkling of a chance at this career, you have to be quick and alert at all times. Got it?" His eyes were piercing mine, and considering the way the rules were presented, why ask? It seemed a given – get it or get out.

"Yes sir, Mr. Rey...I mean Jonathan. I wanted to tell you, I'm eager to work alongside you. I have admired your writing for years. I have brought some samples for you as well," I said reaching to open my briefcase.

"It's okay, I don't want to see what you can write at home sipping a cup of tea between soap operas. I will read your pieces when we have a deadline and two hours to write tomorrow's cover story. That's what journalism is about. You must have some talent if Ms. Morien sent you to me." He looked me up and down, sized me up in a matter of 10 seconds. Last time someone did that, they asked for my number. Not this guy. "You've got a good look – non-threatening, nice smile, and clean. But you seem nice. You're gonna need tough skin to make it. Number one – never let them see you upset, as you are now."

If there had been a forklift, it would have come in handy to help pick up my lip. Within five minutes of talking to this man, I had been shut down and read like a stop sign. I'd heard this was a field where no handouts were given, but wow, this introduction had taken me aback.

"I understand sir, I mean Jonathan," I said, trying to hide my astonishment. "I'm not upset, just digesting everything you said. I'm nice, but I have thick skin. I'm not as soft as I seem, iron fist in a velvet glove – as my mother used to say."

He showed a slight grin. "Hmm, we'll see, Ms. Faith. For today, we have a full itinerary. So, drop your briefcase, grab a pen and pad, and let's go investigate." He rose and walked to his desk and grabbed a folder and keys. He walked to the door and held it open for me.

"Thank you," I chimed. A gentleman under the gruff – who would have thought it? Off we went, this time past the same cubicles, only this time a few heads turned, looking my way and nodding. Jonathan exchanged pleasantries as we walked briskly through. I thought of saying "Good morning", then I remembered, *show up, shut up, and keep up.* Nah, maybe not.

~

Day 1 was rough. Jonathan was no joke. Three different stories we worked on; at least five places we visited where he questioned politicians, citizens, business owners, etc. At each location I was to take extensive notes of the conversations, transcribe them this evening, research any prior histories, and have reports for him first thing tomorrow.

What had I gotten myself into? I had been wondering that all day. However, as tired as I was, I loved the rush of the business and the excitement of the investigation. As I walked into the house with Haley, I started to think about dinner.

"Whew, Haley, it really could be a pizza night! But daddy doesn't like pizza. Guess we'll have to throw something together." Haley smiled and said, "Pizza!", waving her hands in the air. There was nothing like that smile, and I couldn't resist it. I grabbed her up and kissed her as we peeped in the freezer. One frozen pizza left. "Pizza it is, Haley, and we'll make steak for Dad." At least it wasn't as much to cook.

Just as I was pulling out food for dinner, the phone rang. "Hey Mama," I said after glancing at the caller ID.

"How was your first day, baby? You get a story yet?" she asked.

"Ma, it was good. Super busy though, and I have work already. Not one story, but three! I'm going to be up all night."

"What?! Three?! Wow baby, I knew you'd be a great journalist. What are they about? Probably that scandal with the mayor, right?"

I laughed because my mama was known for being assertive in everything she did. "No Ma, they aren't my stories – they're Jonathan's. I take notes and write up a report, and he reviews it and uses it for *his* story. And I can't tell you what they're about! That's breaking confidence."

"Girl, I'm your mama – who can you tell if not me? And why do you do all the work for him? You ain't a slave!"

"I'm not Ma! This is an internship, so I am doing, like, on the job training. I get my own story after three weeks," I clarified for her before she marched down to the Sun herself.

"Okay, I was about to say…," she said with an attitude.

"But I'm trying to get dinner ready and Haley just got in, so I'm going to have to go. I have a ton of work to do," I explained.

"Well, you don't sound like you have time to make dinner and take care of Haley. I can come over and give you a hand," Ma offered.

"Oh okay, Ma. You can, but I will probably do some work, if you don't mind."

"Whatever, baby. I'll be there in a few," Mama said and hung up.

Relief, overwhelming pressure, excitement, fear, exhaustion. Was it really possible to go through the entire gamut of emotions simultaneously? Apparently so, because it was only 5:45 as Mama walked in and they kicked into high gear.

Mama was a welcomed hand. With Haley being in the prime of terrible twos, there was a lot to deal with besides my regular duties. "Now Faith," Mama always said that. "You show me what you had planned to cook, and I'll get it started and play with Haley while you start working."

I reached into the freezer and tossed the frozen pizza out. "Ta dah!" I laughed. "That's for me and Haley. I got a steak and some mashed potatoes in the frig. I was gonna make a salad too for Lucas."

"Now, wait a minute. You mean to tell me you're cooking two meals? Why make more work?" Mama asked as she looked in the refrigerator. "You only have one steak, just do pizza and salad and make it easy," Mama suggested.

Sigh. Here we go – this is why I almost told Mama to stay home. It is tedious to explain how and why I do things. Sometimes she doesn't get it. "Ma, Lucas doesn't like pizza. Last time I called in an order after a long day, he refused to eat it. I just went ahead and made him dinner anyway. After he works all day, he wants a home cooked meal," I explained.

"What about after you work all day?" she said with her hands on her hips. "There has to be give and take. Now that you're working too, there may be some evenings you can't cook a gourmet meal. If he's hungry, he'll eat."

"You know what, I'll just do dinner Ma and you watch Haley. It won't take long."

Mama shook her head. "No, I came to help so if you want to do both, I will. Just seems silly to me," she shrugged her shoulder. "It's silly, ain't it, Haley Whaley?" she tickled Haley and Haley cracked up.

Mama just didn't know I didn't have energy to fight over dinner. I learned to pick my battles. This was not a battle worth fighting.

A half an hour later, I'd finally sat down to write up notes and work on story number one when Lucas walked in. I sprang up to greet him at the door. "Hey Lucas, how was your day, dear?" I said as I reached to kiss him.

"Fine," he said, turning his head to set down his keys, avoiding the kiss. "What you so happy for?"

"I had a good day at work. I got three assignments already, and stories and notes are due tomorrow. But I'm determined to get it done so Mr. Reynolds can have a good cover story," I said as I hailed him into the bedroom.

"Who is Mr. Reynolds, and why you doing his stories?" Lucas turned and looked at me suspiciously.

"Nobody, Lu, relax. He's the writer I'm assigned to but not just any reporter, he's the best. If I can make it with him, I'm guaranteed a job."

Suddenly Haley began chanting "pizza, pizza," and Mama began talking. Lu looked up wild-eyed. "Is that your Mama? What she doing here?" I could tell this could get heated and I had to calm him down.

"She offered to help with dinner and Haley since I had so much work to do. She won't be here lo..." But Lu had already stormed out to the kitchen. He scooped Haley up.

"Hey baby, hello Ms. Brown." They locked eyes and the tension immediately skyrocketed.

"Lucas," Mama said dryly. "You ain't gotta pretend to be happy to see me. I ain't staying long. Just came to help Faith on her first couple of days." She pointed towards the oven. "Your dinner's in there."

"How nice, thank you. I don't think Faith and I will need you to help anymore. Faith can handle Haley and dinner on her own, can't you Faith?" Lucas turned to look at me.

I had walked in at the exact moment of the question, but I was split. I needed help, Lord knows I did, but I couldn't dare go against Lu. "Well, it was helpful because I was kind of tired today and I got a lot of work. I was gonna just eat pizza with Haley and I knew you don't like it, so Mama offered..."

"Shouldn't be no problem with everyone eating pizza, you ask me," Mama interrupted. "Pizza on the table, that's what you eat. But that's just my opinion." She shot a look at Lu, then me.

"No one asked you, Ms. Brown," Lu said abruptly. "Now, like I said, you can handle this, can't you Faith?" His voice was stern, and I knew this would not be over soon. Haley was squirming as he tensed, and I took her from him.

"Of course, Lu," I responded, then turned to Mama. "Mama, thanks but we'll be fine. Why don't you take some pizza and I'll call you later?"

"No baby, you keep that for yourself." Turning to Lucas, Mama continued, "FYI, I know Faith can handle this but you gonna have to ease up since you both working. Pull some of your own weight."

"Ma, come on, let's get your stuff so you can go," I pleaded. Lucas was standing with fire in his eyes.

"This is my house and I got this. But thanks, have a nice night," he said through clenched teeth.

As I walked Mama out, I asked, "Why did you say that? You know he has been the only one working. I'm trying to help and get a job, but you can't jump on him like that."

"Humph," Mama said, "If he had sense, he'd realize what a good wife he has and do more for you. You don't speak up, but I will."

"Ma, I'm trying to keep the peace. He's a good provider, and he does when he can. Now go on home, and I'll call you to-morrow." I hugged her tight. "Love you."

As I turned around I thought, *Here goes nothing*, as I walked back into the war zone.

"So, you gonna let your Mama say all that to me? You know we don't get along and you invite her over with all that mouth? Faith, I don't want to hear that when I get home, you understand?" His voice reverberated fear with each word. "One of these days I'm gonna tell your Mama off, then she will know who runs this house. You handle Haley and the house because that's what we agreed to when you took the job – not your Mama coming here."

"Lucas, I know that," I pleaded. "I got it, but I may need a little help for these few weeks. We may have to sacrifice and eat some quick meals, or you may need to help me with Haley so I can write."

"You know how *I* help! I pay the damn bills! Your writing ain't paying nothing. So, the way I see it, you need to let me come home and relax so I can make enough money for this house." With that, Lucas grabbed his plate and went in front of the 40" flat screen TV. "Haley can sit in here while I watch ESPN, after I eat."

Wow, a concession. I guess he had a point. I wasn't bringing in any money, but it was going to take a miracle to keep up with this home and professional workload.

~

Living and Learning

If it's one thing I've learned over the last 32 years, it is never under-estimate the power of favor. I can remember when it was time for Lucas and me to move into our house. We had no idea how we'd muster up the credit score, a down payment, or a house in our budget that would not look like a run over shack from Alabama. Each house we viewed confirmed my doubts and the fear that we'd be stuck living as guests in our cousin's basement forever. As if God Himself had heard my thoughts, unexpectedly we got a call about a house that had just come on the market in our price range and in a neighborhood that we felt safe raising Haley in. Upon seeing it, we knew it was the one. God's favor was with us every step of the way, from preapproval to inspection, to moving in.

It's easy to forget or allow fear to make one doubt the

power of God. Perhaps, that is why I am so nervous about my assignment with Jonathan. In one breath I was encouraging myself and saying this could be the start of an amazing opportunity, a course change on my path of life. And in the next breath I was kicking myself, saying don't be stupid, he'll never like your work. But I found a slither of strength and faith to go into his office with my work this morning.

"Good morning, sir," I managed to say with a smile, even though my stomach was in knots.

"Morning, Faith," he uttered in between reading the front page news. "I hope you have some notes for me. I need to write a story that's more captivating than this one I'm reading!" Jonathan chuckled slightly to himself, amused by his realization that his writing was light years ahead of his competition at the Chicago Metro News. He quickly set down the paper and looked at me over his glasses. "So? Do I have to wait for an invitation?" he inquired.

Fidgeting, I reached into my briefcase Mama had bought me. It was times like this I was glad I had a quality briefcase, so I could at least appear to be worthy of such an assignment. Nervously, I pulled out the manila folder upside down and my papers went flying. Oh God, I thought, I'm going to crawl into my shell and hide right here. As I knelt to grab the papers, Jonathan walked over and gently touched my arm. "Hey, relax, Faith. I don't bite...on the second day." I apprehensively glanced up at him. Seeing the sincerity in his eyes, I smiled embarrassingly.

"I know sir, I mean Jonathan, it's just that I want so hard to do right. This is my first time back in the journalism field since college and I don't want to blow it." Amazing how nerves will inspire a confessional speech.

"Well, let me see what you came up with for starters," Jonathan reached for the papers as I finished organizing them. Sauntering to his desk as he read, I breathed a sigh of relief and said a quick prayer. "Lord, I need your help, please." I glanced down at my hands and realized they were trembling with fear and anticipation of Jonathan's reaction. *Deep breaths*, I thought.

I despised the fact that I appeared weak and anxious in front of him. That was the last impression I wanted to give.

In between reads, he murmured, "Hmmmm, interesting", nodded his head, and I saw his eyebrow raise a couple of times. But nothing concrete. *Say something already!*

"Faith, I don't often say this but – I'm impressed. First day out, you took copious notes, reviewed fine details, and created what appears to be a somewhat thorough account of the day's activities. Not bad for a rookie. Of course, there's room for some improvement, but overall, well done."

"Really??" I'd never been so surprised in my whole life. Speechless, overwhelmed with gratitude, validation, and confidence that there was hope for my career, my life.

"Do I look like I would lie?" Jonathan asked.

Even I had to laugh at that. "Never. Thank you, Jonathan. That means so much to me. And you can count on me to do whatever it takes to improve."

"Sounds good...let's get started with our day. I need to write these notes into a story, and I'd like you to review a file or two that I had on the investigative report about public school funding."

"I heard about that a few weeks ago, in a special segment on the news. You mean we are covering that story also?"

"Well apparently, after doing some research and questioning, which you will see in the file, the entire story was not told. You will find in this business that there is the story the public is told and the true story that the public could never handle. People say they want to know what's happening, but if they were privileged to the entire gamut of information we discover, most people would go into shock at the appalling actions of public figures and those they 'trust'. Our job is to tell more than the TV, but less than that which would send the world into a depressive downward spiral," Jonathan explained. "You'll see once you get into the file. Of course, you know everything we do here is confidential. One leak could produce chaos on a variety of levels. But knowing the truth, or as close to the truth as we get, can warp your view of society. Just remember – I warned you first."

"I don't scare easily, Jonathan, nor do I find many things shocking. In my life, I've learned to cope with just about the worst this world can bring. And believe you me, I know most people cannot handle the truth. It's like looking into a cracked mirror and seeing it whole. We must give the illusion that all is well, even when it isn't." Pondering this statement and its ironic parallel to my life I continued, "Yes, even when it isn't."

He nodded in agreement and turned to start in on his articles. All was definitely not well at home, but that was irrelevant at the moment. I grabbed the file from Jonathan's desk and walked over to the couch where I would begin to decipher the case of the public school funding, bit by bit.

Knee deep into the file, surrounded by a sea of papers, I looked up and sighed. This story was so much more complicated than I thought. From the beginning, it seemed to be a simple miscalculation on the part of the public school district. Yet, as I read Jonathan's notes and the testimonies of various school officials, the stories did not add up. One person was covering for another who had spent funds that were allocated to a program that was nonexistent. And we wondered why our children were suffering! Better yet, it was our job to wrap this up into a package for the public and tie it with a nice neat bow, letting them know their tax dollars had been everything but embezzled, and little Johnny would succeed, even though his school barely had enough money to pay ComEd.

"Whew!" I said accidentally out loud. Jonathan sat upright from his computer and looked at me.

"Want some lunch?" he asked.

"Yes, my brain is in dire need of refueling. What's to eat around here?" I asked.

"There's a diner not too far that I like to go to on Tuesdays. They have really good soup and sandwiches, and it's a welcome break from the office. Care to join me?" Jonathan asked.

Standing up immediately, I grabbed my jacket and purse.

"Absolutely."

Two blocks north and to one block east, we found our-selves at a café on Michigan Avenue. *Bien Sur* was far from your ordinary soup and sandwich joint. Approaching the doorway, I was amazed at the ability of ambiance to transfer someone to another world. Curved awnings sat perched over a patio with diners outside, sipping tea, eating croissants, and chatting as if they were not in the midst of the fifth largest city in the United States. Inside, the music was calmingly Parisian. Murals on the wall showed the once brick lined streets of Paris, with black antique lamp posts, buildings of marble and stone lined with painters of all sorts capturing the essence of France. Stepping into this café, it was uniquely different and not at all what I ex-pected of a man like Jonathan. Looking around I turned to see Jonathan watching me as I took in the sights. "This is a little European oasis. Not the kind of place I'd expect you'd like." It was out before I knew it. Oops. "I mean…you just seem more like the city type, not the relaxing French type."

Jonathan snickered. "Faith, it's only your second day. There's an abundance of information you have not been privy to yet. I like the city, but it's good to have a dose of peace every now and then. City life can be exhausting. This is a nice change, and they really do have good soup."

"Well, I guess we should order then." I was starting to think that the Jonathan I saw yesterday was not the real Jona-than. Perhaps that was the newspaper façade that he puts up, or maybe it was just a bad day. I glanced up at the chalkboard menu, ordered a tuna sandwich and mushroom soup, and met Jona-than at the table he was already holding for us.

"Good choice," Jonathan remarked as I sat down my tray. "I used to get the mushroom soup, but I'm hooked on tomato bisque now." The commencement of lunch was a welcome relief, because I did not know how to approach conversation with him as of yet. Thankfully, he sensed it and broke the ice.

"So, tell me about your background, Faith. You said you

haven't been in journalism since college. What experience did you have before this?"

Now my accomplishments were something I had no problem sharing. "Well, I guess you could say it began in high school. I took a journalism class and my teacher, Mrs. Collins, recognized something in me as a writer and asked me to become a part of the newspaper. I wrote a few pieces and even submitted a few poems. I wasn't a lead writer, but I helped with layout and Mrs. Collins often had me edit the final copy. There came one moment when I knew I wanted to be a journalist. It was junior year and I remember we were working in Mrs. Collins' office after school as we normally did, and out the blue she said, 'Faith, I have a job for you, an important one.' I figured that she wanted me to fix a last minute article for the paper, so I didn't think anything of it. I was surprised when she told me I would be interviewing the legendary, poet laureate of Illinois, Gwendolyn Brooks."

"That must have been an honor to be given that opportunity," Jonathan commented noticeably surprised.

"Oh, I was awestruck by the chance to meet someone who had become an icon in my African-American literature studies. But my stomach was in knots the entire time," I laughed recalling my fear. "It was an awesome experience though. She was so personable and down to earth and funny, but her words were as deep as the ocean and carried the strength of the Nile. I never forgot that moment, the excitement of interviewing and capturing the essence of a person in a story. From that day on, I knew I wanted to write."

"So, you majored in journalism in college?" Jonathan asked.

"No, actually, I started out in education. I figured I'd be an English teacher like Mrs. Collins. But after a while, I realized that getting a secondary education degree was not my passion. So, I changed majors in my junior year when I left MSU and came home to Chicago. I was finishing my major courses and about to start an internship when I found out I was expecting and everything got put on hold. I got married, had my daughter Haley, and

I stopped writing."

"What made you start back?" I couldn't believe he was interested in hearing my life story, but since he just kept probing, I figured I should not be short with him.

"Haley is two-and-a-half years old now. Before this, we… well, my husband, wanted Haley to stay at home. He didn't really want her to go to a person's house or daycare. But money is kind of tight and I was getting restless at home. I've put my dreams on pause for long enough. I thought it was time to do something to help the family and start back on the road to writing. So here I am." I had to cut it short or else I'd slip and say something he had no business knowing. As it is, Lucas would have a fit if he knew I was talking this much. My face must have given me away, because at that moment, Jonathan decided to dig deeper.

"Interesting story. Judging by the look on your face, there's more to it. But I won't prod. It's rude. That's one of the first things you learn as an investigative reporter. You have to know when to ask questions and when to stop. Most people will expose themselves when they are ready, but if you push too hard they will close up, and it'll be easier to squeeze water from a rock than to get an answer. I do appreciate you sharing with me so far though, Faith. I believe we will prove to have a productive few weeks together."

"Thank you, Jonathan. I must say I misjudged you the other day."

"How so?" He seemed defensive at this remark.

Attempting to smooth things over I said, "I probably was so nervous that first day that I was just sensitive. I thought you were pretty cold and heartless that first day we met. And after I saw that other reporter run out all disheveled, I figured you would be a difficult person to work with. On the contrary, you seem much the opposite."

His face relaxed and I could see him trying to recall the events of our first meeting. "Oh, you know you caught me at a rough time. I don't pretend to be a Mr. Feel Good guy, but I do genuinely care to know a little about the people I work with.

When it's business, it's all business, though. And time is money, so I can be a little tough when it comes to our assignments. Overall, I would say I'm fair and honest, sometimes overly so. But in this business, that goes a long way. It's the reason why I'm still in it. People trust my word, and that will get you into places V.I.P. passes never will."

"I'll remember that. I guess we'd better get back to work. Thanks for lunch. I appreciate it, and I will put it on my list of new European escapes." He smiled and nodded as we stood to head back to the office, back to the reality of life in the unruly U.S. city of Chicago.

~

The first week working with Jonathan was like being in school all over again. When he spoke, I listened and took excellent notes to make sure I didn't miss a thing he was saying. Although he had assigned me to the public school story, my role was primarily to be his research assistant and shadow him throughout this world that was so surprisingly new to me. Each day was fast-paced, and I was thrilled at the opportunities I was given to be so close to breaking news.

Within seven days I had met all the news anchors I so customarily watched as if they were part of the TV, but now they were men and women that we spoke to on a regular basis as a source of information. Jonathan was so well known that most of them came to him to ensure that their information made the front page. Not to mention, Jonathan was pretty easy on the eyes, and it was evident that some of the reporters would like to be on the front page of his life, not just the Sun. One thing I admired about Jonathan as I observed him was that he never was rude to the women, and he politely declined their invitations without trampling their egos. I suppose that is why they kept coming back. His confident rejection was a most attractive trait. Having become friendlier over the past week, I ventured to make a comment on this observation.

Jonathan and I had just listened to the head reporter

of ABC News, Marie Young, concerning the upcoming school budget release. Ms. Young and Jonathan stood to the side after the report, and it was clear she had more than news to tell him about. As her eyelashes fluttered and she gently touched his arm, Jonathan seemed to be extremely uncomfortable by this advance, though he just calmly took a step back. After quickly wrapping up the conversation, he motioned for me over the crowd. As I walked over, Ms. Young decided to follow his line of sight, and when she saw it was a woman, she stayed in place to size me up.

"Marie Young, Faith Simmons, my new intern. She's actually the one who will be doing the majority of legwork on this story." Jonathan held his hand out towards me as if he were presenting me to her. If I had been a piece of meat and she was a dog, I would have been a goner. Her glance went from my head to my toes, and the turn of her lips meant that she was not pleased with me. Yet, through her obvious discontentment, she held out her hand and managed to smile as if the camera had just clicked on. "Pleased to meet you, Faith. You're at a real advantage getting to work with Jonathan." She looked at him as if to say "it should be me."

"Pleasure's all mine, Ms. Young. I am definitely learning a lot from Jonathan." I smiled back, although I couldn't bring myself to say anything more substantial. Being fake was not my strong suit. Thankfully, Jonathan was ready to leave also.

"We'll catch you later, Marie. Keep me posted on any new developments," Jonathan said as we turned to walk away.

"Oh, I surely will Jonathan. You keep me posted on that proposition also," Marie winked as she turned to leave, making sure I saw the wink. I chuckled inside, but it was clear that Jonathan had not returned the wink.

"She's very interesting in person. Not at all like she is on TV," I remarked, attempting to break the silence.

"That's an understatement. She's definitely one to watch. Over the years Marie has given me a ton of information that would have easily ended her in the unemployment line. But, unfortunately, some information comes with a price." Jonathan shook his head as if he were trying to forget Ms. Marie and her mannish ways.

"Don't tell me she expects you to sleep with her to get information?" I asked in disbelief. If so, Jonathan definitely was the exact opposite of what I'd expected.

"Ha, never! She'd do much more than wink if I even hinted at that. I guess you could say I have to put up with her unwanted advances, and maybe even flirted every now and then. There is no way I'd ever sleep with a source. For one, if you fall out, you lose the source. Two, it makes things awkward, and most women want more than they let on at first. I'm too busy to be settled down at this time, especially to the likes of Marie Young."

"She definitely seems like the stalker type." I laughed, remembering her look at me with the wink. It was a shame how so many successful women did not realize their worth, and no matter what their title or the name on their pair of shoes, they were no better than the women on the street selling their bodies for money. "You mind if I ask you a personal question, Jonathan?"

"Shoot, as long as you aren't coming on to me." Jonathan said with his eyebrow raised, unsure of where I was going with this line of questioning.

"That's hilarious. No, I am married," I said, flashing my ring. "You ever been married?" I asked.

"Yes, I was married once, a long time ago. Early in my career, but it didn't work out. I found I didn't have enough time to dedicate to my marriage and the Sun. And I guess the Sun was my priority at the time. So, my marriage went down the drain." Jonathan seemed slightly rueful and reflective as he shared this story.

"Don't I know about that? I've only been back a week and I'm finding it so hard to balance my life at home and the time I spend working on assignments here. I would never neglect my family. I love my Haley, but it's hard to find the energy after working all day."

"From what I've seen so far, Faith, you are a hard worker and you are talented. You will go far in this business if you keep it up. But know that everything comes with a sacrifice. Some facet of your life will suffer. The question is which part."

"Well, my husband seems to think that is happening already. I can't let that happen. I'd never hear the end of it." I said, flashing back to the last episode Lucas and I had about work.

"Well it takes a strong man to allow his woman to work in this field; it can be dangerous and stressful. And most men don't want their women to be more concerned with anyone but them." Jonathan spoke with the wisdom of having been in the situation before.

"That is probably what I am most apprehensive about. What if I do make it? I can't be worried about it now; I'll deal with that when I have to. Enough of this talk, aren't we late for our next appointment?" I asked, trying to change the subject before I began confessing to this man.

"What appointment is that?" Jonathan asked confused.

I laughed as I grabbed my briefcase. "The appointment with my car, for the ride home!"

Jonathan couldn't help but smile. "Okay, I guess we've done enough. Go ahead and head home. Don't want that marriage in trouble."

"Right," I thought. "We want to have a peaceful night." It was my wish as much as it was my cry for help.

On the drive home, I thought about Jonathan's conversation about his marriage. I know that oftentimes when women go back to work, the most challenging aspect is balance. My granny used to say, "a woman got to always take care of home." Even though she worked as a nurse during first shift, she still managed to come home, cook, clean, help the kids with homework, wash clothes, and still love on her husband. That made me tired just thinking about all of that. Women 50 years ago just seemed to be bred differently. It was taught that a woman had certain responsibilities and men expected they be met.

In retrospect, it was a much slower paced time also. Women weren't expected to work; they worked if they chose to. Everything was not a rushed and hurried event. If you look at families today, we're always on the go, eating in our cars, working two jobs just to survive; no one person making enough money to support the household, and the cost of living has gone up. The added stress to women's lives on top of the regular responsibilities can sometimes take its toll. That's why I admire couples that have stayed together and managed to balance this equation called marriage. As I sat thinking about this, waiting for the light to turn red, my phone rang. It was Ms. Robinson.

"Hey, Ms. Robinson, how are you? Everything okay with Haley?" I asked.

"Well, actually that's why I called you, Faith. She seems to be running a slight fever and I wanted to tell you. You may have to stop and pick up some Tylenol. She's been kind of fussy today; maybe she's coming down with a little cold."

Great, just what I needed, another thing on my plate. But my Haley always came first, and I needed to make sure she was okay. "Of course, I'll stop and get some. I'll be there in about 30 minutes. Thanks for calling."

"No problem, baby," Ms. Robinson said. "And you know if that fever doesn't break, she may need to stay home a day and rest. You know she can't get any rest around here with these other children."

"Okay, I will talk with Lucas. We will work something out." I sighed. This was not going to be a peaceful night. With Haley fussy and sick, I would probably not get much work done. But more importantly, what would I do about Haley staying home? I definitely couldn't miss a day. I was only working three weeks. "Granny," I said aloud, looking up into the sky. "How did you do this?" If my husband was the nurturing sweet type, this wouldn't have been a problem. Yet, considering the previous week's incident with Mama, I couldn't call her. Somehow we'd have to work this out. Somehow.

Walking into Ms. Robinson's house, it was clear that my Haley was sick. Her eyes were low and lacking the usual vividness they had when she would see me. She reached for me and my heart melted. "I just hate seeing my baby sick, Ms. Robinson. I think she'll have to stay home tomorrow."

"I know, Faith, I don't like to see any of my little ones sick, but it's probably for the best that she gets some extra mommy love and stay home," she said rubbing Haley's back.

"Okay, I'll give you a call tomorrow and let you know how she's doing. Thanks so much," I said as I gave her a hug and picked up Haley. *Now off to paradise*, I thought.

Thankfully I managed to beat Lucas home. My mind raced as I tried to figure out how to call Jonathan and explain the situation, possibly forfeiting my one opportunity at a foot in the door to my new career, or finagling a way to get Lucas to stay home with Haley. Neither one seemed promising, so I figured I would try Lucas first. I could feel a pounding headache coming on as I weighed the consequences of this decision. Just then, the phone rang.

"Hello," I mumbled the weight of the decision in my voice.

"Child, what's wrong with you," Mama asked with concern.

"Hey Mama, nothing, Haley's sick, running a fever, and I don't think she can go to Ms. Robinson's tomorrow. I'm trying to figure out how I can explain that to my new boss, considering I'm only there three weeks. I don't see how I can take a day off."

"You're right you can't come in the door asking for a day off. I'll just come over and watch her for you. Or you can bring her here. Do you have some medicine?"

"Yeah, I just picked it up. But you know, Ma, you don't have to."

"Now Faith," she interrupted. "That's my grandbaby and that's what grandmas are for. You bring her over in the morning and I will watch her. It will be just fine. You just take care of her tonight so she can try and break that fever."

"Thanks, Ma. I'll call you in the morning before I come over. Love you." *What would I do without my Mama?* I thought. She truly comes through for me whenever I need her. That was a load off of me and I quietly said, "thank you God."

As I began to get Haley situated and her food warmed up for dinner so that she could take her medicine, I heard the door unlocking.

There has never been a time, probably since the first few months of our dating, that Lucas has come home and given me a kiss hello. He made it clear early on that he was tired when he came home and wanted to rest when he came in the door, or at the most, eat. So, it was not unusual for me to hear him come in but not see him immediately. I just figured that was the kind of man he was and there was no use making an issue of it. One of the things my friends had told me when I decided to get married was to pick my battles. This was not one that I chose to fight. I had enough things to fight with Lucas about.

Amazingly, tonight, Lucas came in the door with a bunch of peach roses, my favorites, and gave me a kiss on the cheek. It so took me by surprise, I almost dropped the plate I was putting Haley's food on.

"Heeeyy baby," he said through liquor-soaked breath. He'd been drinking, which meant he was feeling hot and I was bothered. Not a winning combination in this house.

"Wow, those are pretty flowers," I managed to say as I continued to fix Haley's plate. Lucas went over to Haley and scooped her up in one swoop and started kissing on her.

"Hey daddy's baby," he said in between kisses. Haley wiggled away and began to cry. "What's wrong Haley? Daddy just wants to give you some love." The closer he held her, the more she screamed.

"Lucas, she's got a fever, she's sick. Just put her down. I'm fixing her food so she can take her medicine and go to bed."

"Awww, she's sick. How she get sick, Faith? Probably one of those nasty ass kids at Ms. Robinson's." The liquor was beginning to talk.

"Come on Lucas. Don't use that language around Haley. She just caught a cold. Ms. Robinson called me on the way home from work and said she wasn't really eating, and she thought she needed some rest and to stay home a day. She could have gotten sick from anywhere."

"Yeah, right. My baby ain't been sick in over a year," he said, placing her on the floor. Haley began to cry louder. I ran to her and picked her up. "Oh, it's like that Haley. You only want Mommy, huh." Lucas came up to her in my arms.

"Lucas, quit...you're scaring her. She's just not feeling good. She needs to rest." I walked her into the family room and sat her in the playpen.

"She's scared of me? How the hell is she going to be scared of me, Faith? I'm her damn daddy!" Lucas screamed and I jumped at the sound of his rage.

"Lucas, look, just calm down. She's not afraid of you; you just have to talk a little softer, okay baby. She's not feeling good and probably a little sensitive. Let me feed her and get her taken care of and we can sit down and eat." I tried to soothe him and diffuse the situation. The vibe in the room had quickly turned volatile and there was no way I could deal with both of them at once.

"Whatever! All y'all women are sensitive. Where's my dinner?" Lucas walked into the kitchen to see what was cooking.

"Give me a minute and I'll bring it to you. Just relax on the couch for now." I managed to lead him to the couch and get him to sit. Although the situation was calm at the moment, I had to tread lightly.

Feeding Haley and cooking for Lucas took up the rest of the evening and by the time I got her to lay down I was exhausted. Needless to say, I had not done a lick of work.

"Faith," Lucas bellowed from the family room, "Come here." This could mean only one thing. The liquor was in full effect and I was going to have to oblige him to keep him calm. An all-nighter was on the way.

"Yes, Lucas," I said in the sweetest voice I could manage. If he had been sober, he would have seen right through it. Luckily he wasn't.

"Hey girl," he said with a beer in his hand and grabbing me to sit down. "You know you are so sexy with your thick self."

"Okay, Lucas, thanks. But I'm tired, baby. I want to go to bed. Don't you want to go upstairs?"

"No baby, sit with me *here*." This was more of a demand than a request, and when Lucas was drunk, it was clear that arguing was not an option. So, I sat with my hand on my forehead trying to shield myself from his next advance. There was nothing worse than the drunkard Lucas, and I knew where this was headed.

"Give me a kiss." Demand number two. I kissed him quick, and he took a longer kiss.

"What's wrong, you don't wanna kiss me?" He belched as he spoke.

"Yes baby, you know I love your kisses," I kissed him back. Not worth fighting this battle.

"Let's do it." Demand number three.

"Lucas, I'm tired. Let's wait till the morning. I need some rest for work tomorrow, and you need to sleep it off. You know I want you to remember it."

"Faith, I can't wait. I want it now. Come on, give me some." Lucas tugged at my blouse and began to unbutton it.

The next thing I knew, I was a prisoner, captive under his drunken weight. Glancing up at the ceiling and faking enthusiasm, I shed two tears as he found his enjoyment in my vulnerability. There had to be more to life than this. There just had to be. As I turned over and headed upstairs, he patted my backside as if to say good job and passed out on the couch. I crept up to my bed, curled up beside my pillow, and cried myself to sleep.

Most mothers can tell when their child is hurting. It must be an innate inbred connection from being together for 9 months that triggers their protective instinct. Now that I am a mother, I can understand this sixth sense that all mothers have. Therefore, it should have been apparent to me that my Mama could see the scars in me. Although I didn't wear the pain of my marriage on my face and was an expert at hiding my miserable existence from the world, there comes a time when the weight of burden becomes so clear that strangers can see it. So, it shouldn't have surprised me when Mama noticed it the next morning.

"Now Faith," she started as usual. "What in the world has gotten into you? You sick too?" Mama asked, frowning as she took sleeping Haley from my arms the next morning.

"Nah Ma, I'm okay. Haley just had a rough night and I didn't get much sleep," I lied.

"Humph, that no good husband of yours should have gotten up and helped you. I bet he didn't, did he?"

I almost laughed. The thought of Lucas helping was comedic. I chuckled and said, "Of course not, Ma. He was tired from work, so I just let him sleep." That was one way to explain it.

Mama turned to her bedroom and went to put Haley down, all the while, fussing. "I don't understand this new generation of men. Even though your daddy wasn't always home a lot, when he was he did everything he could to spend some time with you, especially if you were sick. And I never had to ask for help. That child belongs to you both."

I sat down on the couch and the tears just began to flow. Tears of frustration from years of neglect. Most people think that abuse is physical, and it can be. But the abuse I had endured from Lucas was mentally draining. The constant need to keep the peace and make things right for him was beginning to take its toll on me. I didn't want to cry, but my soul was aching at the thought of this being my reality forever.

"Faith, Faith, what's wrong?" Mama ran to my side and put her arm around me. Smothered in her bosom, I sobbed, and the sound of my cry rocked my entire being. She rocked me and held me. "Tell me baby, did he hit you? Did he? Because I'll kill him!"

"No Ma, he didn't hit me." I said through the tears. "I just don't understand why I have to live like this."

"Like what, Faith? Tell me what's wrong, baby." Mama's face was stricken with fear, agony over not knowing what was hurting me. I wanted to tell her, but I didn't know where to start. She began to pray, "Lord, I thank you for being my all, my rock, my sword and my shield. Lord I thank you for my Faith, my baby. You know all about it, Lord." I sobbed harder. "You know whatever it is, and I know that this is not a coincidence that she came here to me. Lord I pray that you would touch my baby in the name of Jesus, bind up every wicked thing that comes to steal, kill, and destroy. I speak life over my baby, strength, peace, in the name of Jesus. She will come out of this, whatever it is. Lord, we walk by faith and not by sight. That's why I named her that, Lord, because I believe you can do all things. Bless her now, keep her now, love on her Lord, in Jesus name, Amen." Mama rocked me and held me, and in that moment, I could feel all of God's love pouring into me through my mama. I never felt so safe and so protected in my entire life.

Wiping my eyes, I sat up trying to gather some words that would make sense. "Mama, I'm so miserable with him. I try to make him happy and he just keeps drinking, and he's so mean. I don't want Haley to grow up thinking this is what her daddy should be. Mama I'm tired of this." I gasped for a cry, but nothing came out, just a breath. My chest heaved as I clung to her waist.

"Baby, you don't have to tell me you're not happy, I can see it. I see it in your eyes, and that's not what God intended for you. But you have to pray and ask God to help your marriage, to help Lucas and work on him, and strengthen you. You been praying, Faith?"

"Mama, I don't have the strength to pray."

"Baby, that's where your strength comes from," she said, rubbing my tears away. "When you don't have anything else, you have God. Start praying baby. They don't have to be long prayers for God to hear them. He'll show you what to do."

"I don't even remember the last time he hugged me or told me he loved me. I just make him dinner and keep Haley quiet and try to keep him happy. I don't even know who I am anymore or how I became this shell of who I used to be. And you know the only place I find some peace, Ma?"

"Where baby?"

"At work. I feel so alive now that I'm back to work. It's like I have hope for something better. I don't know why I got this opportunity at this time, but it seems the more I want to work, the worse my family gets. I just want some peace."

"Faith, I believe God can change any situation. And you pray for His will for your life. God has a plan for you, and I believe nothing happens by accident. Maybe this job will show you who you are and help you to find strength for this next step in your life, wherever it takes you."

"I love you, Mama," I hugged her tight. There was nothing like being in Mama's arms. It takes away every fear and every doubt.

"I love you too, Faith. Now wipe your face, you got a job to get to, Ms. Reporter." Mama smiled, handing me a Kleenex. "And put some powder on so you don't look like you've been crying. Don't worry; it will be okay, baby. I believe it will."

"Thanks Ma, for everything."

Driving to work I was forced to have a moment with myself and God. It seemed that the car was becoming my own personal safe haven, and the drive between dropping Haley off and getting to work was therapeutic. Usually I would turn on my radio and blast some neo soul – some Jill Scott or John Legend –to get me in a happy state of mind. But today they were not doing it for me. So, I turned off the radio. I didn't want to hear about love or sad songs. I just wanted some quiet in my mind. And in my tranquil moments in the car, I began to think about what Mama said. And then my thinking became talking.

"It will be okay! I don't see how this can ever change. God I don't know why or how I ended up here. I know I have not been praying or anything like it, but I hope you can hear me. I remember the days I used to go to church and pray like a pro, but I feel powerless right now. This is not the way I planned it to be. I was supposed to have a happy marriage and a good family. Who did I end up with? The drunkard! And I don't even have the strength to fight him. I'm tired of walking around scared and miserable, and I refuse to allow Haley to believe this is as good as it gets. God I need some help. I don't want to give up on my marriage, but I don't want to stay miserable either. Please show me what to do. Thank you. Amen"

"Now, Faith pull it together," I said wiping away the last tears. "Put some powder on and go in there and do your job." Glancing in the mirror as I drove into the parking lot, I fixed my makeup and put a little concealer over the bags under my eyes. "You *will* have a good day," I spoke as I grabbed my briefcase and hopped out of the car.

"Good morning," Jonathan greeted me as I stepped into his office. "I'm glad to see you're early, we have some breaking news this morning and no time to lose. Let me brief you. Have a seat."

Jonathan motioned for the couch and grabbed two manila folders off of his desk. I recognized one from the public school system case I had been working on. I had been so busy last night with Lucas that I didn't even watch the news. So, I knew notes were in order.

Opening the first folder, he began. "Remember the public school program that I had you researching the other day? Well, there have been new developments that just surfaced last night. Mr. Emerson, president of that department, was found dead in a hotel last night. Apparently, he was at the Hilton for the scholarship banquet and had gotten a room for the evening. Reporters said that he had taken a walk outside of the party with a gentleman from the school board and wasn't seen again until they found the body. Foul play is suspected and there are no suspects as of yet."

"Oh my God," I gasped, remembering the research I had just finished. This man was no ordinary Joe. He had worked his way up from an assistant to president of one of the largest branches of the school system. He was recognized for his work in providing opportunities for students to participate in after school sports, extra-curricular activities, and job placement. I recalled from his bio that he had a wife and two children and was a public school graduate. "Wow, is there any reason to suspect foul play?"

"Well according to my few leads that I spoke to at the news station, there were some documents concerning the budget of his program found in his room and considering they are under investigation, it's rumored that there may have been some information that should not have gotten out."

"So, what happens now?" I inquired, wondering what our role would be in this investigation.

Jonathan smiled, "Now, you get a taste of real investigative reporting. Our number one goal is to get the story before the next paper does. Today, reporters will be questioning most of his staff and family, so we start where no one else will." Jonathan had a glimmer in his eye, as if his adrenaline was already flowing and he was on the hunt for his next victim.

"And where is that?" I wondered anxiously.

"We start with the help." Jonathan beamed. "Get your pad and let's go." No sooner than I'd come in and sat down, we were off and on our way. I welcomed the change of pace and scenery because just that quickly I had realized that there was no time for tears. There was a job to be done whether all was well at home or not. And I was determined to get it done.

As Lucas attempted to drain out of me every bit of joy I had daily, my work and my Haley overflowed with the pouring out of love and dedication to them both. Since the announcement of Mr. Emerson's death, there had not been a dull day at work which left me no time to consider my life at home. It was almost as if I buried my head in the sand and came out only to work and play with our daughter. Lucas complained and fussed, but it didn't seem to bother me as much. My mornings and evenings in the car had grown less congested with sultry singing and more filled with my confessions and requests to

God through prayer. Sometimes I just thanked Him for getting through another night with Lucas. Other times I prayed for clarity and peace of mind. I don't know if it was all the praying or my renewed zeal in this internship, but every day seemed to bring a little bit more of my smile out and I felt better. Something was shifting in the atmosphere.

Shifts dictate change, and change is unwelcome to those who are in a position of comfort. Lucas was threatened and even annoyed by my new sense of calm, and even his ugliest ranting and drunken stupors seemed to roll off my back after a couple of weeks. It felt like I was beginning to find me again, and that's when Lucas began to object to my self-awareness.

Friday nights were no big deal in my house anymore. They used to be the highlight of the week, signaling two days of partying, relaxation, and enjoyment with friends and family. They once were a day I looked forward to all week. They signaled freedom, inhibition, and the possibility of adventure. My Fridays have been transformed to a day of dread. They now signal bondage, captivity, and two full days of making nice with Lucas while keeping Haley entertained. They are exhausting days and Monday can never come fast enough. Go figure!

So, I assumed that today, the third Friday of my internship, would be no different. But this assumption proved to be the exact opposite of the truth. To my surprise, after three weeks of investigating and reporting, Mr. Jonathan Reynolds put in a recommendation for me to begin as a reporter's assistant effective immediately. He said he saw some spark in me that he hadn't seen in a long time, and while my writing could still stand for improvement, with some guidance and direction he felt I would be an asset to the Sun! I was so ecstatic that I jumped up and hugged him immediately and then quickly pulled back, realizing that I had crossed the boundaries. Mr. Reynolds laughed and excused my excitement. Although he was serious, he said he understood my enthusiasm and it should be a cause to celebrate.

Who knew when I woke up this day that I would encounter such a life changing, mind-blowing experience? This was my confirmation, my affirmation, the push that would propel me into a new thing. I decided right then in Jonathan's office that this would be the beginning of a new chapter of my life, and hence it was signaling the end of the current chapter.

It's amazing how clarity of vision can bring such peace and comfort to one's spirit. Just three weeks ago I stood in my shower crying, pouring my heart out to God, and asking Him to help me save myself and my marriage. And now, in the stillness of my soul, I could hear God's small voice saying, "you're free." What does freedom mean to a creature of flight that has been trapped in a cage for years? Every morning she has awakened to find the cage locked and the semblance of light covered by the drape of darkness. The slightest glimpse of illumination was so frightening and unfamiliar that she shied away from even peeking at it. They say that the body will adjust to what it is surrounded by. If there is immense light, the pupils will adjust to let less light in to shield the corneas from damage. Similarly, in a black abyss, the eyes will dilate to allow maximum light to come into the eye. Much like cats, even the darkest places can seem to have traces of light because the eyes have become so accustomed to visualizing darkness. Yet, when the veil is removed, when the sheet disappears suddenly, without warning, what does the body do? With no alternative to its new surroundings, it is forced to adjust – immediately. If the eyes will not be destroyed by the intensity of this newness, they must shield themselves slightly until they have adjusted. And when the time is right... they will open and let the light in.

Although my epiphany had been realized, putting it into action was going to take some creativity on my part. My first thought was escape; pick up with Haley, head into the abyss, and run blindly – toward Mama's house, where I'd be found within an hour. I had to laugh at that myself. Realistically speaking, escape was no longer an option in the flight sense of the word.

With Jonathan having offered me a job, I have to stay in the general city limits, which means moving forward would have to in some way involve Lucas. Something inside of me shifted, but reality reminded me that this shift was not a joint venture. Surely, Lucas will protest at the most extreme level about my permanent job and what it would mean to our routines. Yet, the impossibility of being independent had somehow been lifted. In its place came this new idea "reinvention." If I could not change Lucas and could not up and disrupt my surroundings, something had to change in me. Working with Jonathan has allowed me to recognize strength, determination, drive, and value in myself that I hadn't felt since college. There was no one cheering me on, telling me what I was capable of, or that I could pursue my dream and my purpose. The only person in my ear was my husband, reminding me of my wifely duties and responsibilities and how those trumped any ambitious desires I may have once had. Therefore, in order for Faith to flourish and my sanity to survive, I have to redefine my mindset and mentality. What does reinvention look like to someone who has become a shell of who she once was? It means finding yourself again. Only I have no clue where to begin looking.

I head home and I go through my routines, and every time I pick up Haley, I feel closer to her. I am focused on her happiness and her learning, more so than my pain. When Lucas comes in this evening, I am not held hostage by the mood his day left behind, nor am I concerned with how to pull him out of it. Instead, I am calm and cool. Lucas is somewhat taken aback by this but does not mention it. But I can tell. He has no reason to yell because I don't argue. I am Ms. Agreeable tonight because I understand that this season of being less than is coming to an end. It is an eerie type of peace that has come over me and I know that it is God working on my behalf. I can feel something inside of me that is almost guiding my thoughts and moving my mouth. As I lay down in the bed, Lucas grabs me for his weekly dose of anything but intimacy, and I don't flinch. I don't cry. I know that this will not last. My heart and my emotions are tucked away in a place he cannot reach them. I pretend to enjoy, and when he rolls over, I lay motionless, praying silently asking God how I can physically escape this situation my mind has been freed from.

~

A Way of Escape

"Just let go, let it flow, let it flow, let it flow. Everything's gonna work out right you know. Just let go, let it go, let it go, just let it go, baby...."

–TONI BRAXTON, WAITING TO EXHALE

A wise man once said, "You can't see what's ahead of you if you are busy watching what's behind you." It seemed that my lesson on how to find freedom from where I currently resided was wrapped up in my ability to visualize a reality beyond my present state of being. It's much easier to say, "I'm going to leave," than actually setting the wheels in motion to make departure possible. Mama made it clear to me that she would be there for me and Haley if we needed her, but her burdens were heavy enough as it was and the thought of adding two new estrogen producers to a quite headstrong woman's household did not thrill me in the least. As much as I wanted to just jump overboard, into the depths of the unknown life of independence, single motherhood, and a career of fulfillment, I realized that I had become a dependent housewife, with very little savings with which to start fresh.

So, waking up after a night of Lucas's pleasure and my agony, I decided that I was going to pack my tears away. No more feeling sorry for myself, crying, and asking why this was happening, or just dreaming about what I wanted my life to be and wondering why it was not. Instead I would focus my energies on excelling at work, being a super mom to Haley, stacking my chips in a separate account, and keeping Lucas content and remaining indifferent to his ways. The thought of the task that stood before me was daunting and terrifying. If Lucas ever found out my plans, it would be hell, or as close to it on Earth as possible. Hence, this month's goal was discretion.

For the next several days, I buried myself in my new assignments. Although Jonathan's recommendation was highly regarded in our office, the validity of his judgment and the fate of my future rested in my ability to prove that I was an asset and not a liability to the Sun. Initially, I was working with Jonathan, however, he wanted to afford me the opportunity to work with other reporters. As he put it, "Wouldn't want anyone thinking you're the teacher's pet or that you used methods of persuasion to gain your position." Clearly that was the last impression I wanted anyone to have of me, so I welcomed the break from Mr. Reynolds, as I called him in mixed company to ensure no misunderstandings.

I was paired up with two women who were legendary in their own right with the Sun. Martina Bell was my immediate new supervisor, and she made Jonathan's initial aloofness seem like welcoming arms. Martina was all business, no jokes, no conversation, and no interest in who you are. The only thing that interested Martina was a story that was newsworthy. Whether out in the streets doing interviews or behind her desk writing, Martina's 5'2" Latina personality shone through her soft appearance. Upon first glance, she seemed like a meek, fairly pretty, Hispanic woman. But underneath the surface lurked the makings of a journalism drill sergeant. Working with her for the first few weeks reminded me that I was an assistant. I knew based on our first conversation.

"Hi, I'm Faith. Jonathan assigned me to assist you for the next two weeks. I'd like to say, I admire your work and I look forward to working with you."

Martina looked over her glasses at me, from top to bottom, returned her attention to her computer screen and replied, "I am busy right now. You can start by getting me coffee, two creams, three sugars."

Talk about demeaning. I was taken aback but I agreed. When I returned to her desk I carefully set her coffee down, and she typed as if I was invisible and didn't even say thank you. So, I decided to break the ice with a question.

"When I was with Jonathan, I helped him out researching his stories, gathering information from interviews and recording my notes. How can I assist you, Ms. Bell?

She stopped typing and replied, clearly annoyed, "I type my own stories and do my own interviews. If you want to help me, go to the news board, and find some interesting stories fresh out that I can write about. Don't waste my time with homicides – that's not my division. Politics is okay, but I prefer to deal with stories that deal with national and international affairs. When you think you find something, report it to me before you write my name next to it." I nod as I take notes and smile. She didn't return the smile.

"No problem, Ms. Bell. I will work on that right away," I said as I began to gather my things.

Martina turned around and began typing again, "Good," I heard her say as the click clack of the keys continued. *So much for building a rapport with her,* I thought. I did not let it discourage me, though, I was determined to find the most interesting stories on the board for her to write and force her to recognize my eye for a good story.

One week in, I had found the perfect story. It was not politically driven but had a hint of international government set into it. The current ruler of Egypt was being protested because of his radical ways and it had led to protests throughout the streets of Northern Africa. People of all ages had been taken captive and hostages were being threatened and executed for violations of curfews. When I first saw it, I didn't think Martina would bite. But I brought it to her because of her desire to cover international affairs. The look in her eyes was worth my entire week of tiptoeing around her feistiness and fetching coffee.

"Yes...yes, yes, yes! She exclaimed at the glance over the information. "Now this is what I'm talking about. Good job Faith."

I was standing in amazement that she even remembered

my name. All week there had been little more than grunts and "no, find another story" each time I came to see her. My face was beaming with pride, and inside I silently said my own *"yes!"*

"What do we do now, Ms. Bell?" I asked, afraid that the inclusion of me would be nonexistent.

"Well, we start by gathering all the information that is on the board. This has been going on for 12 hours, so we need to be the first paper to publish. CNN probably has the basics running in their byline by now, but there are no stories out as of yet. Why don't you begin to gather everything you can from the news stations? I'm going to put in some calls to try and contact the U.S. Embassy in Egypt. Let's plan to meet back in two hours and report our findings, okay?" Although it was a question, it was more like an expectation. I was so thrilled that she trusted me to do anything, I blurted out, "Absolutely, I'm on it!" and ran away to begin my research.

As I powered up my computer, I realized it was 3:45p.m. I usually leave by 5p.m. and there was no way I was cutting out on this opportunity. It was time to call in a favor to Mama and Ms. Robinson.

After talking to Mama, she agreed to pick Haley up and call Ms. Robinson. The difficult part would be talking to Lucas and explaining that I'd be home late, which meant no dinner for him. I opted out of talking and decided to text him instead. *"Working late, Mama's getting Haley, you will have to pick up dinner. Be home around 8."*

His reply was much more descriptive: *"WTH, working late? Tell them no and come home with Haley."*

I sighed as it seemed that this conversation would have to be had over the phone. I reluctantly picked up the phone to call and took a deep breath, "Lord, be with me," I said as his line rang.

"Yeah, you get my text?" Lucas said, clearly irritated with this situation.

"Yes. I can't talk long, but I can't tell them no. I just got a new assignment and we need the story out tomorrow. It's going to be at least three more hours before we are done here, that's why I asked Mama to get Haley."

"See, this is the type of shit I thought would happen when you got this job, Faith!" Lucas was clearly on edge and I needed to diffuse this soon or else Martina would overhear, and I didn't need her involved.

"Lucas," I scream whispered, "This is the *first* story I've gotten in over a week and I'm going to take it! It's just a few hours. You can grab food and I'll meet you at home. There's no need to be upset." I tried to calm my voice as I could feel my blood pressure rising along with my tone.

"Yeah, whatever. Tell that man you working with that if you stay late one more night, I will have to come talk to him myself. Cause my wife ain't about to be working up under him all night when you should be home with me!" Lucas clicked off before I could say anything else.

I must have appeared noticeably shaken, because when the mailroom attendant, Erma, walked by my cubicle, she asked, "Hey lady, you okay?" I had come to know all of the non-writers on staff from running errands and getting coffee. Erma was in her mid-forties and had been there for five years. She said she enjoyed running the mailroom and the carts because it gave her exercise and allowed her to interact with people without being too responsible for anything. She was responsible for enough at home with her three kids, and her income was solely to pay for their incidentals, as her husband was a big-wig at an engineering firm downtown. Erma was never seen without her cart, her coffee cup, and her Bible.

"Hey Erma, just had a rough conversation. But I'll be okay," I lied. Lucas had shaken me so that I was unaware that I was hunched over and tense from my neck down to my lower back from the thought of what the rest of the night would be like.

"Honey, I have learned one thing in all these years watching people being stressed out over this job. Paul said it best in Philippians 4:16. Mind if I read it to you?" she asked.

"Sure."

"I can do all things through Christ who strengthens me. We can't always handle everything on our own, Faith, but with God, we can. Just believe in Him and ask for strength. He'll see you through." Erma smiled and patted my back gently.

"Thanks, I sure needed that Erma," I exhaled and felt the tension relax a bit. "Have a good rest of your day."

"I will, you too!" Erma winked and walked away. It seems that God plants people at just the right place and at the right time. I replayed the scripture in my head and realized that I had lost 20 minutes of valuable research time. I couldn't spend the next two hours worried about Lucas. I had to finish my research. And that's just what I did.

At 6:45 p.m., after meeting with Martina, who was extremely pleased with my work, so much so that she brought *me* a cup of coffee, I began to pack up my things and get ready to leave. I was starving and knew I had to pick up some food on the way home before I got Haley and prepare myself mentally for my encounter with Lucas. Just as I was powering off my laptop, Martina walked up.

"Faith, I was very impressed with your work today. I will write the first part of the story, but if this goes the way it seems to be heading, we may have to go out and do some field work. I usually travel alone, but considering you have done the research, I will try and put a bid in for you to tag along, if you don't mind?"

If my mouth was open any wider, I probably would have swallowed a swarm of flies. "Wow, thank you, Ms. Bell. What does field work entail exactly?" I asked.

"Well, usually, I interview and scope out leads here. However, since this story is rooted in Egypt, it may involve travel to D.C. or even overseas."

"Uh...," I stuttered for the first time in my life. I didn't want to decline the opportunity. However, I knew this would cause major waves in my already stormy home life. "I have a two-year old daughter, so I am not sure about the travel. It depends on how long. I will need to know the details first. But I'd like to go, if possible."

"I'll know for sure first thing in the morning and you can make your decision then," Martina answered. "I'll let you know. This doesn't happen often, so if you get a chance like this, you ought to take it."

"I will keep that in mind. Thank you again and goodnight, Ms. Bell."

"Goodnight, Faith."

As I rushed home to avoid a further outlandish evening with Lucas, my mind wandered to the possibilities that Ms. Bell had just presented me with. If I was approved to go on this trip, this could put me in contact with so many different news media and investigative reporters, and also I'd have experience on my resume that most people would never be afforded. Plus, who could pass up a trip to Egypt, even if it was in turmoil? I have always wanted to see Africa.

"Who are you kidding," I said discouragingly, "There is no way that I can leave Haley for any extended time, and Lucas would probably chain me to the bed before he let me go that far out of his sight. "But it sure would be great if I could," I dreamed as I pulled up to Mama's house.

"Hey Ma," I waved as she came to the door with Haley in her arms smiling with her apron on. My mother just loved cooking and whenever she got the chance she was always conjuring up some new recipe. Haley was smiling and clapping as I bounded up the stairs and hugged them both.

"Come on in, Faith, I just got done making this dish I found on Food Network," Mama said as she pulled me into the house eager to have a first taste tester.

"Ma, you know I can't stay. I'll taste it, but I told Lucas I'd be home by 7 and it's already almost 8. I didn't cook dinner or anything."

"Girl, you should stop tripping over what that man thinks. I know things aren't great, but you can't keep tiptoeing around him. Have you been praying on this thing? I just don't think this is where you're supposed to be if you are so scared to be yourself or even stay late at work. As much as your father and I argued when we were married, God rest his soul, I was never afraid to speak my mind or do what I pleased."

"Look Ma, I know. I just have to do this in my own time. I have been praying, and I know I want to be free. But I'm not sure if I want to just walk out now. I have to have a plan and need time to get permanently hired to be able to support me and Haley. There's a ton to consider, Ma."

"Well consider what will happen if you stay, especially with Haley. I can always help you out. If I have to go back to work, I will."

That was the last thing I needed, Mama going back to work after being retired and then working in some Wal-Mart or other store that showed no respect for elders. "No, Ma, I will work it out. I actually got word of a great opportunity at work today, but I doubt that I can do it." I picked up one of Mama's bite-size hors d'oeuvres sitting on the counter. "This is delicious, Ma. But what is it?" I laughed and sank my teeth into the second half and was already reaching for seconds before she answered.

"That is a hand-wrapped spinach and mushroom pie with feta cheese. I learned a trick on how to hide it all in the dough so it's like a surprise bite. Good, huh?" Ma took one and nodded emphatically in amazement at her own creation. "Now, Faith, tell me about this opportunity. You know if God puts an opportunity before you, it's because He has already made a way for it to be successful."

"Well, you know I've been working with Martina Bell at the Sun, and up until today she had little more to say to me besides "get my coffee" or "check the board!" I imitated her and waved my hands like she does, clearly blowing me off. "Today I actually found a story on the board she liked, and she asked me to research it and she got all excited. I think it was the first time she's ever given me a real assignment. But anyway, the story turned out to be about the crisis in Egypt, and after we went over all the details she said we may have to travel there to the Embassy to follow the story. She offered that to me, Ma!!" I was beaming as I said it, and the reality of the possibility of my dream of journalism being actualized.

"Praise the Lord, Faith! That is wonderful! Wow, Egypt. I've never been to Africa, but I always wanted to go. Your daddy felt like if you couldn't drive there, then it was too far to travel to; said we might get stuck there and never see freedom again." She shook her head and chuckled. "I don't know why I listened to that. Oh, but Faith, if you could go, that would be such a moving experience, and I'm sure you'd meet a ton of reporters and make some connections. Who knows where this could take you?" Mama was more excited than I was at this moment. She turned to me and realized my smile had dissipated.

"What is it dear?" Excitement shifted to anxiety and concern as Mama stopped babbling and sat down next to me as I held Haley in my arms.

"How could I leave Haley, Ma? And you know Lucas will never agree to this. Even if I had arrangements for Haley, Lucas would probably go crazy if I told him about this. I don't even feel like arguing about it. If Martina says I can go, I'll just tell her to get someone else." Sinking back into the chair, Haley scooted off my lap and walked across the kitchen to pick up a pot she proceeded to bang. How I longed to be two again where the toughest decision was what toy to play with. No cares, no worries, no stress.

"And pass up possibly the greatest opportunity in your career? Maybe Lucas needs to see that your world can go on if he is not there. And you know I will keep Haley. He won't dare come over here and mess with me, so she'll be fine." Mama took my hand, "Faith look at me. I have watched you suffer with this man for years and have said little or nothing about it, because that's your marriage and I know I should keep my nose out of it. But some men don't learn to appreciate what they have until it's gone. Now you can stay here and feel sorry for yourself and "keep the peace" in your house, what little of it there is, and miss out on God's blessing for you, or you can decide to do something for yourself. Step out on faith, baby. God will handle the rest."

The tears were flowing now, as I listened to Mama. Faith was something that I had been praying for more of; faith to walk away, to know I would be alright. I wish God would just drop what I needed in my lap, but I don't think that's how He works. Apparently, in order to get to that level, you have to believe. It had been years since I had believed in anything coming to me, and the thought of God opening this door for me was over-whelming, yet terrifying. I decided I would sleep on it and see what tomorrow would bring. At least I had enough faith to get through the night.

"I'll see Ma," I said. "Ms. Bell will let me know tomorrow, and then I'll make my decision. Thanks for picking up Haley, I'd better get going before Lucas texts me or calls looking for me. I love you, Ma," I kissed her cheek and hugged her as I wiped my face. I gathered Haley up, we said goodbye and headed home.

How can your name be so wrapped up in your destiny? Faith. It had always been an unusual name amongst friends at school and I often got called Faith Evans, after the popular 90s singer, but not until I was an adult did I truly realize the mag-nitude of my name. The Bible says, "Now faith is the substance of things hoped for, and the evidence of things not seen." – Heb-rews 12:1. That is my mother's favorite verse, hence my name, and why she always shares her deepest feelings with me by beginning with "Now Faith." But truly, faith has not been the driving force in my life. It always seemed to me that luck just seemed to be on my side. When I was almost struck by a racing car at the age of six, I saw it just as being fortunate to be alive. At 16, when I was approached with sex and drugs and turned them down, I just considered that my upbringing with the strict-est Mama in Chicago was enough to have made the difference. Applications for college were completed, then denied, then ac-cepted with scholarships. Never did it occur to me that someone had faith for these things to happen.

My grandmother, Nana Mimi, was always the praying grandmother. But I never learned this until I was talking to her a couple of days before my wedding day. Nana Mimi and I had gone to lunch and I began to ask her about her and Grandpops' marriage and how she had managed to stay with the same man for 40+ years and hadn't killed him yet. Nana Mimi, in her wise yet comforting way, proceeded to tell me about how they had started out and had many problems. "It wasn't always good," I recall her saying. "There were years when I didn't think we'd make it, especially after I found out he had an affair and was running the streets."

I remember thinking how astonished I was to find out that Pops had cheated on Nana. This realization caused me to reenact every argument they'd had, revisit in my mind all the times Pops was out of the house, and for a minute, I resented him. Nana wasn't the easiest person to get along with, but she was a wonderful wife and mother, and certainly didn't deserve that. But Nana, seeing my inner turmoil, quickly righted my thoughts. "Oh honey, no one has a perfect marriage. So, don't think that I didn't love Pops or anything. I had times I was upset with him, but I stayed prayerful. When it got really ugly, I'd talk to my sister and try to talk to him, but most times I just talked to God. I read my word and I stayed because I had faith in God and my husband. I knew that he was a good provider; he loved our children, and me, more than anything. When the good outweighs the bad, you make it work. Faith and communication kept us together. Just remember that when times get rough. And pray on it, God will show you."

It seemed that Nana Mimi's words were never more relevant. And as I recalled her words, I began to pray for faith. As pastor said, faith is putting your confidence, trust, and belief in God. This decision to go to Africa would truly have to be a leap of faith. There was no guarantee that when I returned I'd even have a marriage, a job, or stability for that matter. But everything in me said it was the right thing to do. This trip would be an escape for me – not to escape my problems, but my fears. My fears of stepping out into the world and taking risks had to be faced. Fear is a crippling emotion, and I had become a paraplegic to my insecurities. Yet when I looked at my other options, staying home with Lucas, being miserable, and counting the days until I was ready to leave, taking his abuse in the process, Egypt looked pretty awesome. I told God that if I stepped out on faith and did this, all I wanted was for my Haley to be provided for. I wanted to be able to support us, do enough for her to have a good life, and make sure that she knew the true meaning of love and did not accept abuse as her reality. As I closed my eyes and said Amen, I believed that I was sealing my fate and it was out of my hands. If the possibility arrived, I decided I would take it. No matter the consequences.

"Faith, may I see you in my office for a moment?" I heard Martina say as I hung up the phone at my desk and took a deep breath.

Here goes, I thought. *It's in your hands, God*, I prayed as I slowly arose and walked down to her office. This moment would seal the deal one way or the other, and I just had to trust that it would be the decision I was hoping for.

"Sit down," she motioned for a chair across from her desk as I sauntered in. "I talked to Jonathan this morning and let him know of our possible investigation and coverage in Egypt. Did you give it any more thought last night?" She seemed to be genuinely interested in my opinion and waited patiently for my response.

"Yes, Ms. Bell, I have considered this opportunity. If I were to be honest, I must say that I was humbled at the idea of having such an experience afforded to me. Being a young mother, I had to put my career on hold to start a family, and now that I have rediscovered my passion for journalism, I want to dive in. So yes, I have thought about it, and if the opportunity is still available, I am up for the challenge." Looking at Ms. Bell, it was hard to read the emotion I saw on her face, but it appeared that my words had softened her hard exterior for a moment.

"Well, Faith, I don't believe any intern has ever come into the Sun and within a month or two gotten a chance to work with two of the top people in the paper." It was clear that she had no problems patting herself on the back. "But according to Jonathan, in his words exactly, 'I'd be stupid to leave a young aspiring talented and hard-working woman behind, when you could possibly be the next great thing to hit the Sun.' I respect his opinion more than anyone else here, so pack your bags, Faith... we're going to Egypt." She stood and extended her hand to me.

There are few moments in life that cause time to stop and overwhelm your entire being so much so that you are left speechless. But at this moment, I am at a complete loss. "Thank you, Ms. Bell, you won't be disappointed in me." I tried to hide the quiver in my voice, unsuccessfully so. "When do we leave?"

"Monday, at 8 from O'Hare. And since we'll be working together quite a bit for the next two weeks, we should be on a first name basis. Call me Martina," she remarked, smiling. "Oh, and if I were you, I'd be giving big time 'thank yous' to Mr. Reynolds."

"Absolutely, Ms...I mean Martina. I will do so right now." I turned to walk out of her office.

"And Faith, come back and let's spend the rest of the day prepping for this assignment. We need to be prepared fully for what lies ahead." As I turned to walk away, one tear cascaded slowly down my cheek. I walked out and wiped it away, astonished by what had just occurred. It was confirmed...I was stepping out on faith.

I'd love to say that Lucas dismissed me with no arguments and with his blessings. But it was much the opposite. I didn't know how to tell Lucas at first, so I decided I would just get all the arrangements together with Mama and then let him know. His response was less than grateful, and in actuality, I think he was so shocked at my determination that he was speechless. After I told him how it all came together and that my decision was final, he simply said, "You know Faith, if you do this, you are choosing that job over me. And frankly, when you leave, I can't guarantee I'll be here when you get back."

I suppose if my heart were still set on making things work, this would have floored me. However, I was quite calm. As I packed my things, I told Lucas, "I can't tell you what to do, and if you make that your decision, I have to respect it. When I come back, we will see what happens. As for now, if you want to see Haley, Mama's number is there, and you are welcome to call and meet her somewhere or bring her home with you." I knew that he wouldn't dare try to keep Haley with him without any help, so this offer was merely a formality. After a long evening of silence, he decided to go out, then came in later very intoxicated. He passed out on the couch after I told him he couldn't come to bed, since Haley was in there with me. That was my only saving grace. All weekend Lucas worked, and we slept separately. I was starting to believe that maybe it would just be easier than I ever thought. Maybe God was working this out to be painless.

That was too good to be true. Monday morning, as I prepared to leave, Lucas approached me. "Look Faith, I don't know why you would decide to take this trip and how you expect me to just be okay with it. I am not supposed to have my wife off traipsing around Egypt while I'm left here. If you really loved me, you would stay here and be with me." From anyone else, these words may be touching, yet coming from Lucas it was more like a threat than a plea. He realized that I was leaving and was laying the guilt trip on thick.

"I've made up my mind, Lucas, and I can't back out on this opportunity. If you love me, you will understand and wish me luck," I bargained.

"Yeah, well, good luck leaving your family. Lots of good you are." And with that, I walked out on Lucas and into my new career.

~

There is More

My child sitting at the pool,
Be not disturbed, don't lose your cool

I ask - do you want to be made whole?
Perhaps you've forgotten I've already seen the blueprint
Unfold
and
There is more
You're life's plan surrendered into my hand
Don't you understand?
I wait patiently for you to decide you're ready to be through
Waiting on insignificant idols to deliver what you're due
Because I came that you might live beyond mediocrity
Dreams above and beyond what your eyes can see
Accept my love and ability to do exceedingly and abundantly
There's no limit to my love and generosity
I am asking you to come soar with me
Leave behind those who are bound by their insecurities
Refuse to settle for the hope of what could be
Don't you know our father already has it worked out?
I don't understand what you keep crying about
If you could see from the seat at which I sit
You'd laugh over the trivial circumstances
That are giving you a fit.

You would see your life's not about to end
In actuality, it is just the beginning, my friend
See, in order for you to fulfill your role
It was inevitable that some relationships
would have to grow old
Locations change and friendships rearrange
But it's all for your gain
Because there is more
Facing broken dreams and the devil's schemes
Help me Lord, you implore,
And He answers,
There is more
I know you're staring at physical instabilities
But I've come to remind you of your spiritual destiny

There is more
On the wings of grace you can soar
There is more
More opportunities, more open doors
There is more
You were predestined to touch lives
Jesus came to remind you - there is more.

~

Stepping out on Faith

No experience in life can prepare you for a trip to the Motherland. As a Black woman, I have always dreamed of visiting Africa and experiencing the home of our ancestors with my own senses. Although this was not a dream vacation, considering we were entering into one of the most volatile areas in the world, it was truly an awe-inspiring vision. Lying before me within driving distance stood the Great Pyramids at Giza. Everywhere we turned there were armed militia and people in a frenzy: reporters, protestors, government officials, and the people. In a rainbow of browns and tans, I glanced around and saw the beauty of the African race. Although Egypt is sometimes considered its own entity, separate from Africa, this was still the place where at some point the ancestors of the people in the U.S. had come from. I imagined that I would see them in robes or some other garb which resembled the Biblical times, but to my surprise they were dressed like normal people. I wanted to laugh out loud as I realized that I had been a victim of the stereotypes of Africans in jungle-like conditions or walking around like the children seen in videos for organizations that fed needy children.

The city of Cairo was a marketplace of activity. The streets were lined with beautiful towering palm trees swaying in the wind, and buildings all around, indicating the flourishing enterprises in the city. People traveled in sandals, due to the heat, around the streets talking to merchants and each other. During the day, there was no curfew imposed on the citizens, so it was clear that every citizen was taking advantage of the freedom to move around in the safety of the daylight. Martina made reservations for us at a local hotel in the heart of the city, close enough to the U.S. Embassy to get there in case there was a need to move to safety. Martina was well-travelled, and it was apparent that none of the splendor of Africa was affecting her. Watching her interact with other reporters and maneuver around, I quickly snapped back into reality, understanding that I had to blend in and that I was here to do a job, not sightsee. Although, I was determined to pick up a few souvenirs.

After checking into our room, Martina and I met in the lobby at a small table situated on the patio to discuss our plan of action. "First of all, you can see that we are going to be subjected to the curfew during the evening, so we have to choose to spend our daytime hours wisely. There is a rally expected to be happening this afternoon with the president and some other elected officials to discuss the new policies. It is expected to be heavily populated with protestors, as well as the military, but there is a special section for reporters. After we eat and freshen up, we should head out to make sure that we are able to get a good spot." Martina functioned like a professional at all times; driven and focused, relinquishing all emotion, and channeling her energy into the task at hand. I took notes as she spoke and glanced around every so often to see if anyone was listening to our conversation. Most people there were speaking Arabic, so they paid very little attention to us, as we probably stuck out as tourists or reporters, considering the circumstances.

"Sounds good. Once we are there, are we attempting to get any interviews with protestors or just focus on the speeches of the officials?" I inquired, curious as to what spin we would be putting on the story.

"To start out, we'll just take notes on the speeches. I have my voice recorder so that we will be able to sort out everything and form our articles. In the event that we have a chance to get close to the protestors, our biggest challenge will be finding someone that speaks English well enough to talk with us."

It had never occurred to me that we would not be able to communicate as easily with the people. That could present a challenge. "I see, well I will make sure to listen out for anyone speaking our lingo, and if so, we can speak with them." Martina rose to leave, and I followed suit.

"Well, let me call and let them know we made it and I'll meet you back down here around 1?" I said glancing at my watch. The jet lag was beginning to kick in and my body was screaming that it was the middle of the night, while my watch read 11a.m. So much for rest.

"Great," Martina responded. "Make sure you wear comfy clothing and shoes; we want to be able to move quickly and blend in when the need arises."

I said okay and headed over past the front desk to the elevator area.

Later on that afternoon, Martina and I met in the lobby along with our cameraman and his team. In an effort to blend in with the citizens, I chose a white V-neck shirt with a black blazer on top and a pair of khakis. I looked professional, with a common touch. Martina gave me a once over and a nod. She was wearing blue jeans, a tan jacket and flats, and with her hair pulled back, she could almost pass for Egyptian, unless she spoke and her thick Spanish accent gave her away. As Martina gave directions, I glanced outside the lobby door and could see the Egyptian militia waving protestors along as they chanted something in Arabic. The protestors were orderly, but as we stood discussing our direction, the crowd seemed to multiply by the second. *What have I gotten myself into?* The glitz and glamour of journalism quickly dissipated as I realized that we were walking directly into the mob and could easily be taken into any unforeseen situation. Martina turned back to me and said, "We will be heading towards the front of the crowd, near the stage, where the reporters' area is. Once we arrive, there will be space for us, but it may be rough getting through all the protestors. Remember what you see and hear. There won't be time to write until we are in position, but since we're in the heart of the action, there will be plenty to take in." I nodded as she bellowed out the instructions casually, and my heart raced with anxiety. She turned on her heels and headed for the door. "Oh, and Faith?" Martina spun around, "Don't get separated; we may never find each other."

"Right," I stammered. Just the vote of confidence I needed. The revolving doors to the hotel spit us out into the crowd and what seemed to be order from inside was truly chaos on steroids. Everywhere we turned there were groups of men with Egyptian flags and signs, marching and chanting in rows running through the already compacted crowds. Some women stood around chanting with children in tow, some with babies on their backs. It amazed me how people of foreign nations would carry their children into the most dangerous situations for a cause. Americans, seemed, at least in this instance, to have a little more restraint. We became like fish in a sea of waves swimming through the people as they chanted and moved. We moved and swayed, and I took it all in. To my right about a block down was the stage where microphones were set for the upcoming press conference. In the distance I could make out TV cameras and a small group of reporters. I imagined that many of the others here were also stuck in limbo amongst the crowd as we were, waiting to be dumped at the stage by the moving mass of protestors. I kept my eye on Martina and stayed within a few feet of her. This was the real thing, and as terrified as I was, it was somewhat exhilarating. Who would have imagined two years ago that this sort of opportunity would have arisen for me?

Walking by a woman with a child about Haley's age in her arms, I thought of my family back home. I wondered what their afternoon was like. Mama was probably tending to Haley, and Lucas was at work, surely not thinking of me. Just the thought of him started to give me a headache and made my stomach hurt. I will not worry about that," I said aloud to myself.

Martina turned around, "What did you say?" she said straining to hear me and keep in the flow.

I hadn't realized that was an audible thought. "Oh nothing, I was just thinking aloud. These people don't seem to be worried at all." Although Martina was warming up to me, I was surely not going to spill my guts to her, especially not in our present circumstances.

"No, they know that if they get out of hand this will be shut down, so they know how far to go. We are almost there anyways, so be sure to stay close. The crowd is getting thicker."

And stay close I did, until we reached the designated section for the media. From a helicopter, the reporter's area could easily have been compared to an army of ants swarming on a piece of lost food. The central portion of the media section was where all the mics were set up, and it was clear that our attempt at an early arrival was made in vain. Reporters from various countries - France, Germany, Brazil, South Africa, China, and of course, the U.S. - were set up around the press conference area giving debriefings of the situation. It was clear by the number of empty Starbucks cups in the waste can that these people had camped out their spots since early this morning. "Perhaps, we shouldn't have taken that nap," I said to Martina, as we glanced around at the crowds.

"Either way, it would still look like this. We will just squeeze in and find a spot. Let's go in the direction of the U.S. reporters, over to the left." She motioned with her arm and the cameraman and I followed obediently. As we walked by, I listened to the reporters talking. It's funny how some words cannot be mistaken in any language, like terrorist, protest, and president. It was clear that the entire world was watching to see what would come of this possible dictatorship rule and the protest against it. Walking into this assignment, I knew it could go either way, but hopefully the president would come to his senses at the possibility of his citizens starting a war on the streets of Cairo, and back down. If not, Egypt would be the last place that anyone wanted to be.

Martina, being seasoned at this type of excursion, obviously had many connections among the other U.S. reporters. She hugged one reporter, a tall, blond, rugged Indiana Jones looking man, and immediately struck up a conversation. Even in my short time working alongside of her, I'd never seen her be this friendly. Must be some sort of connection. As I approached, he caught my eye and motioned to her as if to say, "Who is this?" Martina whirled around to see me and quickly waved me off, "Oh this is my intern, Faith – Faith, meet Chris Dowry. He works for the New York Times."

I extended my hand and smiled politely. "Nice to meet you, sir." Chris chuckled and turned to Martina.

"If she's going to make it here Tina, you had better tell her to quit the formal act and relax." He then turned towards me and said, "Hi, Faith. Call me Chris. Nice to meet you also. There won't be many more of us here that we can trust and understand, so consider yourself amongst friends. Even though Tina and I always compete to get the best story out first, don't we?" He smiled and nudged her arm. There was definitely some comradery here, beyond the front page.

"Chris, you know it's all in fun. But I always do beat you!" Martina laughed. I must have been staring at her in amazement at this relaxed, almost normal Martina Bell that I had never seen. "Chris we're going to set up right over there, so we'll catch you a little later, okay."

Chris waved and said alright as we walked away. Before I could even say a word, Martina, who I now affectionately knew as Tina, began to explain. "Chris and I studied together in journalism school. We worked on the same paper for about three years before he moved to New York and I to the Times in Chicago. We meet every so often at these big events and always pick up like it was yesterday. He looks out for me too. So, if we have any trouble, he's someone we can trust."

"He seemed to be very friendly," I said almost inquisitively. I wanted to ask, but it wasn't my business.

"If you are wondering, which I know you are, yes we used

to date. But that was 15 years ago. We are just friends, but if there's anything I need, I can count on Chris. Okay, end of discussion. Let's set up for the press conference." With that, the disclosure was finished, and Martina was back to business as usual. So much for bonding.

As we positioned ourselves for the news conference, I pulled out my legal pad and began to take note of the crowds in our midst. It was clear that there was an electric energy pulsating through the crowd. Although I couldn't understand a word they said in Arabic, their expressions read in plain English. Desperation, urgency, the need to be heard, was seen on so many of the protestors' faces. And some other emotion I could not place. It was seen on the faces of several of the younger men in the crowd, who chanted louder than others and seemed to be making their way forward, just as the microphones crackled and the immensely unpopular President took the stage.

His speech was translated into English and in other areas Spanish and what sounded like Mandarin. As I listened in to the political jargon, Martina glanced over her shoulder at me and motioned with her lips, "Are you getting this?" I nodded and continued to record. After a five-minute welcome, and a fair share of political mumbo jumbo, he began to speak on the state of affairs in Egypt. The crowd roared in disagreement with every passing sentence, and it seemed that with each roar it surged forward a few inches. Security was stationed around the crowd along with gates and the militia and judging from their appearance, they were not at all afraid to make an example of a rogue citizen who may try and cross the line. I looked to Martina, who had also just noticed the crowd and shook her head almost in amusement at their persistence. She did not seem to be the least bit phased, and all I could think of was where the closest exit, if necessary, was.

The speech continued and questions began to be asked by reporters. I knew this was our chance to get in closer and attempt to get a great quote to make our story. Chris had already made his way up front and was raising his hand to be recognized. Martina motioned for the cameraman to move up, and we all began to maneuver our way through the crowd in an attempt to hear and be heard. We had gotten close enough to see the whites of the President's eyes and the team who was selecting the next reporter to ask a question when Martina kicked into full gear. Her petite frame was suddenly scooting through the crowds and up to the front, all the while she was yelling with her thick accent, "Mr. President! Mr. President!"

It's hard to ignore such a strong-willed little Hispanic woman, and she definitely was not the type who would wait for someone to recognize her. She commanded the attention of the team and began to shout her question, "Why haven't you commented on the possibility of a Democratic election?"

Time froze, and for the first time in four weeks, I realized how Martina had achieved such success. Here she was in Egypt, amongst hundreds of well-known reporters, but she had managed to make her way to the forefront and ask the question that had been on the minds of millions for days. I had never admired her before, but I was truly impressed by her gall and strategic approach. So, I began to take notes as any good reporter would do.

The response, however redundant it was, seemed to rev the crowd up even more. The president spoke of his attempt to explain to the citizens his reasoning and to exhort his power over them as the natural correct way of doing things. The citizens shouted even louder, and a group of young men began to wave signs and cloths in the air, in adamant protest. But it was the last words that sent the masses into frenzy. "As long as I am president, there will be no opportunities for democracy."

With those words, the crowds swelled like a tide coming into an evening shore. People began to push and scream towards the president, sending security into a panic as they attempted to hold the crowds back. The gates holding back the protestors were beginning to give way and one by one, people spilled through and began to rush the stage. In an effort to protect the president, the militia stepped up in front of the stage, guns drawn ready to shoot, shouting obscenities at the unruly citizens. Crowds of reporters began to move back away from the stage as well. The position of the reporters' tent was to the right of the stage, but it was clear that the path of the crowd would quickly sway in our direction. I tried to call out to Martina, but she was swallowed up by the moving reporters. I stood on my toes trying to peek over the heads of my peers only to see Chris moving in my direction. "Hey, have you seen Martina?" I asked as he walked towards me.

"No, I saw her at the front, but once she started talking, I turned to walk away. You'd better get back to your hotel, Faith... it looks like it's getting a little hairy here. Don't want to be here if something breaks out," Chris warned.

"Yeah, it's just I don't want to leave her here alone," I replied. Truly it was me who didn't want to be alone in a strange country in the middle of civil unrest.

"Look, Faith," Chris continued. "Tina has been doing this for many years. She's a big girl and she knows how to take care of herself. I'm sure she will head back to the hotel too. If I see her, I'll let her know where you went."

"Okay, thanks Chris," I said warily while nodding in agreement, watching the crowd continue to get out of control. "Let's go Adam," I told her assistant. At that very moment, the crowd burst through the fence, sending the entire area into chaos. People began to charge the stage and it was clear that someone would be trampled and possibly killed in this craziness. I turned around and took off running towards the hotel back through the crowds as they rushed against me towards the stage. Everywhere I looked, there were people pushing, shoving, and crying out in fear. Dust was beginning to fly everywhere as people took to the streets running, and it became difficult to see more than a few feet in front of me. As I worked my way through the crowd, I looked to my left and saw Martina, about 10 people over, attempting to do the same thing. I sighed, grateful that I was not alone, and continued to maneuver my way through. Just then, a young man with his arms flailing wildly was bursting through the crowd and managed to slam directly into me, knocking me backwards. Just as I saw a pair of feet about to stomp down on me, a hand reached down and grabbed me up. I looked up, shocked to see Chris helping me up. "You okay?" he asked. I nodded, still trying to catch my breath. "Good, keep up and hold on to me if you can."

I don't know if it was his height or his determination that managed to make the crowds move, but it did, and suddenly it was as if the sea was parting and people were beginning to let us through. After about 10 minutes, Chris made a sudden dart off to the left, and we were able to stop. I could now catch my breath. I bent over, hand on my head and my chest heaving up and down. It took everything in me not to keel over at that moment, but somewhere in my agony was a feeling of gratefulness. I was almost trampled, and I managed to get out. Realizing Chris was staring at me, I quickly straightened up. "Thank you so much. I couldn't have made it out of there without you, Chris."

"No problem, Faith. You know your way home from here? I'm sure Martina's probably there or almost there by now."

"Yes, I see the building from here. I can make it okay, I think. Just take it a step at a time."

"I'm going to go with you to make sure. You have a few scrapes and scratches, but nothing severe. Come on...you can lean on me if you feel weak."

"Thanks, but you really don't have to," I said unconvincingly.

"Yes, I do. Tina would never let me live it down if I left you here. Plus, you look like you need a little help walking after that guy hit you. You jumped up quickly, but that's probably your adrenalin still going. I can't have you falling out in these streets. So, let's go."

Chris hadn't appeared to be Martina's type at all. Sensitive, generous, and helpful all described him, and not one ounce of these described her. *Maybe opposites attract*, I thought. As I limped back to the hotel, I considered how lucky I was to have made it out alive. "Thank you, God," I whispered to myself, amazed at the events of the day and that I had made it out of them in one piece.

About an hour later, after a long hot shower and a shorter than desired nap, there was a knock at my door. To my surprise, Adam was standing there, minus his favorite person, Martina. "Hey Adam, what's up?" I said peeking around the door with my robe on.

"Sorry to bother you, Faith, but we have a little problem. Martina wants to see you in her room."

"Now? Okay, why didn't she call or come here herself?" I asked slightly annoyed at the fact that she couldn't even get up to come to me. We had both had a trying day.

"Well, she would but she can't. She's um...hurt." Adam, who seemed to always be composed and calm, was clearly rattled and distraught. His anxiety came as a shock and I could feel that sense of panic arising in me also. *Deep breath*, I thought.

"Okay, give me 10 minutes and I'll be there."

Adam and I arrived at Martina's door and I knocked gently. "It's open," I heard Martina say through the door in a muffled voice.

Adam walked in first and Martina sat on the couch with the hotel's doctor on call sitting on the ottoman taking her blood pressure. "Mrs. Hall, you must be still so that we can get an accurate reading. No more shouting," the small Egyptian man said in a thick Arabic accent.

"Well, I had to let them in...ouch," Martina winced in pain as she attempted to adjust herself on the couch. Looking at her, it didn't seem to be much wrong with her, except her face had become a permanent scowl announcing her extreme pain. Funny, I thought as I looked at her, this was much like the face I saw daily, prior to Egypt. "So, doc, what's the deal? We have a story to get and I have to be back on the street tomorrow for the protest at Tahrir Square."

"Oh, I'm sorry Ms., but you will not be on the street tomorrow," he shook his head in sympathy. "Your vitals are fine, but you fell and bumped your head, and it seems you may have a concussion. You must be on complete bed rest for the next two to three days until we can establish that no damage has been done to your brain."

"What? Two to three days? The president will have made his big speech by then and I can't have these two covering it without me!" Martina was shouting irately in a thick accent. It was evident that she did not trust our expertise.

"With all due respect, Tina," Adam began, "I don't want to risk another incident like today. If you get caught in a crowd, you may get dizzy or fall out, or even worse, end up in the hospital."

"Look Adam, you have no idea what I have been through in *my* life! I can take a little bump on the head!"

"Ma'am, if you refuse to stay here, I will have to recommend that you go to the hospital, and the hotel will require it to make sure they are not responsible if anything happens to you," the doctor chimed in.

"Martina, I think you should listen to him. I have never had a concussion, but I know they are serious. We are miles away from home, and, no offense sir, but also miles away from modern medicine. I think Adam and I could handle the coverage if you supervised. We can map everything out and you can even give us instructions by text or on the phone if need be. I think your health is more important now," I added sympathetically, yet firmly.

"What do you know? You've been here what, a month?" Martina's wheels were churning loudly. "If Jonathan doesn't have a story sent to him that's worth anything, we will all be looking for a job. Aye!" Martina waved her hands in frustration and looked at us all standing there watching her as she battled her own stubbornness.

"Alright, I will stay here and rest. But, Adam you are taking the lead on the president's speech, and Faith, you will have to do interviews. We...no...I will make sure we have all the questions mapped out and ready for the event tomorrow. And in a few days," she said turning to the doctor, "I'll be back to normal and out of this stupid hotel room!"

The doctor looked pleased and stood and began to gather

his belongings. "Great, Ms. Martina. I'm sure you will be fine in no time if you follow doctor's orders and rest. Contact me if you experience any dizziness or feel faint. If I don't answer, you will need to go to the hospital immediately," he turned to Martina and held out his card.

"Yeah, yeah. I will be just fine, thank you," she said as she waved her hands and shooed him out of the room before we could say another word.

"I'm glad you decided to rest, Martina. I will be working hard to make sure I don't let you down," I added as I sat on the couch across from the bed. "Look at the bright side — at least you are in a plush hotel with good room service," I attempted to lighten the mood.

"Ha! I've stayed in better. And the only way we will make sure to not let me down is to write a damn good story that will knock Jonathan's socks off! Now, let's go over the questions for the president. You need time to study and prepare. Adam, make sure you take notes, too, in case she chokes out there."

I wanted to look at her sideways and say to her that if I was going to choke, today would have been the day when I was almost trampled. But it would be wasted breath to go toe to toe with Martina. Instead, I pulled out my notepad and began to take notes.

Three hours later, Adam and I were tuckered out. We had gone over the notes from the day's events and managed to create a great intro story to send to Jonathan. Even though I volunteered to write it, Martina insisted on doing a sample story so that I could see the level of article we would need after the president's speech. One thing I could say that journalism teaches you is humility. This was not the profession to get into if you were "smelling yourself" or wanted to show off. Martina excelled in squashing the largest egos down to the size of an ant. Thankfully, working with Jonathan had given me an opportunity to grow thick skin and her smart remarks no longer penetrated my brain. My only focus now was to make sure that the job I was here to do was done and that I delivered a story that not only made front page news, but got my name into the ears of those who were prominent in journalism.

Surprisingly, Martina did not resist our insistence on eating and getting rest after our long session. Adam and I bowed out quietly and opted on eating at the hotel restaurant since we both agreed that our venturing outdoors earlier had sufficed for the rest of the day. We chose a small table, off to the right of the lobby, slightly secluded. I didn't want to hear the conversations of everyone else, I just wanted to eat in peace. In my bed would have actually been better, but I didn't want to leave Adam to fend for himself with Evileen Martina. Adam was not a typical journalism type of guy. At first glance, he looked like a grunge model; plaid shirt and jeans that were clearly larger than his frame allowed and dark hair that always seemed to be tussled under a baseball cap. Although he looked plain, Adam was actually a wealth of knowledge, and I could see why Martina kept him around as we ate. Adam knew everything about Egypt's history, culture, industry, and metropolitan lifestyle. He was the researcher of the paper and came in handy on international trips and background information.

"Adam how do you remember all of this information? It's like you are a walking database," I asked.

"I guess you could say that I just am good at collecting and recalling information. Tina and I have worked together for the last five years, and I am always her go to guy when she goes out of the country or she needs to find out something fast. I kind of think of myself as the informer behind the journalist. I was never really good at writing, but I could research anything you're interested in." Adam beamed proudly at the exclamation of his skills. Clearly he felt that his job was a necessary one. In this case, I definitely agreed.

"Well, we're going to need all that information for tomorrow and the next day. I have never been here and I only got to do a couple of days of research on the situation, so we will have to rely on your knowledge to get this article to be as phenomenal as

Martina wants it."

"Duly noted, no problem. I read a couple of your pieces you did with Jonathan. You have talent. A little polishing and you will be in the same position as Martina. Maybe that's why she's so hard on you. She probably recognizes a little of her talent in you and feels threatened."

The thought of Martina ever being intimidated by anyone was absurd. "Threatened by me? Now that's hilarious! She has more experience and expertise; it would take me years to catch up to her level if I ever could," I said in disbelief and amusement at the thought.

"I know what you are saying, but Martina is difficult to work with sometimes and has had her share of complaints about her. If you could write as well as her and keep people from despising you, you could be her stiffest competition yet." Adam seemed confident in this fact and I was floored. I'd never recognized that level of talent in myself. I thought I was good, but to compete with Martina, now that would be something.

"I am flattered you would say that, but I wouldn't feel right taking her job after she's given me this great opportunity. Plus, she'd hate me."

"You will find that in this field, there are more enemies than friends. Not saying she has to become your adversary, but just remember that everyone looks out for self in this business, no matter who they have to overlook in the process," warned Adam.

The reality of Adam's word sunk into my being as we finished our meal. Throughout college and even in my internship, I accepted and was willing to give a helping hand to those in the field alongside me. It was naïve of me to think that my generous spirit would just saturate all that I had encountered along this professional journey. We all had a goal in mind, which was climbing to the top, and Martina was no different. I had to look out for Faith if I was going to make it, make a formidable impression on the writers of the Sun, and continue to excel in this profession. Because if I didn't, who would?

~

Fighting for Freedom

Riding through Cairo on the afternoon of the rally at Tahrir Square, one of the major areas of disturbance among the revolutionaries, one would almost forget that there was a dangerous protest going on. I had decided to take a short tour of Egypt so that I wouldn't be able to say I had ventured to Africa, only to work in crowded, angry conditions and never see a tourist site. Aside from the protestors, Egypt was actually a peaceful place where people can be seen dining along the Nile in cafes or taking boat rides across the Nile to various tourist attractions. In certain areas just outside of the city, camels and camel drivers awaited eager tourists anxious to explore the Great Pyramids of Giza and bask in the mystery of the colossal creations.

Seeing this portion of Egypt helped me to understand why almost 4 million people visited Egypt annually. It was breathtaking, as if one was stepping out of life and into a history book or a movie set, and someone shouting "action"! History had always amazed me and learning about the development of other civilizations and ideas was inspiring. For a moment, I longed for my Haley. I wished I could share this moment with her and show her that mommy had visited one of the ancient wonders of the world. Even if she didn't remember, the experience alone was one I wanted to share with her. Considering the reaction from Lucas as I tried to take her out of the country, I shook my head. *I'm sure he'd never want to come here, unless they served beer,* I thought to myself. In my mind I decided I would not allow Lucas to disrupt my peace thousands of miles away, but I would take this moment and enjoy it, capture the feeling of freedom in my mind and heart, and never let it fade. Being alone in Egypt was allowing me to clear my thoughts and return to who I was. As I inhaled deeply, a smile spread across my face. Out of the sand, I was reemerging.

Isn't it funny how the most serene moments can be interrupted so abruptly? As I rode the cab back towards the hotel, my phone rang. "Faith, I need you up here now. Where have you been? I've been calling your room all morning." Martina's voice snapped me back into reality and reminded me why I was determined to get this right. I couldn't take orders from her for my entire career.

"I'm headed up in a few minutes. Just gathering some notes. I ran out this morning – I had to go a little further away to find a store. You know...it's that time," I lied. There would be no end to Martina's mouth if she knew I had been sightseeing.

"Well hurry up, we only have three hours until the rally and I need to debrief with you all first," Martina barked.

It was clear that the concussion had not decreased her anger level one bit. "Okay, Martina." I sighed a bit louder than I should have because the cab driver turned around and asked if I was okay. "Yeah, I will be when today is over," I replied.

After an hour of prep with Martina, it was time for Adam and me to set off on the journey to the presidential palace, where the rally was set to take place outside. Martina informed us that speeches were to be made by the leaders of the revolution and possibly a response from the president. Our instructions were clear: get it all on record, interview as many rebels as possible, and get quotes from as many higher ups as we could. Only if we did that, Martina reminded us, would I even have a chance of writing a story that could make the Sun. I assured her that I would be on task the entire time and call her if needed. However, Martina being the way she was, she had already arranged for Chris to look out for us in case we got in over our heads or needed some assistance getting to a secure area. At first I was insulted that she thought we needed a chaperone, but I recalled Chris's help at the last event and figured it wouldn't hurt to know someone with more pull than either one of us.

Adam and I both had on earpieces that were connected to our phones for easy use through voice recognition. We promised each other that if we got lost, we'd call one another and stand in a meeting place close to the palace until we reunited. Hopefully, that plan would not have to be called into action, because the idea of rummaging through the crowd again, alone, was daunting, and our task today was strenuous enough as it was.

Entering the palace area was impossible. Once we arrived, there were droves of people as far as one could see surrounding the palace and every possible entryway. Red, white, and black flags with a golden bird flew high along the protestors, signifying the unity against the president. Like before, they chanted in Arabic and shouted out amongst each other. The difference was that the crowd was not a mob, it was simple protestors. Unlike the other area, these people were passionate, yet calm. I didn't feel threatened here at all, and Adam and I began to make our way through the crowd, stopping along the way to talk to a protestor here or there and getting a statement. As we approached the front of the pack, there was a band of reporters standing towards the front cameras taking in the scene and reporters shooting live broadcasts again. Adam and I decided this would be our best spot to stand, as the podium was only about 150 feet away and we could easily get a question out or simply record the speech to get a quote.

Standing in the crowd was a young man about 30 years old, who was chanting fiercely with a woman by his side. She was standing beside him, chanting as well, but looking around nervously to check for her safety. I found it odd that she would feel this way, with the crowd being so orderly. I decided to go over and speak with her. Walking up to her, I locked eyes with her and then her husband, I assumed, and smiled gently. Her look of terror slightly softened, and she looked to him. I came closer and spoke calmly, "I am a reporter and I would like to ask your wife some questions, if it's okay." I held out my pad and pen to show them I meant no harm. "Do you speak English?"

The man nodded at her as if to say go ahead, and she softly said, "Yes, I speak a little."

"Great," I said beaming. "Why are you out here today?" I asked.

The woman's English was broken but her passion was intact. "My husband and I cannot have our own religion in Egypt. I am not a Muslim, but if I say I am a Christian, I die. It is not fair to us. The president wants us all to be Muslim, and if not, we have no vote, no say in government. That is why I am here," she answered fervently.

"I understand. I am a Christian too. I believe it is wrong, and he should give everyone rights. What will make everyone stop protesting? When will this end?" I inquired of them, knowing this would spark a strong reaction.

The husband stopped his ranting and turned to me with such a pained look on his face, as if he had been suffering in bondage for hundreds of years. "My mom, my wife, my children, we cannot walk these streets at night without fear of being killed. If we say we love God, we are forced to hide it or die. When will this end?" he said with tears in his eyes. "This will end when our president understands that we have rights. We are people who deserve to be heard and live freely. We will not stop until we get freedom or a new president! I will die before I let anyone harm my family. I am here to say that is enough!" In haste, he wiped the tears from his eyes, but there was no weakness to this man. My heart ached at the emotion that I felt from him and I could understand now so many struggles through seeing this one. The Holocaust, slavery, even Jesus' death, all resonated in my mind and paralleled this current battle. Even the battle in myself daily.

I nodded thank you and walked away, wiping tears from my own eyes as I realized why I was here in Egypt. This was bigger than a story and a newspaper, I was in my own battle, just like these Egyptians. Against Lucas, the world, my insecurity, and my doubt. And just like that man, I needed my freedom, more than anything else in this world. At this moment, I was willing to struggle, fight, protest, scream, and even die to make sure that the bondage I was in inside myself and in my house did not continue. Standing in the middle of Tahrir Square, I let out a cry and a sound that shook me to my inner being. "Freeeeeeeee!" I had come to Egypt to find the strength and faith that I needed to break free.

My screams were swallowed up in the echoes of the crowd, but it rang on in my soul. I looked up and the world seemed different. At that moment, the only thing I could imagine is exploring the world, writing, and raising Haley in freedom. Although I was nowhere near the safety of the U.S., I felt more safe and secure thousands of miles away than I did in my own home. Adam and Chris had linked up while I was speaking to the couple and walked over to me.

"Hey, Faith I think we found a way to get closer to the palace. Even if we don't get a quote from the president, there are some dignitaries you can interview. Come on." Chris turned and immediately began moving through the crowd, slowly, as this was a much calmer protest, but diligently. I didn't know why he was insistent on looking out for us, except that maybe he still had a thing for Tina as he called her. Either way, I was grateful for his assistance, yet determined to prove myself as well. Martina trusted both of them and if I could show myself worthy of this task, perhaps I'd earn a bit of her respect.

As the presidential advisors and the various attachés came out, we moved within 20 feet of the palace barriers. At the gates were armed security and military personnel. However, to the left was a small section of reporters and some foreign dignitaries speaking to them prior to the president's speech. That was my chance. Before I knew it, I recalled what Tina had done and I took off amongst the crowd, vying for my place among the reporters. Once I was moving I could hear Adam saying wait as he ran to catch up. Almost there, I was shoved out the way by a reporter from the Boston Globe. Unfortunately for him, I had maxed out of "push me around" moments. Maxed out with Lucas and maxed out in life. It was time for me to step up. I squared my shoulders, said God help me, and I pushed through the crowd and in front of the Boston reporter. Before I knew it, I was staring ambassadors from various countries in the face. Adam came up behind me, camera rolling, and I didn't choke.

Calm and with steadiness, I was able to ask questions to three major dignitaries, record their answers, and still catch the president's address. On the way back, we managed to interview a few more protestors, rounding out the day with 10 quotes, four from major figures. This was going to be a groundbreaking story and I was in the midst of it. I had never felt more alive in all of my life than at that moment.

"Wow, Faith, I am speechless. To have gone out for the first time, had to finish the end alone, and return with this... wow," Jonathan remarked in astonishment. Back in Chicago at the Sun's office, I had come in to show Jonathan what I managed to write as a result of our visit. Martina sat next to me, just waiting to jump into the conversation.

"Thank you, sir – it was an honor to have been chosen to go; I did the best I could."

Martina chimed in, "You know after my injury, I had to debrief with her and Adam a few times before they went out, and we were in constant contact during the rallies. I also helped her edit the article, too. It needed a little work." Martina looked proud as she gloated arrogantly, attempting to make herself look necessary.

"Thank you, Tina, for your dedication. I'm sure you had a hand in making sure Faith was successful. I'm glad you are better. But I'd like you to rest now that you are home. Take a few days off."

"No sir, that is not necessary, I am okay; cleared by the doctor in Egypt before we left," Martina retorted.

"I understand but go home. I will call you when I think you have had enough rest. Well done, Tina." Obediently, yet with much dissention, Martina turned to leave the room, giving me a look that clearly stated that had her boss not been there choice words would have been spoken.

"Now, Faith, I have a question for you. Rather an offer. Would you like to become a permanent writer here at the Sun, particularly in international investigative reporting?" Jonathan asked.

At this moment, I could only remember the first time that I had ever walked into Jonathan's office and the fear I felt. I was a different woman then than I was now. I had blossomed back into myself through the internship and job experience. Where I once sat nervous and insecure, I was now sitting in awe of the way God had worked out the details of my journey. There was no denying that this opportunity was designed for me.

"I have to decline at this time Jonathan." The look on his face was priceless. Dejection, confusion, and anger. I had sparked anger in him.

"I beg your pardon?" Jonathan fumed.

"I am truly humbled to be offered this position, but no I do not want to take Martina's position. She is not the easiest person to work with, however, she is talented, and I believe her talent is a valuable asset to this company. I was not raised to step on the toes of those who helped you. So respectfully, I must decline the international position. Plus, with a young child at home, it is too strenuous for me to travel that much."

Jonathan stared at me in amazement. "No one has ever turned a job offer from me down, are you crazy Faith?"

"With all due respect sir, I want to work for you, but I'd like to stay local. I am in no position to demand what I want, so I understand if you have to let me go. But I will stand by my values on this one. If you cannot accommodate me, there will be no hard feelings. I really do appreciate all you have done for me."

Jonathan sat down and chuckled, leaning back in his chair with his arms folded behind his head. "You drive a hard bargain, Faith. But I can see you have made up your mind. Anyone else in this company would have jumped at the opportunity I just offered you, if for no other reason but to simply gloat at the fact that they were able to bump someone out of their position and make more money than 80% of the staff here. But not you. And that, Mrs. Faith, is why I am definitely going to hire you as our new local investigative reporter. Your work ethic and your values are highly coveted and rarely seen. I know you are too valuable to give to any other publication." He smiled, stood, and extended his hand. "Welcome to the Sun, Faith."

Very few times in life does a full circle moment come around in life and allow you to see the evolution of your dreams come to pass. But in that moment, I stood and smiled and shook Jonathan Reynolds's hand with all my strength. One tear slid down my cheek and I quickly wiped it away, embarrassed that I had allowed my soft interior to peek through.

"It's okay, Faith. I can understand your emotion. This is a wonderful day for you. And I am delighted to be a part of it. But I do have one question. How did you choose the name of the article?"

Recalling that day in Tahrir Square, I smiled, remembering the couple I interviewed and their story and retold it to Jonathan. "At the end of that interview, I knew that there was a greater purpose for not just them, but for all of us, and that there would be a constant struggle in life. Yet, knowing all of that, I realized that the struggle is won, not because we fight physically, but because we refuse to stop fighting mentally, emotionally, and spiritually. The battle is won not in the streets of Egypt or Chicago, it is won when we decide that we have found the faith within us to face every fight with tenacity and know that we will be victorious beyond what we see. So, I felt the title, Freedom Found, was fitting, because in Egypt not only was their freedom found, but so was mine."

"Profound, Faith. Thank you for sharing that." As I stood to leave the office, I exhaled as I grabbed my things, knowing that every day would not be perfect, but my fight was fixed and I would be the winner.

Epilogue

For years I had lived in a cage. Closed in by my insecurities, the emotional and physical abuse of an unstable individual, and the lack of confidence all of this created in me. My trip to Egypt was my freedom ride. Although many times along the way I found myself internally paralyzed by the fear that had gripped me for so long, I realized in being away from my toxic marriage, that I could no longer return to it. My Haley was my everything, and together we would forge a new path. Some would say sadly, however, it can also be considered a fortunate outcome that Lucas did not stick around to see what was next for us. In the weeks when I departed, he failed to see his daughter even once. When I returned home, I found our house emptied of his belongings and him gone. What could I say? Was I hurt, was I surprised, was I saddened? In honesty, maybe a little of all three. But one emotion conquered them all – relief. Finally, I had found freedom and would place my faith in God as I embarked on my next chapter.

CHAPTER 3

PLAYING WITH FIRE

HOPE

Some chapters are difficult to endure, relive, or retell, but it is in this expression of pain that I find my purpose, my strength, and my healing. I pray the Lord uses my words to help some other woman realize she can rise above the worst circumstances and come out triumphant...through faith! Thank you Lord for giving me strength to tell my story....

We Meet Again

July 3

It was a bright and vibrant summer's day, the day you walked back into my life. Putting charcoal into the grill, preparing coleslaw, shucking corn, baking the chocolate cake – so many tasks before the guests arrived. As the first people entered, I put on my entertaining airs; I began mixing cocktails and enjoying the company of college buddies. There is nothing like having lifelong bonds that cannot be severed by the demands of life, families, careers, and relationships. The friendships that were present each had special meaning. Joan, who was like the big sis I always wanted, could always be counted on to give sound advice, even if it crushed the dream I held of love. Joan came with Elsa, who was known for her shoot-from-the-hip bluntness that was only topped by her exquisite use of profane language. The two of them were sure to liven any gathering with their presence.

Later Dan arrived, who without shaming his exceedingly large ego, was also the life of the party and one of my best friends. We met by chance in the cafeteria, sat and talked once, and have never separated. Despite everyone's insistence, Dan and I remained strictly platonic. We got to know each other quite well and realized that our bond as allies far outweighed the risk of losing it all to a fling.

Dan and I stood and talked as I looked over to my left to see a car pull up. If I had been told to prepare for what was next, I still don't think I would have been ready. Out of the car steps Anthony, the sexiest man ever to grace the quad or the entire campus for that matter. His sleekness and confidence floated through the air captivating the attention of all who saw him. He wore a short sleeve red polo with blue jean shorts that carefully revealed the legs of a former track star that had stayed in Olympic shape. As he approached me, a wave of heat stifled my being and my smile crept out from under the cloak of amazement and awe.

"Well, hello there," he said with his baritone voice, scanning my body and face for a response. My body was like a magnet being attracted to its polar opposite. No matter the resistance, everything in me reached for him. But I remained calm, masquerading my instant arousal.

"Wow, hello Anthony. It's been a long time," I said and reached out to hug him. His skin smelled of fresh cologne and the essence of a man. I was immediately swept into his muscular arms and I had to force myself to let go.

"Too long," he spoke seductively as he released me and walked into the house. I was in trouble.

After hours of reminiscing, laughing about our Generation X college years, we began to clean up the party. Anthony came and gently took my hand. "Got a minute?" he asked knowing I did.

"I think so," I smiled. "Let's go outside." We stepped out of the side door and stood in the driveway as people congregated in the backyard. I leaned against the house, to stand, but more so to keep from getting weak from his presence.

"I'm really glad I came...you look great. I missed hanging with you all, especially Dan's crazy self."

"Yeah me too. This was just like old times," I chimed, trying to lighten the mood. "So, where have you been hiding for the last few years? Seems like forever since we hung out."

"I know. I've been traveling doing some freelance work, and I came back last month to help my mom with her real estate company. Decided I needed to be back home in Atlanta."

"I see." He stepped closer and put his arm just over me and leaned in closer. I could smell him, and I did not trust myself. But I didn't move either.

"So, I think now that I'm home, we may be seeing more of each other." He looked into my eyes like a man thirsty for trouble.

"I'm sure that could be arranged. You have my number now, so use it." I replied slyly.

"Sure will, sooner than you think." He leaned in and whispered in my ear, "Do you know there's something I wanted to do for a long time." His lips brushed my ears and I felt myself tremble. God, I was not winning this battle.

"W-what is it," I stammered, looking into his eyes.

With that he leaned in, wrapping his arm around me and grabbed my face, pulling me in. When our lips met, they fit like puzzle pieces and I found myself holding on tighter as he kissed me with eight years of built-up anticipation.

"Umm, what's going on here," Dan interrupted, bringing the kiss to an abrupt halt like a needle being lifted off a record.

Anthony laughed. "Oh, I was just leaving, saying my goodbyes." He smiled at me and I couldn't wipe the grin off of my face. "Be sure to talk to you soon," he said as he turned to Dan, giving him the man code handshake, also called the grip. "I'm out. Thanks for the invite." Anthony walked off and my eyes followed him to his car. As he drove away, I sighed an awful sigh of passion.

"Dag, it's like that, girl?" Dan asked jokingly.

"Oh, shut up! It's none of your business. Now come help me clean up," I said turning and walking in.

I thought to myself, *you walked back into my life today and it will never be the same...*

Hope is a funny thing. Wrapped up in hope is the desire

for something more, even though all that is visible is undeniably less. People have hoped to win the lottery, or find a better job, to get a day off, or hoped to fulfill their wildest dreams. Oftentimes, people find hope in an idealistic yet blurred state of reality that exists only in the farthest corners of their mind, and when they awaken they are left with nothing but a memory of something they hoped for but never found. Once in a lifetime though, there is just enough hope to bring about something wonderful...out of ourselves.

~

Hopeless

"They say I'm hopeless...as a penny with a hole in it...penny with a hole in it yea, yea, yea...They say I'm no less, than up to my head in it..."

–DIONNE FARRIS

There was no hope for me after that day with Anthony. I dismissed the idea of him reappearing in my life, because frankly, I was without hope. Just months out of a terribly ugly separation, I knew there was no way I could ever fathom being in another relationship any time soon. In fact, I had no desire to desire another man. I just wanted to be free. Until that day, I had no intention of getting involved with anyone; it was simply me and God.

I had found that the best way to clear my head of the tumultuous ordeal I had gone through, with the separation and impending divorce, was to just take some time to examine my life and let God lead me in the right direction. Clearly, my own understanding of my marriage and what it should be had landed me smack dab in the middle of depression alley. With court bills piling up daily for divorce proceedings, that my ex refused to attend, and the constant nagging of bill collectors about the numerous bills that were being left unaccounted for because what was once two incomes had become one, I was exhausted financially, emotionally, and spiritually. It was all I could do every day just to see to my child's basic needs, and thankfully, as a three-year old, they were not much beyond playtime, lots of love and kisses, and a bedtime bath and story.

But when the night came, my despair returned. All the unanswered questions loomed in the darkness like monsters lurking over my bed. Having to deal with all this forced me to move back home into my parents' house, which was like becoming a grown-up and then reverting to childhood again. Curfews and questions, rules, and regulations, after being a wife and running part of a household, was extremely confining and all I wanted to do was escape. My escape for me came at bedtime for my child, and then I would escape out of the house and go to where I knew I wouldn't be judged...Dan's house.

With Dan, I was always myself and he never made me explain why or questioned my doing – he was just there, as a true friend should be. I found that in my lowest point in life, there were very few so-called friends who I could count on. Adversity has a way of showing you people's true colors. But with Dan, there was complete acceptance. Dan allowed me to just sit, or cry, or have a drink, or relax my mind in whatever way I chose. On some nights, my escape took me into a euphoric state brought on by self-medicating doses of marijuana. I knew that it was wrong, and everything in me said I should go home to my child, but it was the only way I could cope. I had lost my house, my husband, and my freedom within a course of six months. It was like a nightmare that you hope you will wake up and find was not real, only it was. In my hopeless state, I began to find joy in things that made me happy; things that were not in my best interest, I understood, but rather made me feel good. And Anthony fit into that category as well.

One evening, not too many days later, I was playing with Joseph, my three-year-old son, outside when the phone rang. Not knowing the number, I was skeptical, so I answered very dryly. "Hello?"

"Well, hello there." The baritone of his voice sent chills through my entire body. *Pull it together girl*, I thought.

"Anthony, is that you?" I questioned knowingly.

"Yes, ma'am. I told you I'd be talking to you sooner than you thought. What's happening?" His voice was confident and full of expectation.

"Oh, nothing much, just hanging with the little one. What's up with you?" I tried to sound calm.

"I was thinking about you. I have been thinking about you a lot. I want to know when I will get to see you again?" he asked.

"When do you want to see me?" I figured let's see where he's going with this.

"How's this week? Friday okay with you? I figured we could hang out, grab some food, and maybe see a movie or something. I just want to see you again." I could hear the anxiety in his voice. There was an undertone of something genuine, yet animalistic.

I wanted to scream through the phone, YESSS! Instead, I kept it cool. "Sure, Friday is good. What time?"

"Let's meet at my place at 7, okay?"

"Sure, sounds good. I'll see you then, Anthony."

"Great, I can't wait." He hung up. *Oh lord*, I thought. I'm in for it now. There was no way I could resist or ignore the awakening in my belly. For the first time in six months, someone made me excited, made me want to see them, and ignited a fire in me. Although I knew it could be nothing, I was amazed that I might possibly find a reason to hope for something good again, even if it was only temporary.

Friday came and put Monday through Thursday to shame with its perfect weather and air of freedom. Pulling up to Anthony's building – yes I had to meet him there because he didn't drive – I was so nervous. All of a sudden this eight-year friendship had the possibility of becoming something beyond that. Even though it was just a date, there was an aura of anxiety around me, and I couldn't help but get butterflies as I rang the bell. I stood for a few minutes, beginning to wonder if something had changed even though we had just spoken a few hours prior, and then I saw him bounding down the steps. *Good Lord, this man was fine!* My mind was telling my body to breathe, but somewhere in between my brain and my lungs the message got lost. Suddenly he opened the door and I exhaled. "Hey beautiful," he chimed as he reached in and gave me a hug and I could smell the oils from before which had been mesmerizing.

"Hey Anthony, good to see you again."

He wore a t-shirt, that was just fitted enough to show me he was cut underneath it, and khaki shorts, which showed off his muscular-toned legs. Anthony's bald head was clean-shaven, and he wore shades on the top of it.

"Likewise, I'm glad you agreed to go out. I was thinking we could go downtown to the new theater by the dock and maybe grab a bite to eat afterwards. How's that sound?"

"Sounds good to me. What time is our show?" I asked.

"We have about 45 minutes to get there and get parked and all. You ready?"

"Sure. There's my car over there. We can head out." Anthony had already explained that since moving back he had not yet purchased a car, rather had been taking the train and public transportation until he got settled again. Normally, I would have never even considered going out with a man who I had to pick up, but Anthony and I had known each other forever, and a car seemed to be the last of the issues I had with him. Or maybe I was just biased.

The entire evening was filled with laughter and familiarity. Anthony had picked an action flick with lots of one-liners that gave us plenty to talk about as we walked around afterwards. A few times I caught him staring at me as if he'd never seen me before, and I felt that there was something underlying in our friendship. Walking next to his 6'3" frame was very comforting, and he reaffirmed his strength by putting his arm around my waist as we walked, opening doors, and holding my hand when we crossed the street. There was no denying that there was chemistry between us, but I was determined to not let it stop at that. Despite my burning desire to stay at his house, I dropped him off at the end of the night and gave him a quick kiss and drove off. It was one of the hardest things ever! I wasn't a mile away when he called my phone, "Were you scared to come upstairs? We could have spent more time together, I was enjoying you," he said in an inviting manner.

"I was enjoying you too, Anthony, but I don't know if I can trust myself around you, yet." I chuckled. "You are hard to resist." I blushed...*did I just say that*? Who was this woman talking and why wouldn't she shut up before she turned the car around!

"You don't have to resist me; I won't do anything to you. Unless you want me to."

Keep driving, I thought to myself. Every inch of my body was awakening with that last statement and I was sure I did not need to be within 300 feet of Anthony anytime soon. "Thanks, and I believe you, but I'm going home. We can get together again."

"I plan on seeing you very soon." There was that confidence resurfacing.

"Goodnight, Anthony, and thank you for a wonderful evening." Driving home I could sense that for the first time in months I had gone on a date, a real date, with a real man, and actually had fun. Maybe this would be the beginning of something new. I had a renewed sense of hope.

"Let me fly away with you, cause my love is like the wind...Give me more than one caress, satisfy this hungriness. Let the wind blow through your heart..."

What began as a first date, soon blossomed into many encounters, each more intense than the one before. What existed between Anthony and me was friendship, comfort, humor, and carefree living rolled into one. And of course, passion. Anthony and I soon found that the resistance we attempted to control was both beyond our control and beyond our desire to be controlled. The next time we met, we realized how much tension was lying between us, waiting to be chopped down with an ax of intimacy.

"So, what's on our agenda for this evening?" I asked as I stood in Anthony's third story apartment, overlooking the park. It was not the first time he invited me up, but because it was daylight, I figured I was safe to come up and trust myself to exercise caution.

"That's up to you, beautiful. I was thinking we could get some cocktails and grub and bring them back here to enjoy some movies and each other's company." He smiled a mischievous smile and I knew that there was more to the word "company" than just being in each other's space, but I was anxious to spend more time with him.

Standing in his living room, I saw all the evidence of a bachelor pad. Very little furniture, one reclining chair, and a simple wooden TV stand with a small older version of a flat screen TV. Beside it stood a black curio cabinet that held knick-knacks, and on the windowsill, a collection of sunglasses that may have only compared to a shelf at a Ray-Ban store. Anthony was notorious for wearing shades, day or night, each one specifically chosen for the right look. As I stood, he offered me a seat and I reclined calmly as he dressed for the occasion. Anthony had no problems choosing just what framed his sculpted body perfectly. Today, he chose a pair of khaki shorts and a loose-fitting polo that stopped short enough on his arms to show his tattoo of a woman's name. As he came into the living room, he caught me staring at it.

"Who's Dina?" I inquired.

"My mom," he laughed. "You thought it was a woman? No, I love my mama more than anything, and I told her years ago that I had her name on me so that she would always be with me, close to my heart."

"Aww isn't that sweet." I smiled and turned away. Before I could turn back around, he was leaning over my chair, arms on the arm rests and his face closer to mine than I had expected it to be.

"Kiss me," he spoke in his baritone voice. I melted into his lips and was transported out of my body and into another dimension. "Damn, I want to have as many of those as I can. I've been thinking about kissing you since that day at your house."

"Hmmm," I moaned. "Me too. Your kisses are intoxicating, Ant."

"Well, when we return, we'll make sure you are intoxicated by me and that cocktail." His lips curved into a sexy smile, and I knew that I wouldn't last long in his clutches.

We left the house and ran to the local liquor store, a place Anthony was clearly a regular because the clerk greeted him as soon as he walked in. After some browsing around, we decided on a bottle of white wine, as he called it, "Pinot Grigio." The words rolled off his tongue as if it was a serum of passion.

"Wine, Anthony? You don't strike me as the wine type. I usually drink red."

"Well, I'm sure you will like this. It's smooth and crisp."

Back at his apartment, we sat close in two separate chairs, close enough to touch as we drank from our glasses. Anthony shared with me his Jamaican heritage, and how one day he would promise to make me his specialty, ox tails.

"Yuck! I don't eat that stuff. But I will eat some jerk chicken," I laughed.

"I know a great place just down the street – we can order it and walk to get it, since it's a nice day."

"You sure you want to walk around here? No offense, but this isn't exactly the best area to be walking in."

"Girl, you are with me. And that means everything will be alright." Anthony called in our order and we leisurely walked the long mile, through the winding side streets to his favorite jerk restaurant. It was a hole in the wall, but I knew that some of the best cooking came from store front shops that looked as if the woman running it had been around for 30 years. As we walked, he held my hand and I laughed like a schoolgirl, enthralled by his conversation and the ease at which we connected. This was so totally different from anything I had experienced before. Here was a man with culture, authenticity, and genuine care for enjoying the small things in life. *I could get used to this*, I thought to myself.

Soon, day turned to evening and after a delicious meal, we sat back and began to watch a Japanese love story of two samurai warriors who were constantly fighting their feelings for each other, but always found each other in the company of one another. At the end, the woman was killed in battle, and the man cried out in agony, as she died in his arms and he professed his love for her. I looked over and Anthony was wiping his face.

"Are you crying?" I asked, wiping my face as well. We both busted out laughing, embarrassingly surprised that we had experienced the same emotional response. At that moment we shared the feeling and understood that love could transcend beyond death. In that moment, we bonded in a way I didn't expect, and before I knew it, Anthony had me in his arms, and I experienced him in the most bare and intimate way. Our bodies intertwined like long lost souls who had once known each other but were reuniting, determined to discover every inch of each other's bodies. As I relaxed in his embrace, my body released a feeling that had never been unearthed in this way. Beyond the physicality of our intimacy, there was a depth to our lovemaking that touched my soul. We lay in each other's arms all night, rekindling that feeling over and over again. And for once, I felt like I had died and gone to heaven.

"Dang, girl, I wasn't expecting all of that from you," Anthony rolled over and kissed my cheek the next morning. We decided to sleep in, considering sleep had not been at the top of the agenda the previous evening.

"Ha, I could say the same. But I'm not complaining." I smiled at him, trying not to appear too lost in his sense of being, although I felt myself getting there.

"Oh no, not a complaint here. I'm feeling fine! Matter of

fact, I think we should shower and grab some breakfast."

"Sounds good, you first." I wanted an excuse to lay here and digest what had just happened.

"See you soon, beautiful," he leaned down and kissed me with such force, I almost forgot that he was on his way out of the room.

"Kiss me like that again, and we will have breakfast in bed." I was amazed at the heightened amount of chemistry between us. Anthony walked away and I was left there to contemplate what occurred the night before. One minute we were laughing, enjoying each other's company, and the next we were face to face. I told myself I was going to hold out, be strong, and not try to rush things. *Well, so much for that*, I thought aloud. Only this didn't feel like a fly by night thing. Anthony and I had known each other for a long time, and we had never explored what seemed to be underneath our friendship. I decided at that moment, that I would live in this moment.

Life has a funny way of turning around and showing you all it has to offer. One moment you can be down on your luck, feeling like you have been forgotten by God, forsaken, and left alone to fend for yourself. And then, in an instant, the storm clouds part, sunshine rears its face, and gray skies are turned into the dawn of a new day. Just three months ago, I was battling the gripping effects of a nasty divorce, wondering if any decision I had made in my life was right, because they all seemed to add up to a doomed future. But when Anthony stepped in, it felt as if I was given a second chance at love, a second chance at happiness, and experiencing the best that life had to offer.

The next few months, I lost myself in the newness of love. Days of long walks, nights of talking and laughing, and spending time in each other's arms seemed to fill every empty place in my heart that had been left by my failed marriage. Anthony's sincere heart was exactly what I needed at that moment. When I felt low and like I couldn't be loved again, he showed me that there was something great inside of me. He'd always say, "You are just genuine. Your heart is good, and your love is pure." Anthony recognized in me what others overlooked, took advantage of, or simply couldn't handle. With him, I could be myself and share my entire being. In return, Anthony opened up to me and told me how he had dealt with insecurities and his fears of not becoming a successful man, which every man feels at one time or another. Our relationship began to grow, and Anthony wanted to meet my son. So, we took him to the park together, pushed him on the swings, and it felt like this could become something more. It was a real love, the kind that doesn't hide behind physical being and emotional fears, but instead went at them head on and embraced every challenge before us. I was living life like it was golden, and it was like being on cloud nine.

One day, after a nice dinner and sitting down to chat in his room, as we often did at night, there seemed to be something on his mind. "What's wrong, Ant?" I asked, concerned because his face rarely ever showed anything but happiness.

"Nothing, just thinking about life. I thought I would be farther than this by now. Here I am, 33 years old, working security, and yes I'm making it. But I don't feel I'm making a difference. I just feel like I should be doing something more." Anthony's voice had a sadness and longing that I knew could only be satisfied in one way.

"What do you think your purpose is here? You are a great man, and I know that God has a use for you."

"You know, I've never been very religious. I don't even know if I have a Bible in my house. But I was raised knowing God. I guess I never really considered what I was here for before now. I just know it is more than this."

"I don't think it's about religion, honey. I really think it's more about knowing God for yourself. There have been lots of times that I have wondered the same thing, especially when I was going through my divorce and I thought things would work out differently. But I realized that I needed to pray. I just asked God to show me what He wanted me to do. And He did, not in the way I expected, but He has a way of touching your heart and letting you know it will be alright. It will be alright, honey." I touched his hand gently and he looked at me with watery eyes. I didn't know how to respond to his, so I hugged him. It was clear that he needed to do some soul searching, and I knew that could only happen alone.

"Well baby, I will stay here as long as you like. But if you need some time, I understand."

"Thank you, you are so sweet. Stay with me tonight, and let's just rest." As he held me in his arms, I prayed for him, silently, and sometimes not so silently, and asked God to touch his heart, give him wisdom and order his steps. In that moment, I felt closer to him than any physical touch could have allowed me to be. And I realized I loved him, with my entire being.

A week or two later, Anthony was celebrating his 34th birthday. I decided that since he had been so down, I would surprise him with a night in a chic, modern hotel, complete with dinner and drinks and an evening of escape. Of course, he had no idea, which made it all the more exciting for me.

"So, where are we going tonight?" Anthony asked as he got in the car after I picked him up from work.

"Well, we are going to run by your house and grab some things, because I'm taking you away for the evening. Tonight, you are all mine."

"Oh yeah? This sounds interesting. You know I have to work in the morning."

"Yes, I do, and we will make sure you make it there. But for now, don't think about that." I reached over and grabbed his hand and he smiled.

"You are being sneaky, what are you up to?" he asked inquisitively.

"You'll see." I laughed. This was going to be a night to remember.

Anthony and I pulled up an hour later in front of a high-scale hotel in downtown Atlanta. I had never been there, but the rooms looked like something out of a modern New York scene. Once we parked and went in, he was on to the plan.

"We're staying here? I know this is expensive, baby."

"You let me worry about that. Today is your day, and we are going to enjoy it."

We checked into our room, and when we entered, it was better than I expected. The room was beautifully furnished with all modern furniture, a computer desk, flat screen TV, and a beautiful king-size bed with a large backboard and a chaise lounge overlooking the window onto downtown.

"Wow, this is nice. Thank you." Anthony said and walked over to kiss me.

"Thank you honey, for all you do for me. This is better than I imagined. I wish we could stay." I said as I plopped down on the chaise and put my feet up. "They have a CD player, I see. I brought something for us to listen to." I handed him a CD from my bag and out bellowed the sultry sounds of Jill Scott.

"Setting the mood, eh?" he said and came and sat next to me. "We may never leave the room." We laughed and kissed, and I was mesmerized at the perfection that was seized in this moment.

After some relaxation and getting comfy in the room, we decided to get dressed and go down to the restaurant for dinner. The hotel restaurant was as chic as the room upstairs, furnished with modern couches and seats, a bar made of silver and glass windows all around. There were business meetings going on and people who had clearly come as tourists and were enjoying drinks at the bar. Anthony and I chose a high-top table near the window and ordered our drinks. Sometime in the night, we began to play as if we were strangers and had just met. It was like getting reacquainted all over again. All I could think was that I loved every minute of being with him, because there was always fun and never a dull moment. After a few drinks, we couldn't stand another minute being more than a foot away from each other, so we went upstairs and continued our night.

The next morning, we stood in the bathroom mirror, Anthony getting ready while I combed my hair. For a moment we stopped and looked at each other. He walked up behind me and held me tight. "Thank you for the best birthday I've had in a long time. This was truly something I will never forget." I turned around and kissed him passionately and showed him that I wouldn't either. "Only wish they had a door to this bathroom – there's no privacy for poops!" We both busted out laughing at this thought. That was what I loved about him. We could be in a moment of intimacy and suddenly find something totally ridiculous to laugh about. I was falling for him, in a way I never imagined.

As we got dressed and left, I looked back at the hotel, capturing every detail of the room, the lobby, the bar, etching it in my mind. I was sure I would never forget this time we had shared, for as long as I lived. It was a beautiful memory, engraved in my mind, never to be duplicated.

~

Walking on Broken Glass

Just as easily as one can be floating amongst the clouds, one can begin to falter and slip through the abyss of the atmosphere and gradually sink back down towards the ground, where fantasy stops and reality hits. Sinking is never a comfortable feeling, rather it lends oneself to grasping desperately at everything within reach to steady the fall or stop it altogether. In these times, some may panic, some may have anxiety, and others simply face the challenge head on, fighting to the end. As Anthony and I continued our days together, there was a gradual sinking to our fantasy island we had docked on. Days and nights together became more sporadic, clouded by extra hours at work, stress at home, responsibilities with my child, or just plain old tired. When we did meet, we still enjoyed each other, but there was something that was missing. Anthony was missing. The same man he was a few months ago was slowly fading, like the picture in Back to the Future, and I could not figure out how to stop it. So, one day I asked.

"Is something wrong, Anthony? You've been kind of distant lately." I looked at him as we sat on his bed.

"Just stressed out at work. I've been working a lot, and just trying to figure out what I want to do." He wouldn't make too much eye contact, which made me wonder what he was figuring out.

"So, what have you come up with baby? You know I'm here for you," I sat up, wanting to be attentive to his problems.

"I'm thinking of joining the Army." Anthony looked up at me with so much seriousness, I was taken aback.

"The Army? The Army? Wow..." I was speechless. What do you say when the man you love and look forward to seeing every day or at least each week tells you he wants to leave and join the service?

"Yeah, I think it would be good for me. Get back in shape and make a difference in the world in some way. I'm not getting any younger you know. And I just want to know my life counts." His tone made it clear that this would boost his self-image and fill the void he had spoken of just weeks ago. The other thing I heard in his voice was that his mind was made up.

"Well, I can't say I would like it. Hell, I'd hate it. But if it's what you want to do, I have to support you." Trying to hide my disappointment and the impending plummet my heart was making to the floor, I put my head down and turned away.

"Baby, come here. I'm not leaving today. I'm not even sure about when. I just went and signed the application and I'll hear back from them soon. Once I know something, you know I will tell you." He wrapped his arms around me and I buried my head in his chest, knowing this was the beginning of the end.

"Grace, girl I need to talk," I called Grace when I got home the next day, practically on the verge of tears that I was sure she could sense over the phone.

"Uh, uh, what happened? Do I need to come over there? Did that fool do something to you?" Grace was always a ride or die chick, ready to go at the snap of a finger.

"No Grace, you don't have to come here, and he didn't do anything to me. Well, kind of, he did. He put in an application for the Army." With those words, I burst out into a stream of tears.

"What? Oh girl, don't cry. I know you are upset, but did he tell you when he's leaving? Lots of people go to the Army...that doesn't mean he'll leave you."

I wiped my face and attempted to pull myself together. "He doesn't know yet, but he's been kind of distant and I just think he might be trying to detach himself first. I was just thinking it was getting so good." I sniffled and shook my head.

"It's not over yet, just be cool and take it a day at a time. It's already October, so you know he won't leave before the holidays. Just wait it out and get through Christmas. I'm sure it will be alright. Just keep your cool, for now."

"Thanks Grace. I'm sure going to try. Yeah, I'm excited about the holidays with him. He was telling me about his parents' house in North Carolina...maybe I'll get an invite." I giggled, excited at the thought.

"Hey, you never know!! If he told you about it, he might be thinking about a visit. I'm sure you are just overreacting, and I probably would too. Especially considering how many of our troops are being sent to the Middle East. But it may not even happen, so don't worry for now."

"True, true. Well, I'll keep you posted, Grace. Thanks again!" I said as I hung up. There were times that I needed to consult with my girls for advice because it had been so long that I'd been out of the dating scene that I felt out of touch with it. Grace was good at listening, and she was very level-headed and less emotional than I was. Talking to her was like sitting on Oprah's couch, and I always cried, then laughed, and felt better afterwards.

As the holidays neared, the time we spent together was more spaced out, but no less enticing. Anthony heard my concerns about our not being together as much and made the effort to see me more often, even though his work schedule was hectic. I was learning to have more patience and realized that life's responsibilities took precedence sometimes over the things we wanted. I wanted nothing more than to spend every waking moment with him, but in reality, I had to understand that the honeymoon phase was over; we were entering the comfort stage. Our time was spent talking and sometimes just being in each other's presence, rather than the hot, steamy first encounters we had. Nevertheless, I was equally enamored with the time we did spend, because it had more meaning to it, seeing as though we had to make special arrangements to be together and sneak away for quiet moments.

I was unsure of what to get Anthony for Christmas though. Gifts are often a sign of where you are in a relationship, and we had not given ourselves a label, per say, rather there was an understanding that we were mutually committed to each other. So, I needed a gift that said, "You are special, and I love you", without actually saying the "L" word. It had not come up in conversation; instead it was more like, "You know I care about you a lot." Men often are afraid that something happens when that word comes out, and I knew I wouldn't be the first to say it, even though I had felt it for some time. After looking all over, I found the perfect silver link bracelet that was masculine enough for him to wear and didn't say too much but said "you're special to me." I was so excited to give it to him, and since we hadn't discussed our family plans, it seemed like I'd have to make our date, just two days before Christmas, the perfect time to give him my gift.

It was a clear winter night, December 23rd, when we were supposed to meet. However, Ant had gotten called in to work and we were not going to be able to go out. So, I called and said, "Maybe we can just spend a little time together when you get off."

He replied, "I'll probably end up working all night, but come down to the job. It's slow and you know I have access to all the rooms, so we can hang out for a while here."

Seeing as though I was so excited to see him and I wanted it to be special, I wore a short black dress with tights and boots, so I would look especially inviting and remind him of what he would be missing out on at work. When I arrived at the door, he came to meet me and was pleasantly surprised at what he saw.

"Girl, you look good! Wow!" He greeted me with a hug and a kiss, and I inhaled his scent as he held me close.

"Thank you, sweetie. I've missed you. I wanted to show you what you were missing out on tonight." I smiled coyly as we walked inside.

This was the first time I had ever ventured into his job and to say I was overdressed was an understatement. Anthony's building on the outside appeared to be an older building with character inside, but it simply looked like a big empty office building with almost no activity. We passed a few security guards who said hello and made no point of hiding the fact that Anthony had brought in the best-looking woman they'd seen in some time. We rode the freight elevator up to the 12th floor where there was an empty loft space surrounded by floor to ceiling windows. Anthony had two chairs set up, but we never sat down to talk. Immediately, he reached for me, and as if we had been separated for years, he kissed me with a passion I had craved for quite a while. As his hands moved towards my waist, he pulled me closer and I got lost in the essence of him. Before he could go any further, I stopped him and pulled back.

"I have a little something for you," I said as I gazed into his eyes.

"Oh, I can see you have a lot for me that I've been wanting for a long time." Everything in me immediately came alive, and I knew that if there had been an opportunity, I'd be naked in his arms. Alas, that was out of the question.

I laughed shyly and spoke softly as I pulled the box out of my purse. "Merry Christmas, Anthony."

"You shouldn't have done that. I didn't know we were doing gifts."

"It's okay, I just saw this and thought it would be perfect for you. Open it."

Anthony looked at me with a twinge of embarrassment,

for he realized that he was being upstaged at this gift giving moment, but it didn't matter to me. I just wanted to see the look on his face when he opened it.

"Wow, this is hot, baby! I love it." He slid the bracelet out of the box and held it up. "I don't even know where I will wear this, but I am definitely going to find someplace. Thank you." He leaned down and kissed me, and once again, I was lost in his splendor. After some time, we sat and talked until his walkie talkie went off, and it was another guard telling him he was going on break.

"Well, I hate to cut it short, but it seems I have to watch the door."

I held his hand as we walked back down the long gray corridor towards the elevator. "I know you have to work, I just wanted us to have a moment together before we got busy with the holidays."

"I'm so glad you came to see me. We will have to get together after Christmas to celebrate, just you and me." He hugged me and I gave him one last kiss.

"Definitely, we will. Give me a call after you are with the family and maybe we can do something on the 28th."

"For sure," he said, and he walked me to my car. I got in, thrilled at the fact that I had made his night, and I was looking forward to the time we would spend together soon.

Christmas came and went, no Anthony. No call, no text, no email, nothing. I called and left a message and got no response. The 28th came and went, and for a moment, I replayed in my mind what had happened that night at the job. I thought for sure he had said that we would spend some time together. Maybe he got busy with family. I just chalked it up to the holidays and figured I would see him soon.

New Year's came and went. I began to worry. At night I would wonder what he was doing and where he had gone. My calls went unanswered. My texts, unread. I even found myself driving past his apartment to see if maybe he was home, but nothing. It was like he vanished.

"Grace, I don't understand what is happening." It was January 5, and still nothing from Anthony. By now my worry had gone to depression, and here I was balled up on her couch, wiping away tears, wondering what was going on.

"I don't understand either, girl. You haven't heard anything?"

"No, nothing. It makes no sense to me. I keep wondering did I miss something, but I couldn't have. It's like he's just disappeared."

"I'm sure he'll call soon with a great explanation. Maybe someone died or something. Maybe he's just going through. Let's try to be positive." Grace was the best friend I had ever had, and she had been through the divorce and all the prior disappointments with me. This was different than all the rest because I didn't see it coming. The shock of us not talking anymore was like a blow to the heart, and I felt my world crumbling around me. On top of that, my grandmother had just broken the news that she had cancer and would be undergoing chemotherapy within the next two weeks. It was as if I had become the bull's eye for bad news, and it didn't seem to get any better.

"I'm trying. It's just hard. I just want to know what happened. I just want to know he's okay." I wept harder, this time, an ugly sob that swelled up from my soul rang out and Grace put her arms around me and let me cry.

And that night, I cried a river. For many nights after, my river turned into an ocean and my heart felt like it was sinking in sand. For the next six weeks, I heard nothing. In the eerie quiet of my bedroom, I sank into a valley. I was surrounded by thoughts of *"Was it me? Or another woman?"* I didn't know what to think. In my solitude, I turned to the one place where I always found a release – my journal. I began to pour out my innermost thoughts.

Anger. Betrayal. Trust destroyed. Hurt. Brokenness. Every despicable thing I could think, I thought. Every lonely moment I had was enveloped in memories of Anthony. Besides that, I was in a constant battle with myself to be strong for my granny. She was enduring the fight of her life through this treatment, and I was in a fight for my mind and my heart. In every area of my life, I was losing. And it was tearing me to pieces. Here I thought I had found something special, something great, something fresh and new, and just like that, it was gone–poof – vanished into thin air, with no warning, no explanation, and no blame. Just gone.

Just running cross my mind

How did I get to this point
I feel like I've been rolled and smoked,
like a joint
What was the point
of us
There was no trust
Just lust
and lies
phony alibis
emotions disguised
between wet thighs
Hypnotized by
deceptive eyes
I so despise
the event of our demise
If I was wise
I wouldn't act surprised
Instead rise
Hold my head high
and walk on by
No need to cry
I just wonder why
You never said goodbye...

After six long weeks, came a text. "I'm sorry, I've been

going through some stuff. It's not you, it's me. Please bear with me."

You can imagine how a knife feels going into the heart, but it's the turn that makes it worse. This text sent me all the way to rage.

"You're going through stuff?? Bear with me? What the hell am I supposed to make of that? All this time and that's all you can say? No explanations, no call, just bear with me!!" I screamed across my bedroom. "You are a coward, Anthony! And I don't even want to talk to you."

I sounded like a woman scorned, defiled, rejected, a mad black woman. And I had every right to be. But being angry made me feel better. I began to write about it and wrote every evil thing I could think to say to him.

My journal bled red ink as I scribbled across my pages every thought I had over the past month and a half. But I couldn't bring myself to say it to him. I knew that if I had the opportunity to come face to face with him, the words I was feeling would damage our friendship, and anything we'd ever had, forever. He deserved it – I was sure. But I couldn't bring myself to say it out loud to anyone but the four corners of my room. I didn't know what I would hear from him, all I knew is that I was holding on by a thread and I couldn't understand how I was supposed to bear with him, when I had been bearing the load of a painful heartbreak since Christmas. My heart was breaking as I watched my grandmother slip away, and I felt so alone, even when I was surrounded by family and friends.

In my free time, I drove to the riverfront and sat and wrote. In between writing, and in my low state, I had sunken back into a habit I had long since given up. There was comfort in being numb to my feelings, so I numbed myself daily now with either a drink or a smoke. I hid it from my mother and my child, but when I could get away, Dan was the one I could go to.

"Girl, I told you don't get all caught up. Anthony is my boy, but hey, he's still a man. He used to disappear on us all the time. Just think, we hadn't seen him in years and he just reappeared. I hate to say it, but it doesn't surprise me," he said one day as I was at his house wallowing in self-pity.

"Thanks for the kind words, Dan." I frowned at him, angry that there was so much truth to them, but hating to hear them from one of my closest friends.

"You may as well chalk it up as a loss. I talked to him briefly the other day, and he said he was joining the Army. Did you know?"

"Yea, he mentioned it before. But hell, he could have said something to me. I won't even answer his calls. I'm still too mad; I'm afraid I'll curse him out." Being with Dan was almost like being with Grace, because we had been friends for 10 years, but he was not going to sugar coat anything. Straight no chaser was his motto and even though it was annoying at times, he was right. "I'll talk to him when the time is right."

"Okay," he said as we sat and sipped on some drinks. This was my life now. My, had the tables turned.

The day I decided to talk to Anthony, I was alone in my car, sitting outside writing one night, dreading going home, because there I was engulfed by my loneliness and sorrow and of course, I wasn't able to get any escape from it. As I usually did, after putting my baby to sleep, I drove around and parked and had a smoke while I wrote or thought. That night he called, and I answered.

"Hello," he said hesitantly.

"Hello," my voice managed to say. There was no sense of familiarity at all. Just hurt, anger, and disappointment.

"I've been trying to call you. I have been through so much over this past month and a half, I just couldn't talk. It was nothing you did to me. I just needed some time."

And the outpouring began. "Some time? Are you crazy? You don't just disappear and say nothing because you need some time. WE are adults, Anthony! When you are going through something and there is someone in your life you care about, you tell them! Hell, I've been going through something too! I'm sorry if I can't just bear with you for now. You hurt me. You really, really hurt me." And with that, my voice gave way and the tears began to flow.

"I'm sorry. I didn't mean to hurt you."

"But you did. You don't know what it's like to worry if the person you care for has been hurt or killed or is sleeping with someone else or what. You just disappeared. I'll see you on the 28th you said. No call on Christmas, no text, nothing. I didn't know what happened, and I didn't think that of all people, you would be the one to do this."

"My cousin died. It shook me up bad. I just couldn't find the words to talk to anyone."

"Well, I'm sorry to hear that, but it doesn't excuse anything. While you have been holed up in your shell, my grandmother has been battling cancer. So, don't tell me to bear with you! I've been trying to survive myself. But you wouldn't know that!"

"Baby, I'm sorry to hear that. Is she okay?"

"No, she's not okay. She's in chemo now and I don't know what's going to happen. All I wanted was to be able to talk to you. Tell you what was going on. But you weren't there for me, and I needed you. Who have you been with??"

"There's no one I've been with. I've just been alone. And I decided to join the service. I'm leaving tomorrow to go to basic training. I wanted to see you before I left."

"What? Tomorrow? You know, you are something else Anthony." I sat in disbelief for a moment, floored at the news I had just heard. Now I would truly be alone.

"I don't think I can come see you tonight." As much as I wanted to be in his arms one more time, I couldn't imagine making myself vulnerable to all those feelings I had just been trying to cut off over the past six weeks.

"Please, I would really like to see you. I'm at a hotel near the airport. I have a room and you can come stay the night," he pleaded.

I chuckled in disbelief at the gall he showed at thinking

I would come be with him just because he asked. After all this time, I didn't even know if I could open myself back up to him. I sat and cried as I contemplated what to do. "I can't, I have to work tomorrow."

"Please, I promise I'll wake you up. I just want to see you before I leave."

I breathed an exasperated sigh. The ultimate fork in the road lay before me. On one hand, I could slip back into Anthony's grasp and hope that he wouldn't hurt me again. On the other hand, I could run, and not look back, taking this as the break that would ultimately be the end.

"I can't. I just can't." I fought back the tears and said, "Goodbye, Anthony. I wish you the best."

"I will keep in touch. I understand, and again, I'm sorry," he said with such sincerity that I almost changed my mind. Almost.

After I hung up I just sat in the car and cried. Then I began to write my goodbye note to him. Goodbye in my heart and good-bye in my mind. Goodbye Anthony, for now...

~

A Glimpse of Hope

When you walk away from something or someone that was important to you, goodbye is never permanent. As much as I wanted to forget Anthony and not think of his impact on my life, he was constantly in my heart and on my mind. I often sat and wondered how his training was going, what would happen when he returned, and how I would respond. Three months later, I got the chance to come face to face with my feelings.

I was hanging out with Dan, who had taken up the spot in my life that was once filled with Anthony. After a long night of spades, talking smack, and a few drinks, Dan turned to me and said, "You sleepy?" Normally at 2:30 a.m., my immediate response would be yes, of course, but Dan had a twinkle in his eye which told me he was up to something.

"A little, but what's up?" I figured this was Dan's way of

trying to keep the party going at his house or some other spot that he had discovered for us to go to and kick it.

"Anthony just called me. He's in town for the weekend. He wants us to come see him, but we have to come now."

I hadn't jumped at the sound of his name, but inside I was intrigued. "Come where? He's in town? It's 2:30 in the morning, Dan."

Dan laughed, knowing that these were excuses, yet clearly reading that I was interested.

"I don't know, I can call him back and see. I'm game if you are, that is if you don't have to get up early tomorrow."

I really had no reason to not go. My child was in good hands with his grandma and I was definitely able to sleep in if need be. Besides, when was the last time I'd seen Anthony? It had been over 6 months, and if nothing else, I just wanted to talk to him. "Sure, let's go."

Dan and I set out, heading downtown to some random spot they agreed to meet. When we pulled up, most people were stammering out of clubs, half drunk, or sleepy. Others were cozy in their beds. However, despite it being almost 3a.m., I was wide awake, adrenaline pumping, heart racing, wondering what I would say to him when we saw each other. I didn't have much time to think because as I was wondering what my first words would be, we parked and I saw him standing there on the sidewalk, dressed in full army fatigues, looking more handsome than ever.

I don't know if it was because it had been so long or because it was him, but instantly my body heated up, my pulse was racing, and I was like a school girl all over again, unable to breathe or come up with anything intelligent to say. Of course, I had to look cool in front of Dan or he'd roast me forever. Dan and I hurried across the street, and as soon as Anthony recognized us, a smile spread across his face. As much as I wanted to feel in-different, look upset like a woman scorned, I couldn't do it. The most I could trust my expression to be was blank, even though I knew my eyes were giving away my heart.

"Hey Dan," Anthony said as he gave Dan a fist and a manly hug with the traditional pat on the back.

"You looking good, Ant, all decked out in your fatigues. I see you are a military man for real. I almost didn't believe you were going to do it."

"Yeah, it's for real man. But I love it. I'm in great shape and the young guys all look up to me. Plus, I may get to do some traveling, hopefully within the country though." As I was listening to their conversation, I made it a point to sort of stand back off to the side of Dan, so that I was not directly in Anthony's view, but not quite hidden either. But there was no hiding from him. After their brief exchange he turned to me.

It was clear that he felt as nervous as I did about our meeting. While he wanted to smile and I wanted to jump into his arms, we both went gently into our first hello. "Hey there Ms.," Anthony said and smiled. I couldn't resist. With the first sound of his voice, I was like a magnet drawn to my opposite, helpless against his pull. I walked toward him and said, "Mr. Anthony," and before I knew it I was in his arms. He held me tight and close, and I whispered in his ear, "It's good to see you."

He responded, "I missed you, girl." It was all I needed to hear to melt in his arms. I felt like I could freeze this moment in time. But of course, Dan was still within 10 feet of us. "Uh, uh, um," Dan cleared his throat. We slowly pulled apart, yet our eyes were still locked on each other. Dan attempted to strike up a conversation and we talked about Anthony going to Texas to do additional training and made small talk about what had been going on with us. Although it was the middle of the night, the street lights shining down seemed to be like sunlight shining on our meeting, and I was amazed at how the anger I felt, the rage, the hurt, all was lying beneath the surface, but seemed irrelevant at that moment, because all I could remember was how much joy Anthony and I had experienced together. I wanted to lose myself in these memories, but something Dan had told me continued to ring in my ears – "chalk it up as a loss." As much as I would have loved to fall back into Anthony's world, he had made some life changing decisions to join the Army, walk away from those he cared for and loved, and even though I knew I was important to him, his life was going in another direction, and I didn't think there was a place for me in it.

After two hours of talking, we said our goodbyes and Anthony agreed to keep in touch with me via Messenger and through texts while he was away. I gave him another hug and promised we would keep in touch. I figured, there was no need to sever our friendship, because who knows where life will lead later. As we turned to get into the car and Anthony walked away, he blew me a kiss and waved goodbye. Little did I know it was the last time I'd ever see him.

~

One Short Forever

Today I went for a walk
Just needed to take a break and get away
Clear my mind of the trivial burdens of life
And I ended up at our favorite spot
Overlooking the waves on the edge of forever
The endless water stretches before me
And I remember how we used to sit here and dream…

Dreams of a better life, dreams of love
You had a way of making me feel all my dreams would come true
I know that in reality all dreams don't
But when we were together it seemed
That life's rules didn't apply
You made me feel safe
And I opened myself to you
I revealed my inner wants and desire
We shared wine and discussed our future
Never needed another, we would turn off the phone so we could just be together…

Do you remember our good times?
Do you remember how you used to hold my hand and stroke my hair?
We laughed at the simple pleasures
Danced with no music, just the melody of our hearts…

As I sit and dream
I wonder do you ever do the same?
When you see the restaurant where we shared foreign delights,
When you walk past the store where we bought wines,
When you see my picture in your phone,
Do you wonder where I am?
Was all that we shared an illusion?

Cause our spirits seemed to dance in the sun
And delight in the warmth of security
Your masculine hands perfectly fit around every part of my body
When we kissed it was if it was the Fourth of July each time
And how amazing you felt when you would enter into my realm
And take me on a fantastic voyage to ecstasy…

I wonder if it is wrong to still want you
Is it a crime to want the dream to be a reality?
I wish you were here, to share with me this wonderful memory
I can see you smiling, wanting, and walking towards me
To embrace me passionately
Your beautiful body overflowing with heat…

Can we share this again?
Not forever, but just once more
How I'd love to wrap my legs around your waist and hold u tight next to me
No questions asked, no explanations necessary
Just the two of us…
Let's go back for a day or a night

To that perfect forever overlooking the sea of dreams
My body craves you like an addict yearns for a fix
It doesn't have to become a habit
One short forever is all I want to share with you, again...

~

Shattered Dreams

*"Look into my eyes and you can see my soul. If you see my smile,
you would think that I'm whole. But in truth my heart is out of
control, because when you left, you left a hole I can't close."*

Almost immediately, Anthony contacted me via the web. Thanks to MySpace, Facebook, IM, and every other technological site designed to keep you connected to those near and far, I was able to talk to Anthony more now than I had when he was here in Atlanta. It started with just small talk, short conversations like, "How are you?" and "How's training?". I wasn't able to delve into deeper conversations at that point, and I didn't want to get wrapped up with him again emotionally, just when I was beginning to find some level of stability with him gone. Nevertheless, I looked forward to his messages and our talks online. It was cool to see his updates of what was happening, what he was watching, movies we had seen together, and music we had enjoyed together. Somehow, even though we were miles apart, I felt like we were still connected somehow each time he shared a thought or memory.

There was still no answer to what had happened in the six weeks or so that we hadn't spoken. I often wondered and wanted to ask what he did for all that time. But I never did, not to Anthony anyway. And it never came up with Dan, until one day we were out with a group of our old friends from college. We met at a party of a mutual friend and it was like a mini-reunion. Our girlfriend, Joan, who also went to school with us, happened to show up at the art gallery we stood in. "Hey Joan," I said enthusiastically, giving her a big hug. She had been one of those friends who was like a big sister, the advice giver, and just a great listening ear throughout college. Although we had all gone to school together and were around the same age, Joan always seemed to be an old soul, full of wisdom. There was nothing she couldn't read on my face or in my actions when we were together.

"Hey sweetie, it's so good to see you. You are looking great. How've you been?" She asked in her Jamaican accent.

"I've been good, just trying to maintain. You know a lot has been going on lately." My voice betrayed the smile my face showed.

"Hmmm, seems like we need to talk I see," she picked up on my underlying unease.

"Yes, we do." I grabbed a glass of wine and we took a walk over to another side of the art gallery, away from the crowd. "It's been a rough couple of months, with losing my grandmother, dealing with the divorce, and you know Anthony is gone now too. Just been hard," I tried to smile, but there was a tremble in my throat as I held back my emotions.

"I know sweetie, it has been hard. But you are still here. Just keep the faith, it will get better."

"I'm trying to, I really am. It's been nice talking to Anthony again, you know he went to the service."

"Yeah, I heard. I actually saw him not too long before he left. Didn't Dan tell you?" She looked puzzled as if she figured I had known this.

"Uh no," I responded unknowingly, looking around for Dan who was across the room schmoozing with some old friends as he always did at these type of events.

"Well, maybe we better talk to him too." Joan said as she waved Dan over.

"What's up, Dan? You didn't tell me Joan had seen Anthony too before he left," I said immediately as he joined us. Dan seemed taken aback by this new information, almost like a child that had been caught red-handed.

"Uh, I didn't think to tell you." There was clearly an elephant in the room, and no one wanted to be the one to say.

"Well, honey, I don't know how to say this, but I saw Anthony at his reception."

"What reception? He had a going away party or something?"

"Not exactly."

My heart began to race. There was too much hiding in this conversation, and I seemed to be the only one not privy to the secret.

"Anthony invited me to his wedding reception. He was seeing a woman who was pretty well-to-do, and she insisted on them marrying before he left for the service. They did one of those made for TV weddings in her apartment and he was able to invite a few people and I went," Dan explained. "I was as shocked as you probably are right now because I knew you two had been serious. When I brought up your name and asked did you know, he said to please not tell you, and let him."

I felt instant chest pains and shortness of breath, as the room began to spin. There have been few times in life that I am at a loss for words, but this qualified as one of the biggest. I looked at Dan and he nodded in affirmation and looked sympathetically at me. I didn't know whether to cry, be mad at them both for keeping it from me, or to just run out. I guzzled my glass of wine and managed to get out the words, "When?"

"Just a month ago, sweetie. It isn't official, but I believe it will be when he returns. It was a TV show that will air in the next few months, but I guess it will eventually happen."

Air. I needed air and I ran out the room down the stairs to find it, as my emotions burst forth into tears. I stood outside in the brisk air, as my tears turned to sobs and my entire body began to shake. I had loved this man to the core. Even though I knew it was not going to work at this present moment, I always had hope. And just like that, it was gone. And I had never been more crushed.

"Hey, honey, I'm so sorry to have you find out this way." Joan came up behind me with my coat and hugged me as I sobbed into her shoulders.

"I loved him, Joan. I suspected something, but marriage?

How could he? And never say anything?" So many questions raced through my mind. "Who is she?"

"This won't make it any better, but she is white. Apparently a little older, someone he met from work."

"Well, that explains a lot. The six-week sabbatical, the distant phone calls, not hearing from him for days. I just can't believe this."

Dan came out shortly after and put his arm on my back. "I'm sorry I didn't tell you. I just didn't know how. I figured he would have said something by now. But I knew he hadn't because you seemed so happy to be talking with him again."

"He's an asshole!" I screamed. "I can't believe this. Dan can you just take me home?"

"Yeah, I will, let me grab my coat." Dan turned and went back inside.

"I told him he was wrong for not saying anything and he owed you more. I know he felt bad, honey. But that doesn't excuse it." Joan rubbed my back as I shook my head in disbelief.

"Nothing could excuse this. But thanks for telling me." Suddenly, my heart was a stone and my face revealed no emotion at all. I was cut off from the world. In my own private hell, and no one could get me out. "See you later, Joan."

"Call me if you need me," she called as Dan and I walked to the car.

~

Late night thoughts...My heart hurts

I died last week
Heard the flat line beep
As you turned to walk away
With the love you said would stay
I loved you from my soul
And you came in and stole
My essence
My strength and presence
In such a short time

Never will you find
Another woman like me
Look in the mirror and see
Yourself for the demon you are
Could have loved me from afar
Instead of hurting me up close
I thought I needed another dose
But I think that my system
Just had a toxic embolism
Blood popped, a heart stopped
Because of you
I wish you could feel as blue
As midnight feels
When a thief stabs you and steals
Your last dollar
Don't it make you wanna holler?
But my mouth wouldn't open
I was ready and hoping
One scream and shout
And all of you would pour out of my body
No longer would I be in a trance
Or this f-d up circumstance
Of having been misled
Then left for dead
On the side of love's highway
Your lucky vengeance is not my way
Of handling this
One day you'll find the one who fits
But God is one who never forgets
I'll still be around to watch you cry
When your heart is hung out to dry.

~

In the days ahead, I retreated into myself. It was the only place that I felt safe and that no one could hurt me. My heart felt like it had been ripped in two and I had no use for love ever again.

Love had hurt me, let me down, and betrayed me. In the daytime, after work and before going home, I sat near the edge of the water, near the pier, daydreaming, writing, crying, and numbing myself with my new best friend, Mary Jane. With her, I could escape into this other place, where the pain of my circumstances could not pierce my soul and I could write anything that I felt. Sometimes it was hate – the hate I felt in my heart for Anthony's betrayal. Other times it was love – all the love that we had experienced rolled into marks of black ink on a page. At night, I would escape to Dan, who was a silent friend, cracking jokes and carefully skirting the issue of Anthony, but enabling me to shrink further into my cocoon of self-pity.

Weeks went on like this, and at times I felt there was no hope at all for me. Here I was facing a failed marriage, failed relationship, lost my house, lost my grandmother, and I was left with a job, responsibilities of being a single mother, and attempting to walk through life with a smile on my face, yet I was numb inside.

Meanwhile, Anthony and I had stopped corresponding because I had nothing else to say to him. There was no room for small talk, and I didn't trust my emotions to tell him what I felt without a thousand expletives coming out all at once. Dan tried to tell me to move on, just forget about him, and at first I didn't want to hear it. I wanted to remember all of these horrible feelings and never forget so I wouldn't feel them again. But they were devouring me. On the days I felt good, I managed to go out with my mother or friends and feign happiness, or attempt to smile, simply to feel like I was still alive. In the meantime, I threw all my leftover energy into my job and I focused on being the best executive I could be. My projects were coming out great, and my boss actually suggested a possible promotion. Although I was proud of my work, there was a void left inside of me that nothing was filling.

One day, my mother, in her wisdom, came to me and said, "I think you should come to church with me." I laughed, not at the idea of church, but at the fact that she didn't know half of what was going on with me. I knew if I even attempted to seek God, I would be thrown out on my rear for the sins I had been constantly committing each day. "Thanks, mom, but I will have to see if I can." She didn't push the issue and I didn't either. For months she would ask on and off, gently suggesting, as she knew her child was hurting, but I never took her up on the offer.

Instead I sunk further into myself and retreated to that which made me feel good. Sometimes, it was going out for a drink or two or three, or smoking myself into a state of euphoria, or so I thought. Rarely, I wondered why God had allowed all of this to happen, but I didn't truly seek answers. I needed closure from this situation. And the day came when I would get it.

Almost a year later, Dan told me that he had talked to Anthony and he was home temporarily before he was being deployed to Iraq. Reality sunk in. Anthony was back. Anthony was leaving and may never return. Although there was still hurt in the place where he once filled my heart, I wanted nothing malicious to happen to him. As far as he knew, I wasn't aware of what had happened, but I'm sure he had figured it out based on my refusal to respond to any of his messages. However, I wasn't sure what I would say to him if given the chance. It seemed irrelevant to curse him out for what had transpired over a year ago, but I wanted to get it out so that I could be at peace.

Late one night, after driving around, smoking a few cigarettes as I usually did at night, now that I had pretty much slowed down on the Mary Jane, I got a call. It was Anthony.

"Hey there." I heard him say cautiously. I wanted to smile, scream, and shout, but I merely responded with the same.

"Hey, long time." I said dryly.

"I know, it has been. I don't know if Dan told you, but I'm leaving soon, going overseas."

"He did. When do you leave?" I asked, curious, but at a loss for anything else to say.

"Tomorrow morning. I go to Georgia, and then fly out next week to Iraq."

"Wow," I gasped unexpectedly. "What made you call me?"

"I couldn't leave without talking to you. I've missed you and I was hoping you would see me before I left."

With that, I busted forth like a tsunami of rage. "You missed me? Was that before or after you got married? You hurt me Anthony!! In the hardest time of my life, you stabbed me in the heart like I was a dog on the street. I loved you and I was trying to make something work with you. And I have to find out that you got married, on TV? You couldn't even tell me? Do you know what that felt like? Why the hell would I want to see you now?" Tears flooded my eyes and I pulled over to avoid getting into an accident.

"I'm sorry. I'm sorry."

"Huh, you're sorry! That's all you have to say?" I screamed.

"I was confused, and I didn't want to tell you, because I cared about you. I really did. It wasn't my idea, but I did it for her. But we never actually got married. We actually broke up about six months ago. I didn't have the heart to tell you because I knew you probably hated me."

"I don't know what I feel. I thought I was okay now. But it just all came back." My heart began to slow as I took deep breaths trying to calm myself down. "I just want to know why?"

"There's no reason why. And no reason would suffice. I know you probably don't want to see me, but I am going off to war. I don't know what will happen. And I don't want to leave like this. I want us to at least be okay before I go." He pleaded with sincerity and for a moment I felt sorry for him. After all, I didn't want him to die and I still have hate in my heart. But I didn't trust myself to be around him. My head was in a tailspin.

"I never stopped having feelings for you. Even when I was mad enough to hurt you, deep inside I still wondered how you were. It just hurt me so much, what you did to me. I know this is big, you leaving the states. The war is dangerous, and men are dying every day."

"I was hoping I would see you." He pleaded again.

"I can't see you, Anthony. Not today. I just can't."

"I understand. I figured you wouldn't. But can you at least talk to me while I'm gone. I miss talking to you."

"How would I do that?" I asked, afraid to even open up to the possibility.

"I have email and instant messenger, and I can write you," Anthony said. "It will be pretty hard being out there with all guys. I will need to hear from someone who I can talk to when it gets rough out there."

"I guess so," I said, reluctantly. "You better be careful out there. Don't go trying to be a superhero."

"I've been trained and I'm in the best shape of my life. I'm ready to go kick some ass and I don't plan on dying on the other side of the world." Anthony said jokingly.

"That's not funny, Ant. I want you to be safe."

"I will be. It will be better knowing I can talk to you."

"Well, you know where to find me. The same place I've been for the past year."

"I know, I know. Well you take care of yourself, beautiful. And I'll talk to you soon."

"I will, Anthony. Be careful and we'll talk soon. As friends."

"I'd like that." He said and hung up. And I cried myself all the way home and to sleep.

~

Reimagining Hope

I sometimes wonder what made me cry that day. Was it hearing his voice that brought back so many memories? Or was it the fact that I wanted to tell him in so many ways how he had hurt me, yet I still wanted to protect him from the hatred and anger that I felt? In essence, I think it was the combination of my emotions balled up into one snowball that hit me like a ton of bricks in my chest. Over the past year I had endured such pain, and it seemed the one person that I felt comfortable enough to expose myself to had in turn shown me the same result as life's circumstances. And then there was the fear. What if something happened to him while he was away? I couldn't bear the thought of not being able to talk to him, even if it was just in passing or to tell him how mad I was, I still wanted him to come back safely so that I may be able to do it. After the last tear fell and I managed to pull myself together, I looked at this as an opportunity. A chance to get in touch with me, what I was feeling, and to write it down. Normally, my expressions came in poems, where I would just pour out like a pitcher onto paper ever feeling I had. But in the midst of this episode, I began to hear music. Songs of love, adoration, and questioning God's plan; they all began to pour out of me. For hours at a time I would sit at the computer and just let my fingers go, expounding every feeling I had, rolling them together into a lyrical explosion of my inner being.

At the same time, I decided to reenroll in school. I had finished my bachelor's after having my son, and I figured, with my idle time, what better thing to do but to pursue my master's. So, every night I sat at the computer, listening to lectures of mundane professors who tried to dress up the business world in a nice package. In between assignments, Anthony and I talked. The first correspondence was merely niceties: "How are you? What's new?" But as the time progressed and the moment for his overseas departure came closer, our conversations became more weighted.

In essence, we rekindled our once pure friendship. Anthony would tell me of the training drills he had gone through in the day, and I would share the excitement of the boardroom and the many meetings I had attended. Our interaction was light, but friendly, and it was a joy to see that we could once again speak freely, without the anger and disappointment clouding my way. I understood the journey he was taking, and although I didn't condone his choice, the last thing he needed was a mother figure telling him what he shouldn't be doing. We even discussed possibly seeing one another once he returned from Iraq. I believe he appreciated what we had begun in our correspondence and that was confirmed when I received my first letter in the mail from him, it read:

What's happening, baby. I'm sitting here drinking a Gatorade and eating a PowerBar releasing some stress for once. I am officially on my way to Iraq. We've graduated from training and it feels great! I feel great! I'm finally where I want to be body wise. I'm in the best shape of my life; 210 lbs. of lean, mean fighting machine! I can't wait to see you. How about dinner, a movie, and a nightcap at a fancy hotel? That is if you can handle it and you are ready. How is work treating you? Well, Ms. Hope, you keep going and never lose focus on that prize. I can't believe I'm a United States of America Army Soldier. But anyway, I guess I will go now. I've been up for over 24 hours and I'm going to take a nap. I'll write you later on. Love always, Ant."

Inside was a picture of him in uniform, that wonderful smile, and a few of his fellow troops posing with weapons. It truly touched me that he felt compelled to write, and even more that through his letter I could feel his energy. I smiled at the thought of seeing him again and returned a letter to him.

This went on for months, via instant messenger, letters, and texts. Once he was in Iraq, each message became a stressful event for me. I found myself praying and asking God to cover him and keep him safe, away from harm's danger. Sometimes he would tell me he could hear the bombs in the distance going off, and I feared for his life. But he never did. He always said, "I'm coming home, baby," and I believed him. Whether it was two minutes or 20 minutes of conversation, I cherished every minute of it, and I looked forward to the next.

After a few months, Anthony told me that he would be

coming home soon for a quick stay, about a week. I was over-joyed at the thought, and I couldn't help but think that somehow we might rekindle our romance, even if for just one night. But more than anything, even though he was single, I hadn't for-gotten what he had done, and I wasn't about to be naïve. Our friendship had blossomed once again, and I told Dan I wanted to throw him a party when he returned. Of course, Dan, who was always ready for a party, agreed and we began to plan the guest list and decide who would host. Talking to Anthony one day, I mentioned it to him.

"Ant, so when you come home, since I have moved into my own place, Dan and I decided we are going to throw you a party, you know like old times."

"That sounds great! You know I don't need a party, just some one on one with you."

"We'll see about that, but for sure we are going to all get together and celebrate you being back.

"I can't wait, baby. I gotta go. I'll let you know when I'm coming home."

I was so excited after that message, and I began to think of all the things we could do, planned the arrangements, and even considered what could happen between us. Every week, I looked forward to hearing from him about his return, but all of a sudden the messages stopped coming. I figured he was busy fighting for America, serving and protecting our country. I knew he wouldn't hesitate to let me know when he was coming. Then one day, Ant sent a message that said, "I'll be there in a few weeks." It would place it right around Memorial Day or a little after, and I was super excited because I would have the holiday off. If the weather was nice, we could even barbeque. I called Dan and mentioned it to him, and he said to keep him posted. This was going to be the best time ever!

In between our talks, I continued to toil away at my stud-ies every week, just weeks away from graduating with my MBA; I tried to be sure most of my assignments were complete. Since

I had been talking to Ant, I also had gotten the urge to take my mom up on her offer and go to church. I figured if I was praying to God and asking for His help, I should at least show up at his house.

The first time I went, I was very nervous. It had been years since I stepped in a church. Needless to say, I had done my share of sinning continuously. Walking in the door, I felt like everyone could see me and see what I had done. It was as if the ushers could smell the weed on me and taste the liquor pouring from my veins, or the men I had dealt with in my hurt moments. My first time going in I walked in with my head down. But a woman at the door greeted me with the biggest smile and a hug and said, "Welcome, darling. I'm so glad you are here." It was as if God had reached His hands out to greet me Himself, and I immediately felt like I wouldn't be judged in this place. The singing at this church, which was Baptist, reminded me of my days in the youth choir as a girl. I found myself clapping and singing along to the songs I had heard before and even standing up during one. The feeling was not shame at all; rather acceptance, a feeling I had felt from very few places in my life that I was proud of. Hence, I returned, week after week, sometimes without my mom's prompting.

One day while walking through the main hall, a middle-aged woman approached me with a stern look on her face. I wondered what I had done to her or where she knew me from to get this kind of reaction from her. Yet, her voice showed her true spirit. "You need to join the music ministry," she belted out without any hello or introduction.

"Uh, okay," I responded, taken aback, but not terribly shocked. I had considered joining the choir before, but clearly someone of my caliber and negative experience should not be singing up there.

"My name is Tammy and I am the young adult choir leader. Rehearsal is on Tuesday at 7pm. Come a little early so that we can place you in the right section."

"Ok, I will," I said so quickly, I surprised myself.

Two weeks later, I found time to go and I joined the choir. At first, I felt like everyone was watching me. I had to introduce myself and even recite a scripture. Luckily, those years of Sunday school my mother made me attend had paid off. My mom, who was in the senior choir, remarked how proud she was of me and for the first time in my life, it seemed like things were beginning to fall into place. I had my own apartment, after getting a divorce, my child was doing well, I was finishing my master's, and the possibility of Anthony and I was still on the horizon. I began to thank God regularly for what was happening in my life, and in turn, I was convicted over and over any time I decided to try and smoke or hang with the old crew. I didn't stop completely, but I knew the time was soon coming. Dan would tease me constantly about my newfound commitment to Jesus, saying, "Oh look at the church girl. Somebody can't hang out because she has church in the morning."

I would laugh and retort, "You need to bring your tail in there too!"

Dan always had the same response though. "I go to bedside Baptist. The Lord knows my heart. I don't have to go to church to know God."

I would always shake my head at this, knowing that one day Dan would come around. But much like me, it had to happen in his own time, not by the persuasion of others. God has a way of bringing a person to him when He is ready, and even if you plant the seed and encourage a person to go, God gives us free will. The decision lies in our hands, even though God already knows when it will happen. I believe God brought me to Him just in time, because he knew I would need all of His love and strength for what was to come.

~

Hopelessness

"I stumbled on this photograph/It kinda made me laugh/It took me way back/Back down memory lane

I see the happiness... I see the pain/Where am I... back down memory lane

I see us standing there/Such a happy happy pair/Love beyond compare/Look-a-there look-a-there

The way you held me... no one could tell me/That love would die... why oh why

Did I have to find this photograph/Thought I had forgot the past/But now I'm slipping' fast/Back down memory lane"

~ MINNIE RIPERTON

It was a normal Sunday morning, as usual; I had sung in the choir for the first service and was coming down to the kitchen to get a snack before the next. My mom and son were close by discussing what we would eat after church as we did every Sunday. Normally on Sundays, I turned my phone off and did not check it because not many people called on Sunday morning. Most of my friends were still recuperating from partying the night before. But on this day, I had put my cell on vibrate and it began to go off right as I walked toward the vending machine. I turned to my mom and said, "Let me take this, it's Dan. I wonder what's up."

Dan rarely, if ever, called me on a Sunday morning. He was probably the last person I expected to hear from. But something told me to answer the phone. And that something did not feel good.

"Hope, where are you?" Dan's voice sounded shaky and immediately put me on edge.

"I'm at church, of course...what's wrong, Dan?" I tried to sound light-hearted, but I was nervous all the same.

"You may want to sit down." Immediately my heart dropped. What could be so pressing that he called me at 10 am and I needed to sit down for. I told my mom I'd be right back and walked over towards the corner of the room.

"Anthony was in a hit and run last night, near downtown.

He didn't make it. He's gone."

"WHAT??" I couldn't believe what I was hearing. "He's not even here yet, he told me he'd be home in a few weeks." This had to be a mistake.

"Well, apparently he came home and was going to tell us. But I just talked to his guy, and he confirmed it." Dan's voice began to shake. "I can't believe it either."

"What do you mean, he's gone? What hospital is he at?"

"He's dead, Hope." Devastation. Shock. Overwhelming pain hit me in the chest as if a truck had run into me. Immediately, the tears began to fall.

"What happened?" I asked through the tears. By now my mom had walked over to me and all I could do was shake my head.

"He was crossing a street and some guy hit him. They say he was unconscious at the scene, but he had internal bleeding and he died at the hospital. I'm waiting to talk to his sister now."

"Oh my God!! Oh my God!" That was all I could manage to say. I had to hang up. Then I collapsed into my mother's arms. "It's Anthony...he's dead." The tears came and would not stop. The world seemed to be in a tailspin, and everything from that moment on was a blur.

People began to walk up to me and ask what was wrong. All my mother said was, "Her very close friend was killed last night." From everywhere, arms reached out to comfort me, but there was no comfort in this pain. I sat down and cried, and cried, and cried. All I could think was, "*Why, Lord, why?*"

The agony of this reality was too much to bear. Sobs rang forth from my soul as I grasped the truth of what I had just been told. It couldn't be true. No, I was planning his party. We were going to be together again. This was impossible. But it was real.

About five minutes before service started, my mom asked, "Do you want to sing? Maybe you should sit in the audience?" I shook my head no, because I needed to be surrounded by those who could hold me up. I needed to be in my place in God's house to bear this news. As soon as we got into the choir stand, the tears continued. I sang, I don't know how, but through the words came tears and all I could do was cry. Anthony was gone, forever.

Every minute seemed consumed by grief. There was not a song that came on the radio or a message I received that didn't send me into tears. My mom, who had lost a friend at a young age as well, understood my pain and became the one person I could lean on at this time. Dan and I got together and all we could do was cry. In one instant, life had taken a turn. It is amazing how you can be so high on life one moment and come crashing down into a valley the next. With all my church going, the only comfort I found at that moment was in my grief. When it was too much to bear, I went to Dan's and we sat together lost, attempting to find solace in each other, or a drink, or whatever else we could find. To no avail, the grief did not dissipate; it intensified. Like reliving a nightmare, every moment I felt like I was numb to reality, it came back and slapped me in the face.

Two days after hearing the news, I dreamt of Anthony. He was his usual handsome self, only he was in a hospital gown walking away from me. From the back of his gown, I could see blood and I could tell it was coming from somewhere inside. All I could do was reach for him; I wanted to talk to him, to ask him if he was okay. At the final moment, he turned to me and said, I gotta go. I love you, Hope. As I awoke, I smiled, knowing he was with God and knowing he loved me, and in the same moment, I found myself in a river of despair, because I knew I would never see him again.

The hardest thing was the days leading up to the funeral. Dan, Joan, and I talked and said we would all attend. Still in disbelief, we just knew there must be another Anthony that was at the root of this tragedy. Although we had seen the news reports, it was not real to us yet. Dan and I met that Saturday, and he decided to drive.

"Hope, I don't know how we are going to get through this." Dan looked at me and for the first time in my life, I saw that Dan was not as strong as I had thought. Even though they weren't the best of friends, Dan and Ant had a special bond, and I could see he was hurting and terrified of what lay ahead. He had stopped smoking cigarettes, but as we drove, he showed me the box of Newports he bought, just in case we needed one. I had slowed down too, but today, I didn't trust myself at all. All night I had been praying, "God help me get through this." I couldn't imagine seeing him in a casket, not hearing his voice, not seeing his smile, or not feeling his touch...this was surreal, and there was nothing that could have prepared me for this.

When we arrived at the church, Dan and I walked arm in arm, slowly to the door. As we got ready to enter, Dan stopped to have a cigarette. All I kept saying was, "God give me peace that surpasses all understanding." I knew that God would help me keep it together, but I didn't trust that I would be okay. I was never the type to faint, but I had also never lost one I loved so dearly at the age of 35. Dan and I walked in together and quickly found Joan who was her usual strong self, attempting to smile but hiding her pain. The crowd was immense, and it was standing room only in the small dark chapel. I could see the line of people going up to view the body. Around Ant were pictures of him in uniform, one which I had seen from the letters he sent. People were all in a trance, awed at the tragedy that stood before us. As we approached, we got separated and I feared my reaction as I approached the casket. Usually, I wouldn't go up to view the body, but this time I had to. I had to know this was real and I wouldn't believe it until I saw Ant's body. As I got closer, I was grief stricken at the reality of it all. There was his mom, his brother, and sister; and Ant lying peacefully in the casket. He looked tanned, probably from the many months in Iraq, but it was his normal peaceful expression; it was him. As I walked away I held my face in my hands and cried. My Anthony was really gone. Dan and I walked to the rear and I laid my head on his shoulder and sobbed. I sobbed so hard my body shook and I wondered if I would be able to get it together to sit through the service.

Somehow, we managed to find a seat. Everything was a blur. From the eulogy, the reading of the obituary, and the songs. All I could do was hear his voice and remember every day we had spent together. To know that it had all ended, and I had not even had a chance to say goodbye, pained me so. One of our friends got up during remarks and attempted some jokes that Ant used to say that made me smile for a moment. But I quickly lost that as I remembered I would not hear them again. When it was over, Dan and I sat in the car and smoked a cigarette as he said, "It really was him," and wiped a tear from his eye. Although it was a beautiful day in May, when most families were celebrating and enjoying the sunshine, all I could see was gray. But I prayed and I prayed as we went to the cemetery. I knew I had to be strong for Dan. Lined up along the gravesite were his fellow Army men with their guns, ready to salute this man who had honored his family and his country with his life. I found it immensely ironic that the entire time Ant was gone, I feared him losing his life in battle. Yet, it was painstakingly taken at the hands of an unknown driver who would never be identified in his home city, Atlanta.

The sounds of the 21-gun salute shook me to my core, and as the casket was lowered, I stood next to Dan gripping his arm for dear life. When the last tear fell, I turned to Ant and told him goodbye and walked away; for this goodbye would be the last I would ever say.

Back at the house, surrounded by family and friends, the mood lightened, and people began to eat, drink, and recollect their fondest memories of Ant. Although I was no longer in tears, thanks to the strong drink Dan had brought me to calm me down a little, I was still very sad. I had paid my respects to his family and was standing around talking with friends as a man approached us. He began to talk and ask how we knew Ant. Dan, being the vocal one, told him we had all gone to school together, and as we introduced ourselves, Hudson, Ant's best friend, recalled the names he had heard before. As he looked to me, he asked what my name was. I told him I was Hope. Astonished and seemingly touched, he said to me, "So you're Hope?" For a moment, his eyes lit up as if he had solved a mystery he had long since given up on.

"Yes, I am. And you are Hudson. Ant truly loved you; he always said you were his best friend who was with him through everything." To my surprise Henry responded in the like.

"And I've heard much of you. It is a pleasure to finally meet you. You meant a lot to him." With that he turned and walked away, and I got the greatest gift I could ever receive... closure.

Since Ant died, nothing could replace the void that was left with his passing. Oftentimes, in remembering his voice or his favorite song, I would hear him laugh and smile. For many months thereafter, I would cry at this memory. For nights on end, I would reread our conversations I had saved from instant messaging and begin a new one, only to remember he was not on the other side to receive it. But by the grace of God, as the months passed, the pain became slightly less. I was able to look at pictures and smile; reread his letters, laugh, and ponder the possibility of what could have been with hope in my heart that he was resting safely in the master's arms, and I would one day love someone in that way again.

CHAPTER 4
FORGED IN
THE FIRE

JOY

Finding Joy

"Joy, joy, God's great joy. Joy, Joy, down in my soul. Sweet beautiful soul saving joy, Oh joy, joy, in my soul."

~ WHITNEY HOUSTON

It took a long time for me to find joy. I was always searching for happiness, affection, and loyalty, but now that I have joy, I know I have something the world can't give, and the world can't remove. I came to this place reluctantly because to find my joy I had to step out of comfort. To find my joy I had to step out of familiarity and into the unknown. The hardest part about change is not knowing what comes next. But that's where faith comes in. I remember what God promised me; what He showed me. Although at the time I realized change needed to occur, I was too afraid of the unknown to take the leap of faith.

It was a cold day in December, as I stood outside on my porch overlooking the land I had sacrificed everything for, the land I had purchased through my own hard work and discipline, and thought, *this little piece of God's masterpiece is mine.* In the past I never actually understood the value of owning land. My grandparents, God rest their souls, always spoke of owning your own. My grandfather owned buildings, cars, and stocks. I wasn't as concerned about these things as a young adult, but in hindsight, had I known the capital and wealth that was stored up in land, I would have invested sooner. My house, my little lot and a half situated in a pocket of peace amidst the hood of the world, gave me peace because I knew the blessing it was to me. At the end of the day I may have to fix some things myself or hire someone, but it was what I made it to be. It was my safe haven, my oasis in the middle of the desert of urban society. It wasn't that the business of life bothered me, and in a strange way the presence of my people, however developed or undervalued, reminded me of the road that had been taken to reach this point. I endured hardships as the third child of five, the true middle child, never quite knowing if I fit into the perfection of my oldest sister who had graduated top of the class at Stanford or my oldest brother whose creative genius had gotten his art showcased around the country. Yet, I was nothing like my younger twin brother and sister who had dedicated their entire beings to medicine after being diagnosed with a rare condition that kept them at doctor's visits regularly the first 10 years of their lives. I was stuck in between them both, meandering my way through much of my teenage years, attempting to locate some calling or purpose unique to me.

My parents were the epitome of patient with me, always encouraging me to try something new in hopes that their one child who had yet to figure out life might stumble upon something meaningful. I can never thank them enough for the multiple investments they made into my new adventures – yoga for a while, criminal justice, psychology, and I even made a go at law enforcement. Unfortunately, none were my niche. Yoga landed me in the hospital with a sprained neck after attempting to perform a headstand gone wrong. Needless to say, having your students call you an ambulance pretty much disqualifies you as an instructor. I didn't have the dedication for criminal justice or psych – which were much more intense than portrayed in movies and shows like "Silence of the Lambs" or "Law and Order." Law enforcement could have worked had I not partied the night before the test. The unfortunate part was that I wanted all of these avenues to work, but they just didn't drive me.

But in my determination to measure up to my siblings I never gave up. I simply regrouped and looked for my next opportunity. Around my mid-20s, family gatherings became like dreaded dentist visits – you knew you had to go, but you never knew what painful questions or surprise lurked nearby. I some-how always ended up surrounded by my aunts and uncles, well meaning, yet with immensely probing questions. "What are you doing now?" knowingly insinuating my last endeavor's failure. Or the resurfacing question: "Any special person in your life?" It was like my life could only be defined by a job or a spouse, never just by me. For years I would leave family functions slightly in-ebriated or a moment away from tears because of my plethora of non-accomplishments. I would have avoided them altogether if I knew it wouldn't crush mom and dad.

And then suddenly, in the midst of what I would call an in-between gig, I began to feel something inside of me activate. It wasn't quite an epiphany moment, it happened over time as I ran a portion of the after-school program. I found myself smil-ing, more excited to see my children at the center and my co-workers. My path was finally leading me into my purpose.

Every experience in my educational career had been tu-multuous. I wasn't an honor roll kid, but I never flunked out either. What surprised me most about this new journey is the fact that I would end up right where I never thought I'd be – in school. Yet, now my role has changed. I have gone from being the student to being somewhat of a teacher. More like a leader. A builder.

On my morning drive to work I often listened to my favorite gospel station. Although I didn't consider myself reli-gious, early on I found comfort in God's word and the music seemed to calm my spirit. His promises came alive in each lyric, and in every melody I could lose the troubles and stresses of what my life showed me and be encouraged that God had more for me. Pulling up to work at Clayton Middle School, I found re-newed love and purpose as the children smiled and said, "Hi, Ms. Joy." It was funny to see them as happy to see me as I was to see them. No matter what was bothering me, one of their hugs or high fives always lifted me.

As I walked in the front door and stopped to sign in, I was

greeted by one of the other after-school teachers. "Hey, Ms. Joy! How's it going?" Ms. Green always had a smile and a hug for me every day. Her spirit exuded light and peace, and I was always thankful to have a person like that on staff with me.

I hugged her and said, "Hey, Green! Girl I'm good, about to get ready for this afternoon. I'm excited to see what the children came up with." Ms. Green started an entrepreneurial class with the after-school students that had blossomed into booming businesses. This was the first day of their pop-up shop for all to see their self-made products. Nothing is more rewarding than seeing the students proud of their own accomplishments and learning valuable life skills that could bloom to businesses in their future. One of my main goals was to enrich the students' lives in a way that stayed beyond our program.

"I can't wait! I hope they sell out!" said Ms. Green as she walked down to the room where students were setting up.

"I'll be there soon, with my wallet," I chuckled as I walked away beaming.

The after school program was filled with middle schoolers from a variety of backgrounds, but what they had in common was that they were all labeled "at-risk." In my program, I had redefined that term to uplift our students. In the outside world, "at-risk" referred to students who were in circumstances that could prevent them from being successful educationally, emotionally, or socio-economically. I told my students that you can redefine that word. So, we say we are at risk of becoming greater than anyone in our neighborhood, achieving knowledge beyond the school walls and gaining wealth in ways that included yet surpassed money. I wanted our children, especially our children of color, to know that they had power over their lives and situations and that the only limits they had were the ones they put on themselves. It was fulfilling work, something I lacked in all the other professions I had tried. And for that reason, I had stayed on and was currently entering my fifth year with the program.

After checking a few emails, I decided to go down and

check out the pop-up shop. I could hear music down the hall and students were all over the hall heading that way. On a normal day we averaged 350 students or more, and today we opened the center to the public to encourage business. Parents, teachers, and students spilled out into the building all for the benefit of the children. I had to be sure to speak to them all and take plenty of pictures to memorialize such a great occasion.

Inside the room, which doubled as a lunchroom and meeting place, tables were set around the perimeter with students adamantly pitching the reasons why their customers should buy their goods. Overall, there were about 15 tables of students, each with a line of interested consumers. I approached the table to my right and saw one of my favorite students, Kera.

"Hi Kera, how's it going?" I asked with a smile. "I see you have some beauty products here. Let me hear about them." Kera was one of my students I had watched blossom from a shy, yet confident young girl, to an outgoing and mature young lady. I was sure she would be a lawyer or hold a political office because she was sharp and always looking to have a voice in what we did at the center.

"Hey, Ms. Joy! I have created an all-natural hand cream with different scents. The cream is proven to keep your hands moist even after washing because it is made with Shea butter and essential oils." She proceeded to do her Vanna White impression and moved her hand in front of the containers to show them off.

"Wow, impressive. I'll have to try one out. Do you have a sample?"

"Sure do!" She took a tray with many small containers and allowed me to choose my scent. I went with citrus; it always was refreshing and uplifted my spirits.

I rubbed a dab onto the back of my hand. "Ooh silky," I exclaimed and we both laughed. I could see the pride she had in her work, and I genuinely liked it. "Okay, I'm sold, how much?"

"A small container is $5, the larger one is $8."

"Such a steal! Give me two smalls; I'll give one to my

mom." She gleamed as she bagged it up and I gave her my $20 bill. "Thanks Hun, let me not spend all my money walking in the door and go see some of your friends."

"Thanks, Ms. Joy!! Have fun!" She smiled as she handed me the change and went on to the next customer.

"Wait, let's take a picture with your product. This could be your advertisement!" I said as I pulled out my iPhone. We took a quick selfie as I held up her product and I went on through the room.

My next stop was Daren's table. Daren was my rough-around-the edges, wanna-be, hard kid. Many of his after-school teachers had a hard time with him, but we had established a trusting relationship in his many visits to my office. He was truly a child I loved, because beneath that hard exterior was a young man waiting to be validated. He and I talked about his dreams of opening a strip mall and his management style. Although he could be a little abrasive, Daren was that student I knew had so much potential, he just needed to be seen.

"Sup, Ms. Joy...you ready for this?" Daren's energy was contagious. No one could negate that and seeing him so excited made me smile inside.

"Hit me! What ya got, Daren?" I replied as we did our handshake. Part of our connection was that we had our own handshake no one else knew and it helped him to trust me, even on difficult days. One thing this job has taught me is the value of building relationships. Once people can see you and know that you see them, there is a safe space that you create. Daren and I had that.

"I have here something I know you'll need. Check out my inspirational planners. Each one has its own saying, and I have one just for you."

I nodded my head, impressed as he handed me a spiral bound journal that had one of our after-school slogans on it. It read, "Caution-greatness inside." My eyes lit up at the artwork he had added; much like a construction site, he had drawn a horse with black and yellow tape across it on the cover.

"It's 100 blank pages for you to keep notes in. And I know you are always in meetings taking notes and thinking up new ideas. I thought you'd like it." Daren looked up at me with those bright eyes and smile, and I couldn't help but hug him.

"Daren I'm truly impressed! This is amazing! You drew the cover?"

"Yep, Ms. Green helped me to get it produced on cardstock that's more like cardboard so it's sturdy. You like it?" he asked, eager for my answer.

"I love it!! We may need to reproduce these for all the students. Well done sir!" I gave him a fist bump and he gleamed. This was amazing to be a part of. I was so full of joy I wanted to cry because here was a child who others wanted to throw away, and I knew in that moment he would become someone great. "I'll take three for my team!" I exclaimed, grinning.

"Wow that's what's up! Okay, let me get you a bag. I'm halfway sold out of those now!" Daren turned and bagged them up as I handed him a $20 bill. "Keep the change," I said, and he was shocked. But I knew the value of sowing into my students and this wasn't the time to be stingy.

It was days like this that gave me renewed zeal and really solidified my sense of purpose. Seeing the children find a skill that would last with them beyond this time in their life made me feel great. Not because of me, but because of what paths could open up for them as a result. I was truly grateful for my team that helped me, especially Ms. Green, who would go above and beyond to do anything for the children.

After visiting a few other tables and speaking to staff and parents, I left out of the pop-up shop to take a call. As my phone rang, I looked at the caller ID and saw it was my oldest sister, Annette, who was calling. "Hey sis, what's up?" I answered.

"Joy, where are you?" Annette said in a frenzied voice.

"Um...hello sis, yes I'm good, how are you? I'm at work, what's up?" I said cautiously, because she rarely ever called this way, it was usually about something Mama and Daddy were planning or to see what was new with me. Naturally, I was concerned.

"Sorry…hi sis, can you get to the house in like 30 minutes? We're having a family meeting." She sounded even more frantic than when I first picked up.

"Yeah I have to wrap up this pop-up shop and I can come. What's wrong?" I was getting more on edge as the conversation went on.

"We'll talk when you get here. Just come as soon as you can," she said and then hung up. I stood staring at my phone, and every thought went through my head. *Was something wrong with Mama or Daddy? Or did the twins have some new health challenge – even though it had been years since anything like that had happened.* My mind was reeling, and I just said a quick prayer. "Lord, let everything be alright when I get there, Amen." I grabbed my things and locked up my office, then went to find Ms. Green to let her know I was leaving.

Driving to Mama and Daddy's house, I put on my gospel and tried to not worry. What could this family meeting be about? In the past we had family meetings from time to time to announce big changes or to discuss plans for holidays. We had just gotten through the holiday season, so I knew it wasn't that. My twin sister and brother were both doctors with their own practice just outside of town. Perhaps they needed to share something with us about the business. My oldest brother was living in New York pursuing his career, so there were just four of us who still lived close. I shook my head and turned up the music, crooning to the sounds of Brian Courtney Wilson, and drove on, determined to not be upset and to believe that whatever was going on would be okay.

I always felt a bit of nostalgia driving down the streets towards our childhood home. So many days we had all rode our bikes up to the local park and played outside for hours until the streetlights came on. Every person in a Black family knew that the streetlights coming on was a universal sign to take your butt home before you got in trouble. We never had many friends growing up, with it being five of us; we were our own little clan. Sometimes a girl from school or one of the boys' friends on the basketball team would come over to the house, but for the most part, it was just us. My oldest sister Annette was always Mama's number two. She was in charge when Mama wasn't around, and she made sure we all knew. I wouldn't say Annette was bossy, but she definitely exercised all of her power over anything. I remember once asking her if we could go get an ice cream cone while we were at the park and the ice cream truck pulled up. Annette gave us this long lecture about spoiling our dinner and that we weren't supposed to be spending a lot of money, so when we got home we'd better make sure we ate everything at dinner so Mama wouldn't be mad.

Although she was tough as a big sister, she was also equally fun and loving. Annette would coordinate races between us, and if one of us got hurt while we were playing or if someone was mean to us, she was the first one at our side ready to go to bat for us. I remember thinking she was being overbearing at times, but now I know it was only her effort to make sure Mama and Daddy wouldn't get on her case about not being responsible. I think at times Annette loved being in that position, but other times, she would tell me she just wanted to not have to do so much for us all and just be a kid. Although we are both involved in our careers, we make time at least once a month to catch up and have lunch together. She was always supportive of me finding my way in life; patient but always encouraging me to hurry up and get it together. I chuckled to myself; you had to love Annette for who she was, even if she still sometimes talked to me like Mama number two.

As I turned on the block of our cul-de-sac and pulled into the driveway, my twin brother and sister were getting out of the car.

"Hey, Joy!" My sister Naomi ran over to me and gave me a hug as I got out of the car. Naomi and I were the closest of all of my siblings. As children, even though she and her twin, Noah, were attached at the hip, she longed for girl time more often than not. Annette was much older and didn't really want to be bothered with the "little girls", as she called us, so Naomi and I did a lot together. We were only three years apart, so we experienced many firsts around the same time. I can remember getting ready for my first date with Naomi in my room, helping me pick out an outfit to wear and watching me comb my hair, while Noah made silly faces at us and teasing us. I was there for her first date, and I did the same. Naomi looked up to me as the girl closest to her, even though she was more grounded than I ever was and at a much younger age. It made me feel good to have her in my corner when I couldn't figure out what to do with my life; we would sit on the phone for hours laughing and talking as she listened to my stories of yoga gone wrong and my next career idea. Her and Noah had always wanted to be doctors after overcoming their childhood illness, and I always thought of her as fragile because of it, though she never really was, I still wanted to protect them both.

"What's up big sis," Noah hugged me and tickled my side as he always did. We had a playful relationship, probably dating back to the times that he would make jokes and come up with all these fantasy scenarios when we were kids. In a way, I believe it was his way of coping with all of the doctor's visits and medication they were on up until they were about age eight. But we came to know him as the jokester of the family, despite his immense intelligence. Naomi and Noah were both honor students all through school, no matter what they faced. There was never a dull moment when they were around, whether it was talking about their latest patient, Noah cracking jokes, or Naomi finishing his sentences. It was a rarity to see either of them angry or upset. I always looked forward to seeing them in between our busy schedules.

"Do either of you know what's going on? Annette called me and she didn't really sound like herself," I said as we all walked to the front door.

"I have no idea," Noah said. "I'm hoping it's not a family trip idea or something like that. You know Mama was talking about that around Christmas and I really don't think that's a good idea. We're all over 30 and with our own lives. It seems a bit much to do. Maybe a family outing or something. No telling."

"Yeah it could be that," I thought aloud. "I bet Mike won't come home for that either way. He's too busy trying to make it big. Hosting gallery events and the like."

"It was a struggle just getting him to come home for Christmas," Naomi chimed in. "I doubt it if he'll want to do anything else for a while."

"You're right, Sis," I laughed and shook my head. "Well let's go see what Mama #2 is up to."

The three of us walked to the door and rang the bell of our old home. It seemed that every time I came back to visit, it got a little smaller and a little more nostalgic. Mama and Daddy were now in their late 60s, and Daddy was still working part time at the post office. But nothing was like coming home. Mama always had a cake that was just baked this week or some dinner she had put on and welcomed us back with open arms. There had been some rough times when I dreaded coming back because of scrutiny and everyone wondering when I was going to get my life together. I never had the courage to skip a family gathering like Mike did, but I often left early because I hadn't become comfortable in who I was. Over the past few years, it had subsided slightly but there was still a little apprehension inside of me because I was fearful of being judged. Having the twins with me made it better and I was glad that we had arrived together.

Mama came to the door dressed to the nines as she always was. Even at 67 she was the epitome of class and style. I remember wondering how she did it; raise five children, take care of the house and her husband, and keep smiling. It was rare that we saw a hair out of place or heard her angry, although when she was, Daddy knew how to sweeten her up. I know it wasn't always easy for Mama, but she made it look easy. I figured when I found someone, they had to at least measure up to what Mama and Daddy had shown me. Their relationship was what I wanted to have for myself.

"Hey, my children," Mama said with her arms wide ready to hug us all. We had a big group hug and almost fell over laughing at the four of us trying to get in the doorway. As I walked in the front door, I realized coming back to this house always brought a variety of emotions to the surface. In one case, this house symbolized safety and security. Yet, this house also represented my launch and preparation for the next level. Mama never pushed me to hurry up and leave so I stayed for many years after high school in my dated bedroom – pink spread, flowers, and all. It wasn't until years later that I came home one day, looked around, and said to myself, *you've outgrown this place.* So, I started looking for apartments, and within a week I was telling Mama and Daddy that I was moving at the end of the month. Although they pretended they were saddened by my move, I think secretly they were happy to see me taking this next step. Now as I enter into this house as an independent woman, a homeowner, and someone who has found herself, I am hoping that this is a quick and easy family meeting.

Our house was not much different than when we lived in it, with a new sofa and 65" flat screen TV in the family room, but the same plush white carpet – which I have no idea how she kept it clean with five kids – the same basic décor, built in bookshelves full of books I hardly ever saw anyone touch, and Daddy in his same spot in his recliner watching TV. As we all walked in, we each went over to him and gave him a kiss. Daddy was a cool and calm person. He was the epitome of a provider and protector, always coming in the door with a new surprise or treat for us and Mama. Although he worked long hours when we were young, I can't recall a time he didn't have time to sit down and give each of us some of his undivided attention. Daddy had moved from mail carrier to an office job at the post office and since then his belly had gotten a little plump. Hugging him I squeezed him extra tight and took in a whiff of his scent. Daddy was insistent on being clean and smelling good. After a long day outside, his first stop was always the shower before he sat down to dinner with us. Now as he had turned a little gray and worked only part time, I was glad that he and Mama got to spend more time together and hopefully soon enjoy retirement together as well. One thing Daddy always said was, "I work so your Mama doesn't have to. She's got enough to do with the five of you rascals." He'd always laugh after us and tease us for working Mama's nerves, but truthfully, I think he wanted her to be able to continue to do what she loved most – taking care of her family without the stress of work. Mama always seemed content in the house cooking and baking, even though she had her share of activities. For a few years she took yoga (hence, my daring try at it), she did dance classes, arts and crafts, fitness classes; you name it, she'd done it. I think it gave her a little break and time for herself away from the house. But truthfully, Mama just loved being a mom and a great wife. I don't know that I am cut the same way, but I respect what she did for over 35 years, and I know how to keep house if nothing else.

Noah and Naomi hugged Daddy and we all sat down on the sectional in the living room with Annette and Mama to start our family meeting. Annette, Mama #2, was already in overdrive. "Ma, what can I help you with?"

"I just pulled a peach cobbler out of the oven. It can cool off while we're talking then we can eat it. Y'all want something to drink?"

Noah yelled to the kitchen, "I'll take water." Naomi seconded it. Funny how they were still so twin-like at times.

"I'll take a Coke if you have one ma," I said.

Naomi started in on me. "Sis, you know you don't need to be drinking all that pop." She followed it up with a curled up lip and an "I've told you this before look."

"I know, I know, I just need to make sure I stay awake on the way home. It's been a long week. But I've cut back. I only drink a few a week now, not every day. See?" I said and stuck my tongue out at her laughing. It was nothing like having two siblings as doctors to keep you on track health wise.

Annette and Mama came back with drinks for everyone,

and Mama placed a hot tea in front of Daddy. "Um, since when do you drink tea, Daddy?" I asked.

"Well, I started a while ago. Your Mama and the twins say tea is healthier than coffee, so I'm trying. But ain't nothing like that first cup in the morning." He winked and we all smiled. It was good to see them, even if it has just been a month or so since Christmas. We didn't do many winter gatherings, because of the weather and snow we got in Michigan, being off the lake. But I loved seeing them, regardless, so this was a treat. I just hoped it was a good one.

"Annie, can you call your brother, Michael?" Mama asked. Annie was Mama's nickname for Annette, although she never let anyone call her that except Mama. We used to tease her and sing "The sun will come out tomorrow" every time she did. After a few hard pinches and some silent hits, we cut it out, but it was still cute to hear Mama say that.

"Yes, I told him we'd FaceTime him once we all got together so he could listen and chime in. Let me call him now." As she prepared to call him, I looked and Mama was sitting close to Daddy, but she was handing him the tea cup off the coffee table, which I thought was odd, but she loved catering to him, so maybe this was her new thing. I couldn't help but think that something was off, although I couldn't put my finger on it.

Hey Mike, we're all here," Annette said. Everyone crowded around saying hi and waving and she passed it around for us all to see him. Mike was our oldest brother and he had relocated to New York and opened his own art gallery. My brother has talent, creating beautiful paintings and sculptures, but there was not a real market for that here. His dream was to create artwork that would go into museums or prominent buildings and offices, so he wanted to branch out and try New York with its hustle and bustle and overpriced lifestyle. Mike had a studio that probably costs more than me and Mama's mortgage put together, but he was always a smart artsy guy and it fit with him. Although we didn't see him as often as we liked, hearing his voice and seeing him on the screen of Annie's phone was heartwarming.

Mike was never the traditional family guy, so we didn't expect him to come home often, just holidays and special occasions. He seemed to want a different life than the slower paced suburban life we led.

"Hey everybody," Mike said. "Hi Mama and Daddy. I'm in between meetings; I have a big art show coming up this weekend and I'm trying to prep the gallery. It's been so busy lately and that's a good thing, but I been all over the place. Got some big names coming in and I want to present well."

"Who's coming? Maybe I need to fly out and come too," said Noah getting excited. As the only two boys, they had a special bond growing up. Noah was small, frail, and sickly and Mike always came to his rescue when kids would pick on him. It's funny now that Noah is more overprotective than Mike and the roles are reversed with the 'good doctor' looking out for his big bro.

"Um, just a few of the cast of the new Broadway play, Hamilton," Mike said and smiled wide.

"WHAT?!!!" Annette screamed. "Wow, Mike that's big stuff," said Naomi. I had heard about the play but of course it wasn't in suburban Detroit so there was no way I could see it without driving to Chicago or flying to New York, neither of which sounded appealing in the snowy winter.

"Mike, I wish I could come, I soooo want to see that play!" Annette exclaimed. "A friend of mine was telling me about it and he said it's a must see."

"Well I haven't seen it yet either, but I definitely will entertain them as my special guests this weekend and hopefully catch a big sale."

"We're so proud of you, son," said Daddy. "Doing big things in the Big Apple. My boy." Daddy looked proud and slightly saddened at the same time. Mama just rubbed his shoulder and nodded, but something still was weird. There was a slight downcast to Daddy's words and I couldn't help wonder why. "Sure hope I can see that studio of yours one day."

"Thanks Pops, for sure you can. You can come to the gallery anytime, you and Mama. I can show you around New York City and Manhattan," Mike said proudly.

"And Soho, Naomi added. "I heard that's where the funky people live." She looked at us afterwards because we all turned to her. "Okay, not funky, but you know artsy. Like Mike."

Mike laughed, "Yeah it's cool. Kind of eclectic. So, is this what the meeting is about? Coming to visit?"

Mama sat up from Daddy and got serious. "No, it isn't. I know we talked about a family trip at Christmas..."

"Ma, it's really not feasible with our schedules right now," Noah interrupted.

"Yeah the school has kept me pretty busy. You too right, Annie?" I asked.

"I'm in the middle of a big case at the firm, and I know it'll be a minute before I can get away. Maybe I can in the spring or summer." Annette was a lawyer at an up and coming Black law firm and working towards partner. I knew she was not available. I was shocked she found time to get away and come over today.

Mike chimed in, "The summer would be cool because there's lots to do outdoors and it's not so cold. We could work on that."

"Can I finish saying what the family meeting is about?" Mama raised her voice, which she rarely ever does, and everyone stopped. We were all taken aback, but it was clear now that something was on her mind and it was serious. Daddy rubbed her back as she stood up to talk. All of us looked around perplexed, because this meeting had just taken a turn.

Mama took a deep breath and straightened her shirt that was not out of place – a clear sign she was nervous. "Okay, so I called you together because your Daddy and I have some news. How about you all sit down?" Now I was really nervous. Mama never told us to sit down unless we were in trouble or got some bad news.

"About a month ago, Daddy and I were out to eat; he had taken me to my favorite restaurant to get some dinner.

Your Daddy started complaining about his stomach. We thought maybe it was the food, or some indigestion; you know how that red sauce can mess up your system. Anyway, we came on home, but his stomach was still bothering him. He didn't really have much of an appetite, and then he was having some other discomfort. We figured this wasn't just some acid reflux, so we made an appointment. The doctor thought it could be an ulcer or a hernia, something that he could possibly take meds for or worst case, have surgery. They ran the whole battery of tests. None of that was the case."

By this time Naomi and Noah had sat up straight and I could see their doctors' minds going. "Dad, were you having any bowel changes? Constipation, diarrhea, bloody stools? How come you didn't call us?" Noah asked. "Last time I checked we were doctors." Noah tried to throw in a light moment, but it didn't ease the tension.

"Let your Mama finish." Daddy stated firmly. Noah sat back and with a look that was in between puzzled, hurt, and calculating. Meanwhile, the rest of us were on pins and needles waiting to hear what it was.

"They decided to run some additional tests to rule out some other things. We got the results last week, and your dad and I decided we wanted to get you together to share them in person."

By now you could hear the drip of one lonely drop of water from the bathroom sink down the hall. We were frozen in dreaded anticipation. This couldn't be good news.

"The doctor says Daddy has Type 2 diabetes. He thought it was possibly cancer or a prostate issue, but that was fine. His recommendation is gastric bypass surgery to send the diabetes into remission. And then we'll see what treatment to go with from there. So, he may be taking an early retirement so that we can focus on his health."

I'm almost sure that no one said anything for the first minute after she stopped talking. Then it all came at once.

"Oh my God, Daddy," Annette said through tears and ran

and hugged him.

Naomi and Noah started talking to each other, then Noah turned to Mama. "Okay, I know some great doctors. We'll get a second opinion and find the best ones in the country if we need to. You can beat this, dad. Many people think it's a death sentence but it's not. Some lifestyle changes and surgery may not be necessary. I've heard they have some new holistic treatments for diabetes." Leave it to the two logical ones to start problem-solving.

In the midst of Annette crying, she dropped her phone on the chair and I could see that Mike had paused his video and I knew that meant he was having a moment. Mike and Daddy didn't always have the best relationship growing up, hence his move so far away. But in recent years, he'd come home more often and at least attempted to improve it. I couldn't imagine what was going through his head right now. Guilt. Shame. Regret.

And then there was me. I was in total shock and disbelief. First of all, I am a self-proclaimed Daddy's girl. IF anyone was going to come to my rescue throughout my life or defend me, it was him. And as far back as I could remember he never had been anything but supportive and loving to me. Every thought went through my head: *He can survive this. He's a fighter. My Daddy is indestructible. What if he's not?* Tears welled up in my eyes and I turned to Mama, who had sat back down and was wiping her tears. And that's when I lost it. What would Mama do without Daddy? He was her rock, her joy, her peace. I couldn't imagine one without the other. Immediately, I went and hugged them both and whispered, "We'll get through this." It was all I could do in that moment. My whole world had been turned upside down in a matter of minutes and my head was reeling with the reality of the moment.

One by one, we all gathered around them and began hugging them through tears and disbelief. Finally, Daddy spoke.

"Mike, can you hear me?" he said slowly. We were all so

concerned with our own personal moments, we forgot he was on the phone.

"I'm here, dad," Mike said quietly. I could hear his voice cracking as if he was choking back tears.

"Listen, I don't want y'all sitting around here crying and acting like this is a funeral. It's not. Clearly, it's not what me and your mom expected to hear, but I am trusting that God didn't bring me this far to leave me. I wanted you all here together because you know with your mom and me getting older, I don't want the burden of taking care of me to be on her alone."

"Oh, Alfred, stop that. You know I don't mind one bit," Mama spoke as she squeezed his hand.

"I know you don't baby, but I don't want to wear you out. I need you to be alright when I come out of this," Daddy said to her with a wink.

"Oh my gosh, are you flirting, Daddy?" Annie asked in her condescending tone.

"I am grown, and yes I am flirting with my gorgeous wife of 35+ years. I can do that, and I think I should even more right now. But in reality, we wanted to talk with you all about helping out after the surgery and possibly some of the appointments. The doctor says that there will be times that I feel fine and other times I won't feel up to doing much of anything. Also, there's some adjusting my body has to do after the surgery. So, I'm asking for your help." With that, Daddy shed a tear and wiped it away before it even hit his cheek. But I had seen it – we all had. And in that moment, it was real. I'd never seen my father cry or hardly ever look sad. If he did, he never let any of his children see it.

I stood up and went to the kitchen to process and hide my river of tears that was uncontrollably starting to flow. This was my daddy; I couldn't believe this. Just when things were starting to fall into place for me, this happens. And I just couldn't imagine what Mama was feeling inside. She just sat next to him rubbing his arm as my brother and sister began making calls to some doctor friends. Annie started explaining to Mama what cases she was working on, but she'd try to get some time away. Mike was saying something on FaceTime, but I couldn't make it out. Here were all my siblings, with their busy lives and important schedules brought to a screeching halt. And here was little old me. Single with somewhat of a career, but truthfully, I had the most free time and flexibility of us all. I wiped my face on the back of my sleeve and walked back to the family room.

"Hey sunshine, you okay?" Daddy said as he often did when I'd walk in a room. I took a deep breath and moaned, holding back more tears.

"No, I'm not, Daddy. But don't you worry about me. I'm just worried about you," I let it out and snuggled on the couch under his arm, careful not to press on his stomach, because now my strong tower of a dad had just become a delicate, fragile man in my eyes.

"Aww, my Joy, you always were a sentimental, sappy girl," Daddy said as he rubbed my hair.

"Yep, a big old softie," Noah said as he started cracking up. Leave it to Noah to lighten the mood. "Dad, I have a friend I reached out to who can get back to me tomorrow about some treatment options, if you are open to listening."

"He's really good Daddy, and very holistic," Naomi added. "He's not into treatments that poison you, like all those drugs you see on TV. He had a patient last year with a really horrible diagnosis who has now changed her life around and completely healed. It's worth a try."

"Now y'all, don't be trying to have me drinking no witches brew!" Daddy said laughing. Everyone chuckled except Annie. Mama noticed and walked over to her, as she held her face in her hands.

"Annie, talk to me. Lift your face up, let me get you some tissue." Mama always talked to Annie like she was her mini mom because that was what she was. But in times of hardship, Mama allowed her to be her child again.

"Now, your Daddy's right, we are not about to mourn your

father while he's sitting right here. I had my moment too." Mama turned to look at us all. "Lord knows, I can't even remember what my life was like without your father in it. But after I cried, I turned my face to the wall and got down on my knees and started praying – praying hard. I said, 'Lord, I know you know everything, and you knew this day would come. I thank you for every hardship and challenge you've brought us through thus far and all the blessings we have. I don't believe you brought me this far to leave us, and I have faith that you are a healer. I'm begging you father, have mercy on my Alfred, give him strength to endure this process, and healing on the other side. I know you're able. And strengthen me Lord, so that I may be the helpmate that my husband needs.' As I stood up from that prayer and said amen, I felt such a peace in the room, as if God had come to sit with me himself. And I knew, and I proclaim, this sickness will not end in death. So, dry your eyes children. And let's talk about the plan to get your Daddy well."

Annie sat up and smiled and hugged Mama tight.

"Amen," I replied to her touching story. Mama's resilience was amazing, and I could only hope to one day become the woman she is. "Mama, Daddy, I have an idea. I heard what you said, and I know Noah and Naomi have the practice, Mike is in New York, and Annie has a ton of cases. I have some security in my position right now and I think I have the most flexibility to help. So, if you all don't mind," I said as I turned to my siblings, "I would like to help you take care of Daddy." I turned to Daddy and smiled and winked as we always do.

"I would like that, Sunshine, I'd like that a lot," Daddy replied with a smile and a wink.

"Well, I want to help too," Annie stood up immediately. "What can I do Mama? Daddy?" Annette, no matter her good intentions, always wanted to feel like she was doing the most or first. Although she probably really wanted to help, her need to feel important and valued often fueled her actions.

"Annie, I know you have a lot going on, and we want you to continue to go for making partner. It may be easier for Joy to help right now. But you can always jump in and help her." *Oh Mama, why did you say that?* I thought to myself. Annette could never see herself asking me to help, I would be shocked if she ever did.

"Alright." Annie responded in a curt voice, just like I thought. I couldn't help but shake my head, this was not the time to be self-centered.

"When are they planning for the surgery Dad?" Naomi asked. "We could speak to some of our doctor friends this week."

"It's scheduled for next Wednesday," Mama answered.

"So, you've already decided on it?" Noah exclaimed. He was definitely not into jumping the ball when it came to medicine. "Why didn't you ask us first?"

"Son, the doctor says he's had some great breakthroughs with this surgery with patients with my numbers. He believes it will be less damaging than the long-term effects of medicine, and I may even be able to get rid of it altogether. So, I said okay. I need you to accept that." Daddy looked at Noah with sympathy, because he knew this was hard for him to do as a doctor. But what he was asking was for him to just be a son.

"You can all come if you want and if you can." Mama interrupted as Noah was pacing and walked over to Daddy.

"We'll be there, don't worry," I answered. I was already thinking about how to rearrange my schedule and how to have Ms. Green take over when necessary.

"I have court Wednesday, but I can come right after," said Annette.

"We can clear our appointments for next week so we can help out too," Noah replied. "If this is what you want Daddy, I support you." He leaned over and hugged him tight. Another tear dropped just as I thought I'd stopped.

"I wish I could be there with you," Mike said sadly. "As soon as this opening is over, I'll book a flight home."

"It's okay if you can't Mike, the weather is getting cold and I know the flights will be expensive," Daddy said and motioned for Annie to hand him the phone.

"Dad, I don't care how much it is, I'll make it happen. I love y'all so much and I want to be there." Mike hardly ever came home, but this was different. Even he realized that this was a moment where things had just shifted.

"Sounds good. Let's have some cobbler and then watch this game. Daddy has been raving about this Lions game all day, so we might as well cheer with him."

"Um, I don't think cobbler would be good for Daddy right now, in light of the situation." Naomi interjected.

"Don't worry, I can't eat any sweets right now anyway. I'll just sniff all of yours!" Daddy laughed and we all laughed with him.

With that, Mama got up and started to get her cobbler out of the oven. For the first time, I saw how fragile my parents were. I looked at my siblings sitting there, everyone processing this moment, and I was so filled with love and the need for family. I don't know why it happened now, but I knew we would get through it together. God-willing.

~

The next few days passed in a blur. One moment I was crying and praying, asking God to heal my Daddy, then another moment I attempted to bury myself in work to distract myself from reality. My Daddy has diabetes. Every time I thought of that, I got choked up. Usually, when things were really bothering me, I'd call my girl, Alexis, but right now, I couldn't talk. I was not a big social media person; I would hop on Facebook every now and then to see what's happening with some old friends. Without giving details, I posted, "Asking for prayer." Almost immediately, my friends, my true friends, began to reach out to me asking, "Girl, what's up? Are you ok? Call me."

I couldn't speak at the time, because I was still processing the emotions that came with this new diagnosis. Instead, I texted and just let them know my Daddy was having surgery and I was asking for prayer. That worked for almost everyone, except Alexis. After leaving work two days after visiting Mama and

Daddy, I was driving home, and my phone rang.

"Hey girl hey!! I'm calling to check on you. Now, what's going on?" Alexis and I had been friends for over 25 years, and she knew me better than I knew myself sometimes. If there was anyone I couldn't hide from, it was her.

"Hey girl, I'm okay." I responded, trying to keep my voice steady.

"Umm child, I have known you too long, what's going on with your dad?" Alexis could hear it in my voice, and I figured I may as well tell her since she would keep asking. Leave it to real friends to pull it out of you.

"Daddy has Type 2 diabetes. Mama called us to the house the other day and sat us all down. They are doing a gastric by-pass surgery next Wednesday in hopes to help send him into remission and I told Mama I'd help her nurse him back to health afterwards." It wasn't out good, but the tears were already streaming, and I was gulping back sobs.

"Awww friend, I'm so sorry to hear this," Alexis sighed, "How's your mom?"

"She's strong as a rock – told us to stop crying and acting like we were at a funeral while Daddy was sitting there. Cause you know we all were a blubbering mess," I chuckled, wiping away my tears.

"Bless her! She is right! Stop all this crying, you know my uncle had that same diagnosis and he had surgery and is fine, cutting up as usual. Your dad will come through this."

"Yeah, I'm trusting God, but I'm still scared you know? You know how much I love my Daddy, and to see Mama almost break down for a minute got me too. Even Mike said he's going to fly in to see him. Just seems like everything was going good then bam...this!" The tears welled up in my eyes and my head began to hurt as I thought of all the possibilities.

"Wow, Mike hasn't been home since the holidays right?" Alexis asked surprised.

"Yeah, so you know it's serious cause he can't stand De-

211

troit!" We both laughed because we knew Mike said he wanted to follow his career, but I think he secretly was escaping the monotony of Michigan, and as he said, "ghetto black folks".

"It's going to be okay. I'm taking a few vacation days and I may have to adjust my schedule slightly to work different hours until Daddy is up and moving again. I just don't want Mama to have to deal with it all alone. With Annette, Noah, and Naomi being so busy with work, I thought it would be a good idea for me to be there with him."

"I agree, you are definitely the best one for helping out, just make sure you take some time to take care of yourself. Are you eating?"

"Girl, you know me like a book!! Not much, but I'm getting better. I don't think I ate the first day at all, but I'm going to do better. And every time I look at something sweet, I put it down because I think I may get it!" We laughed together. "Girl I know it's crazy, but it has me thinking about my life too. But I have to be strong for Mama so I can't be falling out."

"Exactly! Okay, well I'll check on you later this week, try and take a deep breath. Run a bath and have some wine! I'll be praying for you and the family. Love you girl!"

"Love you more! Thanks BFF!" I hung up, smiling. Talking to Alexis always made me feel better. She had moved away to Houston years ago, but we still got together at least once a year when she came home. Our lives had gone in different directions; she was married with two kids, running a PR firm; I was single, with no kids, sometimes dating, and just finding my way in my career. In many ways I looked up to her, not just for her accomplishments, but because her character never changed despite what she achieved. She was still my home girl, my ride or die, and that silly cheerleader from the D when it all came down to it. I exhaled and drove home, thankful for true friendship.

When I arrived home, I saw there was a package outside my apartment door from Amazon. That had become my new addiction, and I swear packages were arriving every other day from my late-night shopping binges. My new goal was to spruce up my place so that I could start having the family over or some friends, and maybe even a man one day. My newest arrival was new curtains for my living room that I had just redecorated with hues of gray, blue, and white. Blue was supposed to be a calming color, so I wanted to sprinkle it throughout the places I was the most to help bring more peace into my home. Excited to put them up, I dropped my things on the kitchen counter and immediately opened them up. They were a perfect blend of modern style, mixed with traditional, which summed me up. There were many things that I considered myself to be traditional about – chivalry and dating was one – which may be the reason I was still single. On the other hand, I was opening up more and more to modern viewpoints on many things, based on my experiences. I didn't believe that everything had to be like the old days. It was okay for women to work and be independent, but there was still a need for a man to be the head of the house.

Many discussions with friends over the years had opened my eyes to see that there were lots of ways to function in this new millennium. I just wanted to make sure I held my standards and morals, not compromising totally for anyone.

My last relationship had been with a man who was very unconventional. From our initial meeting, I was turned off by his rigid conversation – which should have been a sign. But underneath the rigidity, he showed me a softer side that helped me to see some value in myself and validate the emotions I was going through as I was establishing my life. However, what I didn't know was that he'd want to be here almost every day, which I definitely was not used to. He was "in between" houses, and at some point got in between jobs too. I began to resent him for sitting in my bed, eating my food, and becoming comfortable with his 'in between' status. After a while, resentment began brewing between us and I was less available emotionally. When we would talk, I wanted to continue to be open and have discussions, but truly he was a narrow-minded person who could at times be mean.

Once he came to family dinner and Mama smiled her Clair Huxtable smile at me, which meant she had much more to say beyond that moment. He bonded with Daddy around football and politics, so he was all good with him. Mama never said anything to me directly, even though her face did. I just kept working at it, hoping that he would move from 'in between' to stable, without me totally being annoyed by him in the process.

Don't get me wrong, it wasn't all terrible. We enjoyed doing things together outside, listening to concerts, watching shows together, and cooking. In those moments, I would say to myself that it could be okay, if...it was the "if" that kept nagging on me. What was the "if" that would make everything okay? If he got a job? If he got his own place? If he was nicer at times? We as women often try to rationalize the ifs and say that we'll be happy if or when this happens. What I've learned, after counseling and a few much needed single years, is that I have to choose to be happy now. If someone is bringing me so many second thoughts and doubt, I have to truly examine what is the next choice for me.

I think the point that it struck me that he wasn't quite the one for me was when I threw a party when I got my promotion. He pretended he wasn't coming or that he'd forgotten, which truly pissed me off, if I'm being truthful. This was a big moment for me, and I would expect him to be there. My girls reassured me that I would have a great night regardless. As the evening progressed, many friends and coworkers showed up to celebrate with me, and still no Malcolm. At some point, I just admitted he wasn't coming and said forget it, let me enjoy MY night. Sure enough, that's when he walked in smiling and grinning, saying "gotcha" with a pan of food in hand. I wasn't happy at all to see him, mostly because that wasn't the time to play a joke. This was an important moment and in my traditional sense, I wanted my man by my side. He attempted all night to be super friendly to people, and I resolved that I would make the best of it. Then he showed his true self.

We were at opposite sides of the hall but within earshot of each other talking. I waved and smiled at him and motioned for him to come to me so I could introduce him to some friends from work. At first I thought he didn't see me because he just shook his head. Then his group moved a little closer to me, so I said, "Malcolm come here, I want to introduce you to some people."

No sooner than I said it, he put his hand up as if to say stop and then said, "Don't summon me". Not only did he say it, but it was loud enough for his group and my group to stop talking, turn, and look. In an effort to save face, he claimed he was coming and that I didn't have to summon him over. My sister Naomi turned and looked in my direction, catching my glare. It took everything in me not to curse him out on the spot, but at that moment I knew I couldn't do it anymore. Too much "in between" and then you have the nerve to be rude! Inside I was on fire and he could have easily dropped dead with the look I gave him. Being who I am, not ever wanting to make a scene, I kept it cool. Once we got home, he tried to be lovey-dovey, but I told him that night to pack his stuff and get out. He had embarrassed me and completely humiliated me in front of my family and friends. After an hour or two of arguing, as he attempted to defend his actions, I washed my hands of Malcolm.

To this day, he still calls every now and then asking to talk. Each time I ignore him. I haven't brought myself to block him yet, but it's coming. I just woke up and realized that no matter how much I wanted a traditional loving marriage like Mama and Daddy's, I had never watched him disrespect her publicly and I knew that was a deal breaker for me. Hence, me remodeling and redecorating for the last couple of years so that I could recreate my place of peace for me first. Although I've gone out on a few dates, even had a fling or two, not one of them sparked me to want to take it further. As my therapist says, it's time for me to focus on me and doing what's best for self, understand myself, my wants and desires, and work on those. At the right time, the right person will come along. And now with Daddy being sick, I don't have time for dating anyway. For now, I think I am in a relationship with Amazon and Netflix, and I'm perfectly happy.

~

It seems that when you are dreading something, the time leading up to it passes so quickly. It was surgery day and I hadn't slept much at all the night before. I spent half of the night watching TV and drinking wine, and the other half tossing and turning, caught between worry and prayer. It's funny how people always say, "if you are going to worry, why pray?" That's easy to say when it's not your Daddy who has diabetes and is going through a high-risk surgery. I believe in prayer, I truly do, and I've seen Mama and Daddy get through a myriad of circumstances on a wing and a prayer. But honestly, I have always been stuck somewhere between worry wart and God will work it out. It's like Jesus gave me just enough faith to not give up, yet oftentimes allowed me to have moments of weakness – forcing me to depend on Him or someone He sent to remind me of the promises of God. Today, as I paced in the hospital waiting room, prayer was the only thing on my mind.

Mama and Daddy had insisted that we pray before the surgery, and since we couldn't all be there at once, it was a four-way FaceTime for us. Mama asked Naomi to pray, as she is very spiritual and much more composed in a crisis than anyone else in the family. I think it's the medical side of her that is methodical and not emotional. Some days, I wish I had that side.

After we prayed, we each kissed Daddy and told him we loved him and we'd see him soon. Mama was the last to see him off before the surgery. She bent down slightly, whispered something in his ear that made him smile, gave him a quick kiss, and said, "Hurry back, I gotta put dinner on for you and the kids." It was the sweetest thing – reminding Daddy of her responsibility to him as her husband and giving him something to look forward to coming out of surgery. I saw one tear fall down her cheek, which she quickly swept away as she turned from him and he waved and gave us a thumbs up as they took him away. After watching him leave, we each retreated to our separate corners of the waiting area.

Noah paced back and forth, checking his watch every so often. It was the doctor in him that I saw in action mentally. He was calculating what was probably happening every 30 minutes and giving a play by play to himself and the air more than anything, but we heard him and realized it was his way of coping. "Anesthesiologist should be in the OR by now. He's probably down."

Next 30 minutes, "Probably making the incision by now and beginning...," he continued on.

From time to time he'd turn to Naomi and they would have a twin doctor mind meld moment. "You think they'll do stitches or staples or both?"

Their minds would go, and this complicated medical conversation would carry them until the next 30 minutes.

Mama sat reading a magazine and I sat with her. Annette was at court and Mike was still in New York; he couldn't get a flight until next week. The silence was so awkward, yet I had no idea what to fill it with. I was almost seeing double from no sleep the night before. Mama kept telling me I looked tired, and I could lie down, and she'd wake me when there was news. Unfortunately, rest was not an option. What if I fell asleep then they came out with a report and I missed it? I'd either get the watered-down version from Mama or the PDR equivalent from the twins and neither would satisfy my need to hear it myself. So, I decided I needed caffeine and food. "Anyone want anything from the cafeteria?" I asked. "I'm going to get a coffee and something to eat."

"See if they have any green smoothies, Sis," Naomi said, "Noah you want one?"

"Nah, I'm good – just a water for me" he replied.

"Mama you want something?" I asked as I watched her flip through a magazine that she obviously was not engrossed in. She shook her head no, so I headed out of the waiting room to get coffee, get fresh air, and to regroup.

There are moments in life that seem to define an era, and to me this was one. All I could wonder was what would life be like now for Daddy? Would he still be the hopeful, faithful, energetic dad he's always been? Would this shake his spirit? I couldn't help but smile and think of what he'd always say to me, "Rain always comes before a rainbow baby, and that's God's promise, that He's always with you." I smiled as I took the escalator down to the cafeteria. That's all this was, just a little rain – more like a thunderstorm – but even so, the sun was still shining and that meant a rainbow was coming soon. I took a deep breath and reminded myself that everything was in God's hands.

Sleep deprivation always led me to eating a little more than usual, so it was no surprise that even the hospital cafeteria smells had peaked my interest and I found myself at the register with two waters, a green smoothie, coffee, a breakfast sandwich, a fruit cup, and a muffin for Mama, just in case she changed her mind. All the rest, except one of the waters and the green smoothies, was for me. I shook my head to myself and chuckled, "This is why you can't lose any weight Joy."

Against my better judgment I didn't stop to get a tray, so I was doing a full balancing act in line waiting to pay. As I approached the register, I dropped both waters and almost lost the muffin. Bending down to pick them up, I found myself face to face with a handsome young man in a lab coat who had just reached down to get them for me.

"Hands full, huh?" He laughed as he picked them up and went to place them on the counter.

"Yeah, picking up things for the family...guess I should have gotten a tray." I smiled and looked up only to peer into the warmest brown eyes and smile I had seen in a long time. "Thanks!" I said quickly then awkwardly turned around attempting to mask the rosiness I felt coming into my cheeks. *Mmmm, mmm, mmm*, I thought. Guess you can find something good in the hospital.

He stood behind me in line as I paid and then he stepped up to the counter. I walked over to the condiment area and grabbed some cream, Equal, a straw, and a fork then started looking around for a bag. As I was looking, the same gentleman walked over to the condiment area.

"Do you need some help?" he asked. I looked up and there was that smile again. Who was this man? Why was he so close to me? Why was I getting warm and nervous? *Joy, pull it together*, I thought.

"Actually, I was trying to find a bag and a carrier, so I don't drop everything again," I said, smiling and motioning to all the stuff on the counter.

"They keep them at the register, but I'll grab it for you" then he turned and walked away. As he walked to the register, I watched him and thought how there were still nice people in the world, and he's one of them. Nothing more.

"Here you go," he handed me the bag and carrier. "I'm Theo, but everyone here knows me as Dr. Jackson," he said as he flashed another smile.

"I'm Joy," I said as I stuffed everything in the bag. It had been so long since a man worth looking at had said a word to me, let alone smiled, that I was tongue tied. "I need to get back upstairs before my family starts wondering where I disappeared to."

"Nice to meet you, Joy. I understand no one chooses to hang out in a hospital cafeteria except those of us who work here and need a break."

"I bet! It's definitely not my choice of hangouts. Thanks again and have a great day." Before I could say something dumb or make a fool of myself, I turned and walked back towards the escalator with just a little more pep in my step. I thought to my-self, *maybe hospitals aren't so bad when you run into fine doctors!*

Back upstairs, we waited another hour and a half before we got news about Daddy. Finally, the doctor came out and said, "Surgery went well. He's in recovery and you all will be able to see him soon. I believe it went well, and after we run some tests after his recovery, we will be able to discuss his treatment plan."

As soon as he asked if we had any questions, Noah ran over and began to give him the third degree about treatments.

"Excuse my brother," Naomi ran over and said. "He's just anxious. I'm sure we'll have time to talk about that later after Daddy's in his room." With that, she rescued the doctor who was surely looking for a way out of Noah's inquisition. "Noah, calm down. That doctor just got out of surgery. We'll have time to talk later."

"I'm just wondering the direction they will take. Based on the research I've looked at, there are some holistic treatments I think we should look into before they go the traditional route of insulin, if that's what they decide," Noah explained.

I turned to look at Mama, who was saying a silent prayer. This was not a great time to have this conversation and definitely the wrong place. "Well, thank God Daddy is okay," I said and motioned towards Mama. Noah got the hint and went over and gave Mama a hug. At least for now he paused his doctor brain to just be a son.

While we waited for Daddy to come out of recovery, we updated Annette and Mike on FaceTime, letting them know all was well. Daddy would have to stay in the hospital at least two days, so we'd all take turns coming to visit. Mama insisted on staying, and the nurse had already agreed to make sure she had a reclining chair to sleep in. Even though we all said she should go home and rest, she refused to leave Daddy's side. I don't think I can remember a time that they were ever separated for any length of time in recent years, and I imagine that she didn't want to even tackle the notion of sleeping alone in the house. We all understood, even though nothing was said. Once you've been with someone for so long, the idea of adjusting to them not being there could tear a person down. I'd seen it happen with our grandparents; G-Ma and Pa-Pa never left each other's side, even when one was sick. It was almost like their connection was so strong that the other felt the sickness too. We'd laugh when one of them would be sick, because the other would immediately express the same feelings. Even though it was a mental thing and probably their way of staying together, it was so cute to see them in love and not wanting to leave each other's side. I longed for that kind of love.

Once Daddy was in a room, we all went in and gave him gentle hugs and kisses. He was groggy, of course, but he managed to flash a smile before drifting back to sleep. After being there for more than eight hours, the beeping of machines and smell of sterilization was getting to us all. Noah and Naomi decided to go on to the office and try to prepare for the patients they would have to squeeze in the rest of the week. I wanted to run by the office and grab some work so that I could come back and stay with Mama, who took one look at me and said, "Joy go home and get some rest. You look exhausted. I'll be okay. They will take good care of me here. You can come back in the morning."

Reluctantly, I agreed. Partially because I couldn't drink another ounce of coffee and expect it to keep me awake, and I really did want to crawl in my bed and release the stress of the day. We all gave Mama a hug and kiss, then I made her promise to call me if she needed anything or if anything changed. Walking out of the hospital knowing my parents were both in there made me realize just how fragile they were as they were getting older. Mama was always strong and kept a good house, and Daddy always took care of her. Now roles were going to be reversed, and I was determined to make sure that they both came through this stronger. I would be their support as we entered into this new era of life.

~

New Normal

After a two-night stay at the hospital, Mama and Daddy were itching to get home. I pulled up in the front and watched Mama wheel Daddy to the curb. He looked alert and was fussing at Mama, saying he didn't need any help getting up, which is always a good sign. "Hey Sunshine, I missed you."

"I missed you too, Daddy and you too, Mama. So glad you are coming home and doing better." The doctors had said that the wounds were healing well and for the next couple of weeks he would be working towards regaining his strength, and then we would meet to decide the next course of treatment. Daddy slowly slid into the front seat as Mama and I supported him.

"You know what I have a taste for? A milkshake!" Daddy thought aloud and turned to me.

"Now you know that is not on your list of approved foods, honey," Mama scolded him just like she did us whenever we were sick. "I'll make you some soup when you get home."

"Ah, what does it matter? They both just slide down and slide out!" Daddy started laughing at his own joke while we shook our heads, then he let out a groan.

"What's wrong, Daddy?" I asked nervously.

"Nothing…just can't laugh too hard yet. Still a little sore," Daddy said.

"Don't worry, you'll be cracking jokes and busting out laughing in no time Daddy. But I think Mama is right – soup it is."

"Ooh it's going to be tough with you two being my nurses! I'm used to being the one who makes the decisions." He smiled jokingly and we headed home. He was going to be back to his old self in no time.

Back at the house, I had rearranged the furniture so that Daddy wouldn't have to walk too far to the couch and made sure that there were no obstacles in his way. Knowing Daddy, he would be trying to get up and move around when Mama or I weren't looking. He was always used to working and being on the move, and now he was being told to sit down; I doubted that we'd be able to make him do that for long without a protest.

Mama began making soup while I got Daddy situated. Certain positions were uncomfortable, and he had to figure out the right way to sit that wouldn't aggravate his wounds. He let out a deep sigh and was sleep before Mama could get all the ingredients in the pot.

"You know your Daddy can be stubborn. We really will have to keep an eye on him because he's likely to try to sneak out for a drive."

"I know...that's why I've decided that I will be staying here, at least until he can move around on his own."

"You do not have to stay here, Joy. I can take care of your father just fine." Mama was just as stubborn as him at times, although she hid it well. She could sweet talk anyone into doing what she wanted when she turned on her southern charm. But it wasn't working this time.

"I know you can, but you need some rest too, Ma. Don't worry, I arranged to work from home and my neighbor will get my mail until I go back. So, you're stuck with me." I stuck my tongue out playfully and hugged her around her back. It would be good to spend some quality time with them anyway. How often do grown children really get to do that? And secretly, I think Mama was somewhat glad to have me there.

"Well, since you'll be here, you can take your old room. It's got a futon in it that's pretty comfy. I used to lay on it after doing my yoga. You wanna do some yoga?" Mama was teasing me because she already knew that dream was long gone. Just in case I had forgotten my neck sprain mishap, the cold weather always gave me an ache that reminded me.

"Real funny, Mama," I chuckled. "Actually, I need to catch up on some emails for work, so I'll grab my things out of the car and go in the room for a while and work. Let me know when the soup is ready, and we'll see if Daddy's up." Mama said okay and turned on her daytime TV shows while she cooked away. Cooking was her solace, her happy place. As long as she could cook up something great for us to eat and watch us enjoy it, she was in heaven. I left her to it and got settled in.

Here I was back again in my parent's house, in my old room, as a caretaker for my Daddy. I believe there's always a greater purpose for being in situations, even if it seems grim. I hadn't figured out the purpose of this time, yet I anxiously waited for it to be revealed to me. I understood that Mama and Daddy were getting older and maybe this was the transition they say happens when your parents get older. It allows you to see them in a vulnerable state, something children rarely do until they are older. Up until adulthood, your parents are always the strength and backbone of the family. As they increase in age, there seems to be more of a need for them to exercise their independence, and as much as we want to allow them that, as children we can see the need for them to have help. Such a dichotomy but I was determined to continue to keep their lives as normal as possible.

Mama had turned my old room into a workout, lounge, work, and playroom. It was funny being back here, in the room that was once painted pink and had posters of all my favorite rap artists lined up on the wall. In this room I had my pink dual cassette player loaded with a fresh tape every Friday night to record my favorite slow jams off the radio. Where the futon now sat, my daybed was once there, and I'd lay on it for hours listening to music or pull out the trundle to have company over for a sleepover. Now it was painted a light blue and white with accents of green. In the corner where my dresser sat was Mama's desk where she sat and did her business. She hasn't worked in years, so I'm not quite sure what business she did, but I knew that she was always responsible for handling the bills and keeping Daddy organized. She also had a small TV mounted after we convinced them to get rid of the tube TV that still sat in the room up until a couple of years ago. Daddy insisted the TV still worked but Noah just wouldn't have it. Noah bought the TV, brought it over and installed it all the same day. Even though Daddy insisted he didn't have to do that, I think secretly he appreciated it. Daddy has always worked so much that oftentimes he didn't do much in the house in terms of fixing up. He'd much rather pay someone so that he could spend his time off enjoying Mama and us.

I only brought one small bag over. Even though I may end up staying a couple of weeks, I know I can always run home and get more things if need be. I sat my bag near the futon and grabbed my laptop out of it to check on some work emails. Even though I was covered at work with Ms. Green and my crew, I still needed to keep my finger on the pulse of the after school program. Thankfully, there were no big events happening right now; simply day-to-day duties occurring. My main responsibility was to ensure that the program runs smoothly. Although I'd miss my students, I could still be impactful from Mama and Daddy's house. Opening my emails, I saw the usual updates and junk mail, answered a few questions, and decided to shut it down and take a quick nap. I climbed on the futon, curled up in the blanket, and tried to rest a little so that I would be refreshed to help Mama and Daddy when I got up.

I woke up from what was supposed to be a quick nap, only to turn over and look at my phone and see it had just been three hours. It felt like a lifetime, but I must have needed it because I woke up like a new woman. After taking a deep breath, I sat up and decided to freshen up and go see what Mama and Daddy were up to. Apparently I had slept through all of the excitement because when I came out I saw Annette in the chair in the living room and Mama and Daddy on the couch.

"Hmm, well if it isn't sleeping beauty. Nice of you to join us, Joy," Annette said jokingly but there was always a condescending undertone that came through her words. I internally refused to acknowledge it, as I was feeling so much better since my nap and I did not want to feel any stress from her.

"Hey Annie," I said. Even though it wasn't her favorite nickname, it was my way of letting her know I was no longer the little sis she could boss around. "Did I miss something?"

"No baby, just a few hours of us sitting here talking and resting, but you needed your rest too," Mama said lovingly.

"Yeah, I did. I didn't realize how tired I was. I haven't gotten much sleep lately with everything going on. How are you feeling Daddy?" I asked as I walked towards him to hold his hand.

"Better now, Sunshine. I'm a little tired, and been dozing on and off, but I got such good company, who would want to sleep now." He flashed his award-winning smile, and even though I could see the exhaustion behind his eyes, it was good to see him trying to get back to his normal self.

"I was just telling Annie she could stay for dinner. Your brother and sister said they may stop by after they close up the office, and we can all call Mike and let him talk to your father. He may have to postpone his flight because his art show went well so he's booked for the next few weeks. I put a roast on right after you laid down and it should be about ready soon." Mama sure could make anyone feel loved.

"That's sad to hear...I was looking forward to seeing him. I can stay a little bit. Plus, it smells much better than my usual Chinese takeout," Annie remarked.

"Annie, you have to make some time to take care of yourself. Working nonstop, even if it is towards partner, is no good if you aren't able to enjoy it. Eating all that take out will make you sick."

"I know it's just that I rarely have time to eat, let alone cook. I was thinking of doing Home Chef just so that I don't have to plan and prepare food. It may help." Mama turned her head towards Annie looking extremely lost.

"Mama, Home Chef is a service where you pick your meals and they deliver it and you cook it. Most of them take about 30 minutes or so but it's all prepared ahead of time to help busy families. I tried one, it's not bad." I attempted to help Mama understand because in their day there was no excuse or allowance for a woman who didn't cook. So, she was completely baffled at the idea.

"What in the world? They know they can come up with some stuff nowadays. Ain't nothing like a home cooked meal, ain't that right, Alfred?" Mama turned towards Daddy, and he grinned.

"Nothing like it, Mama. Speaking of food, I'm getting hungry and that roast sure smells good. What time will the twins be here?" I asked as Daddy started licking his lips. I could almost see his mouth watering.

"Um Daddy, the doctor said you have to take it easy right now with your eating. Mostly soups and soft foods until you are healed. You know that. Roast will not agree with you at the moment," I said to him as I reached into the refrigerator to get some juice.

"You know, I need to hurry up and heal because y'all are messing with my appetite!" As we all busted out in laughter, Daddy cringed again, remembering his pain. "Alright, I guess I'll have some soup for now."

I went to grab the soup and the doorbell rang. Annie went to the door and Mama sat with Daddy trying to console and reassure him that she would cook all of his favorites once he was better.

Noah and Naomi came in fresh from work and went straight to hug Mama and Daddy. "Hey big guy, how are you holding up?" Noah asked. "Have you changed your gauze today?"

"Yes, Doctor. My nurses are taking good care of me."

"Thanks again, Sis, for helping them out. You know we're here if you ever have any questions or need anything," Noah said to me.

"I got this brother," I laughed. "Just call me Nurse Joy." Everyone started laughing, because it was a known fact that my medical skills were limited to treating cuts and bruises. I am not squeamish, but I definitely didn't know much beyond the basics.

"Girl, you are hilarious," Naomi laughed as she came over and hugged me. "Make sure to add that to your resume!"

"Oh, you got jokes lil' sis!" I couldn't help but laugh, and nothing was needed more than laughter right now.

As we all sat down to eat, Mama prepared plates and the usual family banter continued. It felt good to have us all together in the house again so soon, usually it only happened at the holidays. We even FaceTimed Mike so he could see Daddy too. Perhaps some good could come from this after all.

After a filling meal and a little more talking, Daddy had asked for more pain meds and passed out on the couch. He was still in recovery mode, so even though he seemed his normal self, he was far from it. We all knew that this was just the beginning of his ordeal. I was determined to treat him the same, not like he was sick. I believe that what you want to happen can happen if you believe enough. I'd heard of diabetes patients with such positive attitudes and determination that their willingness to live and make some lifestyle changes had outrun their diagnosis. I just prayed that it was the same for Daddy.

Just as we were cleaning up the kitchen and settling in, Noah jumped into doctor mode. "Now that Daddy's sleep, I wanted to share some news. I know the doctors will probably want to go with the common treatments of insulin, but I have a friend who works in holistic medicine who has had some success with diabetes using natural remedies. I wanted to suggest that we look into that Mama, if it's okay?" Noah turned to her seeking approval. I could tell he was nervous. Most of the older generation had grown up on unconventional remedies, but this was different. I had no idea how Mama would react.

Mama looked at him skeptically and said, "Well tell us what you're thinking. I trust Daddy's doctor; he's been our doctor for years. But I'll listen." That was progress.

Noah went on to explain a regimen of a variety of herbs, fruits, and vegetables that he said were proven to almost reset the body if combined. Noah and Naomi had tried some of the treatments with their patients and had seen great results. Some of them had been "cured" of diseases like diabetes, high blood pressure, cancer, and tumors. Noah also mentioned that the doctor would give Daddy a monthly regiment of supplements to build his system and help fight off the diabetes naturally. He'd had two patients that used this method and fully recovered. One was younger and one older. After Noah finished he turned to Mama to get her opinion.

"Well, I don't know anything about these holistic doctors. I remember when we were younger we called them witch doctors – always concocting some weird solution to give to people who were sick. One thing's for sure, your Daddy loves his meat, so good luck on convincing him not to eat that."

Annie chimed in, "Noah, I know you mean well but this is serious! We're not going to play Russian roulette with Daddy's life. Two patients aren't many to go on. I vote no." Annie was always the pessimist.

Naomi chimed in, "Well to be clear, this is just our friend we know personally. He's not the only doctor who stands by this. There have been many with similar results. But we as doctors are taught to prescribe medication, that's where money is made through insurance. However, sometimes the medicine, especially diabetes medicine makes you worse. I've done some research on this and considering Daddy's specific condition, I think it could be successful. When we go back for his checkup, it's worth speaking to his doctor about it."

Annie just shrugged her shoulders and walked to the fridge to get some more water. I decided to ask my question because I didn't want to gamble with Daddy's life either, but I knew what diabetes could do to a person.

"Okay, here's my question. How long does he do this? Forever? When would we know if he's getting better or not? I'm open to it, because I've done some holistic things for myself, just for little stuff like sinuses and allergies. I'm just wondering how we will know it's working." I was cautiously optimistic at the thought of this, yet still practical. My logical mind couldn't completely wrap itself around this.

Noah replied, "Good questions, Sis. We would have to sit with the doctor and go through the details. Just based on what I know, I would recommend a minimum of three to six months and Daddy would have to get retested and evaluated regularly to see his progress. The good thing is the surgeon said the bypass surgery itself had a major reverse effect in terms of influencing his diet and removing some of the weight. We would know it's working if Daddy's numbers become normal and stay normal."

Mama sighed and sat on the couch close to Daddy. I could see the wheels churning in her head, and I could tell she was nervous. This was a huge decision and regardless of how we felt, Daddy was her life partner. Whatever was decided would not just affect him but her as well. They were intertwined in every aspect of their beings and the thought of them not being together made me choke up a bit. This could be a life or death decision for her. At that moment, I wish I could just go to God and ask him for an answer. Sometimes in life, it feels like if I just know what will happen I will be alright. But that's not the way life works. My life was the epitome of that. I wouldn't have tried so many outlets and career moves had I know how they'd work out. Yet, each one taught me something more about myself. In some ways, maybe not knowing was part of the plan to help me understand myself better. Lost in my thoughts, I zoned out for a bit, analyzing all the possible outcomes. Either way, it was Mama and Daddy's decision, so I turned to her.

"Mama, what are you thinking?" I asked.

"You all know your father," Mama began. "Since the day I met him, he was always keen and alert; no one could pull a fast one on him. He would haggle down the prices at stores and outthink the best con man. So, I know he won't go for it if he thinks we're up to something. I've seen what insulin dependency and poor diet can do to a person with diabetes, let alone being overweight. I saw it happen to your grandmother. She started off okay, then lost her toe, lost some of her sight, and no matter how much she fought, those drugs drained her will to fight. In the end, I believe it wore her out. I've seen others survive diabetes, and I know they're all different, but I can't imagine your dad going through that." As she spoke, she teared up and each of us began to wipe our eyes at different moments. It is so hard to see your parents in a vulnerable state, and this was one of the few times we'd seen Mama truly express that human side. In our minds she was always supermom. "I don't know if all this stuff is 100%, but I'm willing to speak to the doctor and your dad about it. Noah the way you say it, it's helping his body regulate itself, so it doesn't get worse and reverses. This doctor friend of yours needs to explain how that works and we need to see some results of others who have tried this. I'm going to pray on it, and when your father has his next appointment, I think the twins should be there with us. In the meantime, I'll begin to work on your father's understanding of the situation. The doctors already said he has to change his diet, so that may be the first step. I'm open to it, but I want to be sure it's going to work."

I was shocked. Never did I imagine Mama going for something holistic. She was traditional in a sense and very much the good patient, following doctors' orders. This would be interesting to see unfold. Just as I was feeling some relief, Daddy stirred.

"Let me get Daddy ready for bed. I think we have some answers to look forward to and we'll see how it goes. Noah, can you let Mike know about it too? I want to be sure we don't forget to tell him everything. As much as I'd love to talk some more, me and Mama need to get some rest too."

"You need any help, Sis?" Naomi asked.

"Could just put the rest of the food up in the kitchen while we take him back to his room?" I asked as Mama went over to Daddy and began trying to wake him up enough to walk.

Everyone started to pack up, and as we were all saying goodbyes, Annie said, "I can help some if you need Mama."

"We're fine baby, go ahead and get home before it gets late. Glad you stopped by. Joy and I will be here so come back anytime." Annie's look was a mix of sadness that she wasn't doing her oldest sister duties of taking over and jealousy that I was. She was such a different person to figure out. I loved her but never understood why she was insistent on being in charge and important. Secretly, I think her ambition to partner was in an effort to validate herself. But everyone knew she was always successful and on top of her career and life. If anything, I was the one who was wandering for so long trying to get it together. I resolved that some things I just would not understand.

Daddy stood and waved sluggishly as we helped him walk to the back. By the time he was in bed, everyone had left, and Mama and I sat in the kitchen for a few talking.

"What a night, huh Ma?" I asked. "Lots to take in."

"Yes, what a night. I really have to pray on all of this. I don't want to upset anyone, but this is very different. Me and your dad have always been traditional but not open to new things. I just want him to be okay and fully recover. God knows I do." I slid my chair closer to her and wrapped my arm around her shoulder.

"What did you always used to tell us Mama? God sees all and knows all before we even understand. You encouraged me every time I failed at a new career with those same words. I probably didn't get it until much later and some injuries, but you were always right. Let's pray on it and trust God."

"Well look at my Joy, wise beyond her years." Mama looked at me and smiled and hugged me tight.

Though I was reluctant to come stay here initially and give up my freedom at home, there was no place I'd rather be at the moment. "I learned from the best." Standing up and yawning I replied sleepily, "I love you, Mama. Let's go to bed."

~

The Turning Tide

Two weeks had gone by since Daddy's surgery and he was getting stronger by the day. His wounds were healing nicely, as Noah put it, and he seemed to be getting his strength back. After our family talked about treatment options, Mama began to prepare more things for Daddy that were on his approved list of foods for diabetes and the holistic methods diet – mainly his favorite lean meats, selected fruits, and veggies. Initially it was all soft foods, but he was getting into small solid meals. In an effort to "prep" him for this holistic possibility, he hadn't had much meat at all and Mama insisted that it was a good move based on his condition. Daddy rarely argued with Mama. He trusted her like none other so if she said it, he was on board, at least 95% of the time. I had been back and forth between my house and theirs the past week as Daddy got stronger, and even went to work to check on things a couple of times. Ms. Green was handling things well, although one of the school administrators seemed to be breathing down her neck more than usual.

After talking to Ms. Green, it seemed that one of the heads of the school district had come by to visit while I was out. Ms. Green handled it well, ensuring him that the after school program was progressing smoothly. He was one of the major backers of the after school program initially, but as of late, he'd been very critical and was examining every minute detail pertaining to it. I wasn't sure what this would amount to, but I needed to keep my eyes and ears open.

Mr. Thomas was not the type of leader one would expect to see in a minority school district. He came from an affluent portion of the suburbs and had worked many years in wealthy communities with privileged students. The school I was in was the exact opposite. Most students were in low-income families, on welfare, or in sub-par housing. The after school program was a haven for the community where children stayed out of trouble. Thanks to the program Ms. Green developed around entrepreneurship and with the at-risk programs we offered, I had seen the attendance rate grow almost 30%, and almost all of our students were finishing school and looking ahead to ambitious futures.

However, every time Mr. Thomas came around, there was an eerie sense of a hidden agenda. Although he loved to hear of the accomplishments of the program, he always questioned whether it was truly necessary and where we could make cuts. It didn't help any that he was white. It never seemed he genuinely cared for our minority students but cared more about politics and money that made him look good. I let Ms. Green know that I would be sure to come in this week to do some checkups, plus I had a meeting with Mr. Thomas and some of the other leaders to discuss the upcoming summer programming. Even though this was the most rewarding job I'd ever had, no one informed me ahead of time how much bureaucracy existed in the educational arena.

Since I had been with the program, I had always worked

closely with a small team. There was Ms. Green, who assisted in any way possible, helping all of us on the team with administrative tasks and setting up events, like the pop-up shop, and assisting after school-teachers as needed. Although she was one of the last ones to join the team, she was certainly one of the most valuable. Mrs. Nether was my immediate supervisor and had recommended me for the position after working with her for a few years in various roles, including recruitment. She saw in me the leadership potential and took me under her wing. Mrs. Nether was my go-to person; if I had any questions or concerns. She always had a listening ear and some wise advice on how to find a solution to a problem without ruffling too many feathers. Watching her handle some of the toughest parents, students, and staff had helped me to learn how to navigate through personalities and opinions that seemed to run rampant at times. However, it was always with ease and diplomacy that Mrs. Nether would have someone in her office to share some constructive criticism, and at times it would get heated, but they'd always walk out laughing. I had studied well and picked her brain about how she did it. Mrs. Nether would always say to me when I asked how she did it, "The key is connecting to people and listening. I always try to be a buffer when there is conflict and hear both sides out. Even when it's a difficult situation, people want to feel heard. I've found that it works well. Don't get me wrong, I've had to get a few together when necessary, but the staff knows me, and we have respect. They will learn you and do the same, and I will always have your back." Those words of wisdom guided me my first few years at the center and helped me to navigate my way from shy timid Ms. Joy, to a strong and confident leader.

Mrs. Nether and I could usually be found with the rest of the team, particularly Mr. Stenson, Mrs. Love, Ms. Chapman, and Ms. Whitmayer. Mr. Stenson had been with the program for many years and was a staple amongst the community, often serving as disciplinarian, coach, and mentor to students over the years. Although he is older in age, he understands the power of relationship and connection. He is a valuable asset to the team. Mrs. Love is wisdom and understanding rolled up in order and love. Although she serves as a liaison between important members of the program and staff, she has mastered how to listen first and then evaluate the best plan to bring all members together in a way that promotes unity and precision. I often have her keep track of important data and information because she is so organized and can present it in a way that enlightens those to the possibilities of what's next. Mrs. Love and I have spent many days in the office together, mulling over how to best share and present information to the community, and I must say we are nearly always successful. There is no need to put on a face with her; she is open and honest and full of integrity when it comes to working with the program. I absolutely treasure her expertise and friendship because many days in between working hard we share stories of our personal lives and have gotten to know each other beyond coworkers.

Ms. Chapman and Ms. Whitmayer came into the team over the past two years and bring a variety of experience. Ms. Chapman is a psychologist who works with some of the youth who need counseling and support. Her days in the program are filled with expanding funding and programming for our at-risk youth, as well as leading seminars and workshops with students about overcoming their circumstances. She is often seen with a crowd of children confessing their life stories. Her psychological mind is helpful in understanding the impacts of living in poverty on the east side of Detroit. Many of our children come from broken homes, abusive relationships, and traumatic backgrounds, and Ms. Chapman assists them in navigating it all. Ms. Whitmayer works with bilingual students since we have a large Hispanic community. Ms. Whitmayer always must cope with the many issues and language barriers she has to deal with amongst bilingual children and their families. She finds ways to communicate through humor and gestures – both of which can be successful –but in actuality sitting in one of her meetings is a little taxing.

Each member of the team brings their ability to the program to assist it in running smoothly. I keep them all together on the same page and share the vision for our program. There have been some heated discussions and long days and nights, but it never fails; we come out successful in our endeavors and I believe that is why I am so at peace with this new career. For once, I can visually see the impact on Black and Brown children and their communities. Maybe I am not making the most money like other directors I know, but the reward of breaking cycles of negative thinking and low expectations is payment enough.

I decided that I would take a quick break from Mama and Daddy and stop by the program. I needed to get a read on what was happening, but more than anything I missed my students.

Walking into the center, I was immediately greeted by hugs. "Hey, Ms. Joy, where you been?" It was none other than Daren, my little buddy who had said hi first.

"Hey Daren, Ms. Joy has been taking care of some family business. But I've been thinking about you and how you're doing. Tell me how are you? You been behaving?"

"Now Ms. Joy, you know I hold it down around here. It's all good. I'm doing alright, had a few moments last week, but it's cool now."

"Oh boy, you'll have to tell me about them later. I need to go to a meeting, but I'll be sure to see you before I leave." I patted him on the back and went on to my office.

I walked into the area where all of our offices were and said "hey'" to everyone as I passed by. Everyone smiled and waved. Even though I enjoyed being away and spending time with the family, it was good to be up and out and back at work in purpose, even if only for a few hours.

As I settled in and began checking emails, I heard a knock at the door. "Come in," I answered as I checked the calendar for any updates. It was Mrs. Love.

"Hey welcome back! Even if just for a little bit." She and I laughed as she sat down.

"I know right?" I answered jokingly. "Feels like I've been gone forever, and it's only been a couple of weeks. I've been checking my emails at least once a day, but I had to come in to catch up. How have things been?" I could count on a straight up answer from Mrs. Love.

"Well, the short version is pretty good. The longer version, well…"

"Oh boy, let me brace myself," I sat up and listened and shook my head. Who knows what drama had happened while I was out?

"It's not that bad. A few bumps with the new classes we rolled out last week. Some of the staff was giving out the wrong information to a few parents, but I quickly fixed that, and Mr. Stenson helped. Enrollment is actually up for a few programs, and…oh, one of the kids, I think his name is Darryl or something – he got in a fight and was suspended for a few days. Girl he is a mess! Cursing up and down the hall while everyone was leaving, I couldn't believe it. But Mr. Stenson took care of him right away and I think he'll be seeing Ms. Chapman too. The only bad thing was Mrs. Nether was in the building and saw part of it, but she didn't mention anything to me. Just spoke to Mr. Stenson and he said he'd take care of it. So hopefully all is well."

"You mean Daren?" I was recalling our conversation just a moment ago when he said he had a "few moments". *Grossly downplayed, Daren,* I thought to myself. I had to make a mental note to speak to him one on one soon.

"Yeah, that's it. I always forget their names. He really seems to need some guidance and help. I can see how troubled he is sometimes. Hopefully his time with Chapman will help." Mrs. Love was thoughtful and always concerned for the children's well-being and people in general.

"Yeah, I will definitely be talking to him. That's my little buddy. I really think he has some potential, but he doesn't always use self-control. I do hate that Nether was in the building when it happened. Ms. Green said that Mr. Thomas had stopped by briefly too. I wonder what all that is about?" The wheels in my head were churning. Although I was very confident in our program and the staff, I always wondered what was happening when the higher ups paid us visits. If it was just a visit, I'd have no problem and welcomed them in. But two in the last two weeks was more frequent than normal.

"I know, I was thinking about that too. I don't have any reason to wonder about Mrs. Nether, but Mr. Thomas is another story. He almost never comes by unless it's to drop off something real quick. But I did see him walking around and talking to someone I didn't know. Maybe it was about some building work, who knows. Maybe we'll get an idea in the meeting today."

"Hopefully so. That's why I came in. I wanted to be present, not just chime in over the phone, so I could see everyone. I know we need to start planning for summer programs too."

"Yes, we do, and I actually got some resources together I'll share at the meeting. I'm going to work on that now and I'll see you at the meeting." Mrs. Love stood to get up and walk to her office.

"Okay, see you then." I turned around in my chair to face my computer and began to think about everything she had told me. It seemed that I had missed a little bit of excitement, some that I didn't mind, but it was weighing on my mind the discussion about the visits. I was hoping to get some clarity at the meeting. I looked up at my sign next to my desk that read "All I need is coffee and Jesus." I said it to myself aloud, "Come on coffee and come on Jesus" and continued to go through emails and prepare for the meeting.

About an hour later, we all convened in the meeting area which doubled as a rec room when students were done with work. The room was once an old lunchroom but has been converted with a basketball rim, an area with some exercise equipment, a pool table, darts, and tables for board games. I sat down at the table next to Ms. Green as everyone was walking in.

"Hey lady," Ms. Green smiles and nudges me. "Good to have you back around here."

"Listen you have been holding it down from what I hear, so I owe you a thank you and maybe a bottle of wine." We laughed and winked at each other as Mr. Thomas walked in. I am truly on edge now, because usually Mrs. Nether runs our meetings, so this must be important.

"Hello everyone, let's get started," Mr. Thomas begins. "I'm sure you all are wondering what brings me here besides your smiling faces." Immediately, I feel the BS starting.

"I'm here because earlier this week I came to the center with a representative from the Mayor's office. Some of you may have seen me walking around with him." A few of them nodded their heads in agreement. *So that's what this is about,* I thought. My wheels were definitely churning.

"The gentleman with me was coming to get a view of our program and what goes on here. Ms. Joy, I know you weren't here, but Mr. Stenson and Mrs. Thomas gave him a brief overview of the program and a quick tour." I look at Stenson and his expression is blank. I can't tell if there is something he wants to share or not, I'll check in with him later.

"The reason why he was looking is because the city wants to set up some summer programs that will be open citywide and expand the reach of our center. Now normally they would look at some of the more prime areas, but the goal of the Mayor is to have state-of-the-art programming available in neighborhoods that would normally be seen as underprivileged. He liked the space and we have entered into an agreement with the city to host their new program, Reaching Beyond. This will service students in high school and prepare them for job opportunities leading to careers. In order for us to accommodate them, I will be reducing the number of programs we normally provide for our middle school students. Therefore, there may be some personnel cuts and some students may have to explore some other options, but this gives us an opportunity to help the Mayor reach a new demographic. I know you have questions so I'm going to open the floor for you all to ask."

I wish I had a poker face because I believe my expression

is betraying me. Did he just say reduce the program, fire people, and move some of our kids? Our team has been working so hard to keep a consistent group of our middle school students here and service their families, and now with one meeting, it's gone.

Mrs. Nether spoke first. Although she's second in command, she's seen the work we've done here and I'm hoping she will speak to that. "This sounds like a great opportunity and I am looking forward to expanding to service older students. I've spoken with Mr. Thomas and I assure you that you all will not be a part of our personnel cuts. This team has done some phenomenal work, so I do believe we can continue to service our community while welcoming this program. I know it's hard to hear some of our students will have to find another place to be this summer, but hopefully they will be able to return in the fall."

So, she knew about this. She's trying to smooth it over and make it not sound so harsh. Epic fail.

Mr. Stenson spoke next. "Will we still be able to sponsor our sports programs?" Of course, this was his major concern, and in the summer, it's his baby.

"Absolutely Stenson," Mr. Thomas replied. We will not be cutting our sports or summer programs, just reducing them."

"Mr. Thomas..." I pause to collect my thoughts. "Exactly how many students are you thinking will need to attend elsewhere?" Fifty students may not be so bad. I could find some spots at local park districts. I am on pins and needles hoping it's not much more than that.

"Right now, we have 15 classes – both academic and extracurricular. "The largest class is about 20," I say as I look to Mrs. Love for confirmation. She nods. So approximately 300 students give or take, but we usually open at least five more over the summer so a total of about 400."

Mr. Thomas replied, "Right now the city is planning to fill 200 slots, so that will be about half of our staff and students."

"Half?" It comes out before I can think. Then I pause. Every thought in my head is on my students. What will happen to them if they can't get in somewhere? Will they be on the streets? And what about their parents? How will we choose? "Excuse me sir, I'm just a little surprised it's that many." I have nothing else to say at the moment because I'm in shock and I'm saddened. Everything I've done over these past five years to build this program and the Mayor comes in and wipes half of it away. For at least two minutes the room is silent. I imagine everyone's head is racing with the news we just received. I can't begin to fathom how this can affect our kids and how I will share this news with them. They'll be crushed.

"I know it's a lot to process right now, but Mrs. Nether will be working with the team to determine what the next steps to informing our community are and ensuring both programs and space is ready to go in the next couple of months. I will be in touch periodically and I'm always available if you have any questions." With that, Mr. Thomas turned and walked out, leaving us to bear the brunt of this new burden.

"Two hundred slots?" I just kept shaking my head and repeating it. I couldn't believe it. Over the last five years we had worked so hard to grow our program and with one conversation it was going to be reduced to benefit the Mayor's agenda.

"Well, at least it will help some other kids," Ms. Chapman remarked.

"Yeah, but these are our community students, our babies who we've built relationships with. They will be crushed." I was still in disbelief.

"How will you decide who to cut?" Ms. Whitmayer asked.

"I have no idea. I'll start thinking about it tonight, I guess. So many of our staff depend on that summer money also; maybe I can convince Mr. Thomas to allow some of them to take the city jobs." I stood and began to pack my things up.

"Are you leaving?" Mrs. Nether asked. "We can start working on it now if you want."

"If you don't mind, I'd like some time to process this and we can meet later this week. My dad has an appointment so I can't stay." I replied soberly.

"Okay, that's fine. I'll send a meeting invite out." Mrs.

JEANINE A ROGERS

Nether and everyone stood to leave, and Ms. Green walked over to me and patted my back.

"I know this is a lot, and you are already going through a lot. Just know that God will guide you. It will all work out." Ms. Green always had a word of encouragement no matter the situation. I valued her optimism.

"Thanks, Green. I'll see you all later." The team said bye as I walked to the front, went in my office, grabbed my things, and went to the car. I felt like I was running out, but I couldn't breathe. This was the last thing I expected and all I could picture were the faces of my children who'd be forced out. It wasn't fair, but at the moment my head was too clouded to think through a solution. I'd mull over it and see what I came up with later. Driving away, it was the first time I questioned if this was truly the job for me, and that hurt.

I texted Mama and let her know I was on the way so that we could get Daddy to his appointment. He had a follow up with the doctor, and the goal was to go over his next steps and treatment plan. I was praying that it would be better news than I'd heard at work.

~

Surrender

"Hey guys," I said as I walked into the house. Mama and Daddy were dressed and sitting on the couch. They had clearly been enjoying each other's company because they were smiling and Mama was leaning on Daddy's shoulder. "Look at you two lovebirds," I laughed.

Mama blushed a bit and sat up. Daddy winked and I had to smile. I only wish that one day that'll be the love I'll have with someone after a lifetime of love and marriage. "We're ready, just have to put our shoes on."

Mama stood and started getting her things, and Daddy sat up and looked at me. "What's wrong, sunshine? I know that look on my baby's face anywhere." Daddy always told me that I couldn't hide anything I was feeling from him. It's like he understood my moods before I even spoke.

"Just work stuff, Daddy. I'll be okay," I lied and smiled. I was sure hoping that I would be, because at the moment that seemed almost impossible.

"Mmmm hmmm," Daddy said with his lips curled up. "We can talk about it on the way."

"Daddy, I don't need to add any stress to you or Mama. I just need to think." I didn't want to burden them with my issues when Daddy was dealing with his new diagnosis and the trajectory of his life. My problems seemed trivial compared to that.

"No stress here. You look like you could use an ear and that's what me and your Mama are here for." Loving but persistent, that was my Daddy. It was worthless to argue with him any further.

"Okay Daddy, I'll tell you on the way. Let's go so you aren't late." With that we headed out to the car and started to make our way back to the hospital. On the way I filled Mama and Daddy in on the news from work and how disappointed I was that some of our kids would be missing out on programming all because Mr. Thomas wanted to kiss up to the Mayor.

"It just doesn't make sense. We're doing better than ever, and now they come in, eye our building, and decide some of our underprivileged kids will just be booted out. Not to mention the staff. And there was no negotiating with him. His mind was made up, and Mrs. Nether just went along with it. I think everyone was in shock, but the program is like my baby that I've nurtured over these past five years and watched grow. Just like that, someone with no investment in our community comes in and hacks away a portion of it. I just hate the thought of having to choose who will be allowed to stay and who won't. And the conversations I'll have to have..." My mind drifted off while I was talking, and I could feel my blood pressure rising as I talked about it.

"Well baby, you know the politicians always have an ulterior motive. It's good it's helping some high schoolers, but I know you want your kids to be there with you. Unfortunately, it seems like education is becoming more bureaucratic as the years go on," Daddy commented.

"I can see how you feel it's kind of a slap in the face to all the work you've done, but maybe it's worth considering how this can be a positive change, Joy." Mama was the voice of humility and optimism.

"It just makes me think that at any given time they can just come in, make a decision, not consult with *any* of the people who run the program, and change it. Who's to say it won't be me cut next? I know you think I am being emotional and overreacting, and you're probably right."

"Now don't go beating yourself up like that. You never know why things happen. It's totally alright for you to feel what you feel," Daddy was doing what he always did which was comfort me in hard times. "See what they come up with and maybe talk to your boss about it. Even though it may not change anything, it will be good to let her know that you'd like to be considered in some of the decisions that directly affect your center before they are finalized. That's only fair."

"You're right, Daddy. Mrs. Nether is more open than Mr. Thomas so maybe I'll talk to her and see what happens. Thanks for listening to me vent guys."

"Anything for our Joy," Mama said as she patted my arm. Even though I hardly ever told them about work matters, being closer to them in the house had brought us all closer and allowed us to show more of our vulnerabilities. In some ways, being with them was comforting and reminded me of the times I had struggled to find my way in my career in life and they always supported me, no matter how many times I failed. I pulled up at the hospital front door to let them out and then went to park. Driving through the lot I started to form my thoughts to share with Mrs. Nether. I'd be sure to reach out for a meeting with her soon.

Once I parked, I went in and looked at the directory by the elevator for the floor Daddy's doctor was on. I was pretty apprehensive about going into hospitals, especially after being there to see my grandparents take their last breaths. But Daddy's procedure had gone well, and I hoped that this time it would work out much better. So far so good.

I found his doctor and pushed the elevator button. As the doors opened, out stepped Dr. Jackson. "We meet again," he said with a smile. Immediately my heart started pounding. Damn he looked good in that white lab coat.

"Hey, Doc. Good to see you again." I managed to say without stuttering.

"Good to see you too. I take it you're back with your family?" he asked.

"Yeah, follow up visit from the procedure. Hopefully all will go well today. I'm meeting them upstairs." I wanted to walk on the elevator, but the doors had closed already, and we were face to face. I didn't know what else to say but I wanted to keep talking to him.

"Well, hope everything goes well Joy." He remembered my name! I was blown away.

"Thanks, Dr. Jackson." I said with a smile. "I guess I should be going, they're waiting on me." I pressed the elevator button up.

"Sorry to keep you. Hey, here's my card…call me if you need any medical advice or have any questions. I don't know exactly what's wrong but if you need a second opinion I'd be glad to give it." He handed me his card and his fingers slightly touched mine.

"Wow, thank you so much, Theo. I appreciate that." He smiled at me remembering his name. *Oh yeah, I didn't forget you Dr. Jackson*, I thought. The elevator dinged and I was rescued from saying anything else that may have betrayed my true thoughts. "Well, let me go. I'll definitely give you a call if we have any questions." With that I got onto the elevator and turned around to see him smiling and doing a quick once over of me. Thank goodness I was coming from work and not in my usual leggings and sweater get up. As the doors closed, I waved at him.

Once they closed I couldn't keep my mouth from hanging open. I was in complete shock and much different from earlier at work. This was a welcomed distraction, and I'd almost forgotten about Mr. Thomas. Almost.

Once I reached the floor Mama and Daddy were on, I stepped off and was surprised to see Annette. "Hey Sis, I didn't know you'd be here." I said as I hugged her.

"Got a little moment away from the office, and I figured I'd pop by since the hospital isn't far from work to get some updates. You know we all are concerned about Daddy's health, not just you." Such a snarky response to a very simple statement, but that was Annie. Sometimes I thought maybe she just needs to get laid so she can get the chip off her shoulder. I chuckled to myself.

"Oh, that's funny, Joy?" She asked and looked at me with disdain.

"No, I was thinking about something else." Actually, I was still enamored with my encounter with Dr. Jackson, which was about the only positive thing going for this day so far. Annie shrugged her shoulders and took a seat by Mama. Just when I was about to sit down, the nurse came and called Daddy in. Mama and I had already agreed that she would go in with him, but Noah and Naomi would be on the phone to listen in from a doctor's perspective. Which left Annie and I to bond, oh joy!

"See you soon, Daddy. It's going to be just fine." I winked at him and smiled, and he gave me a thumbs up as Mama held his arm and he walked back to be seen.

Annette pretended to be engrossed with her phone, so I just sat and mulled over the day's events. As I went to take my coat off, Dr. Jackson's card fell out of my purse right in front of her feet.

"Oh, are you here to see a doctor too? What's this?" she pried. I grabbed it quickly and stuck it into my purse.

"No, I ran into a doctor when we were here before and I

actually just bumped into him again on the way up. He gave me his card in passing in case I had any questions about Daddy. So, how's work?" I asked quickly, trying to change the subject. If Annette knew I even had the slightest interest in him, she'd go into full match maker mode trying to arrange a date. She always liked to concentrate on fixing other people and telling them what to do, instead of working on her. Sometimes it was actually helpful, but today my mind was all over and I didn't know that I really even contemplated a date with him. Or maybe I had since I was talking myself out of it before she even said anything.

"Ohhh, so you know him enough to tell him about Daddy? Is this a new prospect on the horizon?" Here she goes.

"No, I don't know him. I ran into him at the cafeteria when Daddy was here before and we had a quick conversation. I think he was just being helpful."

"Well, that's nice but if he gave you his card he must have been interested. What's he look like? What department is he in? Is he single?"

And the Spanish inquisition begins, I thought to myself. "Annie, I don't know. He's ummm, very good looking and I don't know where he works or if he's single. He wasn't wearing a ring. But I think he was just being nice." Even though I was trying to be elusive, a hint of a smile flashed on my face.

"Nope, I see it, you think he's cute and you're interested. You should call him. Maybe you guys can meet for coffee or something. When's the last time you dated anyone anyway?"

"It's been a while. I haven't had much time for it and I'm not actively looking. Calling seems so forward. But I guess I'd have to since he doesn't have my number." I started thinking, and then quickly shook my head. "I have too much going on right now for that. Work is a mess and Daddy; I don't know that I'd have the time."

"I hear you. But if a fine doctor came up to me and gave me his card, I'd call." Annette looked at me and smiled then went back to her phone. Who knows, maybe I might get up the nerve.

As we sat and waited for Daddy, I contemplated what happened earlier at work. The truth is I had to find a way to discuss this with Mrs. Nether and find some programs for my students who would be out of the program this summer. I couldn't imagine the havoc it would reap in their lives to be back out there on the streets with no safe place to go. And I was still in disbelief that a political agenda could uproot what we'd worked so hard to establish. Our program is city funded so I assume that gives them some leverage, but it just seems so unfair. There was a shaky feeling inside of my stomach at what the future may hold and that was giving me quite a bit of anxiety.

"So, what's happening with work? You said it's a mess." Annette asked.

"The mayor wants to remove half of our staff and students to bring in a new program and we just got the news today without warning. I have to work with my boss to decide who will stay and who will go, and we didn't even get a choice in the matter. It is just disheartening knowing the work I put into it to get so many students. Now I'll lose a bunch of them to the streets because of this."

"That's horrible to hear. I don't know a lot about your job, but I know you love those kids. What will you do?" She sounded genuinely concerned and I was glad to be able to talk to her about it. She was good at discussing work matters.

"I'm not sure. I want to talk to my boss before the final decisions are made, but honestly, I don't know if that will help either. It really makes me wonder if they can come in and make these kinds of changes on the spot, who's to say that I won't be next?" A tear trickled down my face and for the first time I realized that I was nervous about my own security.

"Oh Joy, it's going to be okay. You always seem to bounce back from whatever life throws at you. If this doesn't work out, there will be other opportunities. Hey, you could always open your own center. Ever think of that?"

"Actually, no I haven't. That would be a huge project

to undertake and where would I get the money?" Although it seemed like a viable option, the thought of starting from scratch made my head hurt.

"There are lots of companies we work with at the firm who are always looking to invest in community programs because it's a write off. You never know where this could lead you. I could help you if you decide to look into it."

"Wow...thanks, Sis. I appreciate that. I really do." I grabbed her hand and gave it a squeeze. Sometimes Annie was still like a play mom to me and this time I needed it.

Just as I was about to check some emails, Mama and Daddy came out smiling. "Great news girls! Your Daddy's numbers are looking much better since the surgery and the doctor believes that he will continue to recover well. We have some pamphlets to look over regarding some medications he will have to take. But the diet he's been on has helped him make some great strides over the past month. He says he is very hopeful that Daddy can eventually send his diabetes into remission. Praise God!"

"Wow, that's awesome news!!" Annie and I were beaming and went to hug Daddy immediately. Daddy, however, was not so ecstatic.

"What's wrong, Daddy?" I could see through the smile that something was bothering him.

"The doctor said although I'm getting better, he wants me to consider retirement. I don't know if I'm ready for that."

"It's okay," Mama said as she rubbed his back. "We have time to think about it. Let's go home. Your brother and sister may stop by after work and I need to get dinner on."

"I have to go back to work, but I can stop by later. We should call Mike too and tell him the news," Annette said.

We all got up and walked towards the elevator to leave. The day was starting to look up after all. And I was giving more consideration to Annie's suggestion of a new start and making a call.

~

It'd been a week since Mr. Thomas dropped the ball on us, and now I was sitting in Mrs. Nether's office waiting to discuss the changes. As I walked in this morning, I had my points ready to discuss alternative solutions and I'd done some research on some other programs in the area that may be more conducive to the mayor's idea. *Lord, be with me,* I pray silently as I wait for her to come in.

"Hi Ms. Joy. I'm glad you stopped by and I know you had some concerns after our last meeting. What's on your mind?" Mrs. Nether sat down in her cozy leather chair in front of her computer and folded her hands. Here goes.

"Well, I've been researching other programs in the area that have more of a high school presence and space to accommodate the Mayor's program. I wanted to share them with you in hopes that Mr. Thomas may consider us keeping all of our students in house and maybe consider an alternate location for the summer program." I opened up my portfolio and lay out a few flyers for nearby programs with specs I'd put together.

"Currently these two are the most promising as they only have a minimal number of students and ample space to accommodate the numbers that the mayor proposed. In general, the students are high school aged and will provide a better environment for students on their way to college."

"Oh, I see you've been doing a lot of work on this. I understand it was very unexpected to hear a portion of our students would be lost, but I believe Mr. Thomas is quite set with this decision. He's even began to have additional talks with the Mayor, so although this seems feasible, I don't know if he'll go for it. Are you concerned about the students and staff that will be leaving?"

"Of course, because we've worked so hard to secure the programs we currently have. Our parents depend on us for stability for their children. I am not thrilled to have to let anyone go either. But in the end, I want to ensure our children we've invested in have opportunities for success where they live." I seemed to be making good arguments, but by the looks of her face, they weren't working.

"Well, I'll present them to Mr. Thomas and see what he says. However, I think we should still plan for the changes he suggested. If the ball is in motion, you know Mr. Thomas will not look to disappoint the mayor. He ultimately decides what funding we receive and how it's distributed." Mrs. Nether looked like she didn't agree, but also was without power to make any changes. In my head I thought this is what bureaucracy looks like and our children and communities suffer as a result. This is definitely not the arena I want to stay in if every decision will be based on money.

"I understand, thank you for listening, Mrs. Nether. I am disappointed to hear this but hopeful that something good will come of your conversation. I'll be in touch. Also, I'm back to work now that my father is doing better, so I'll be in the office if you need me."

"I'm very glad to hear that. You are definitely the backbone of our program, and I appreciate all that you do for the center. Take care and we'll talk soon."

I stood up to leave and although Mrs. Nether was available to listen, it was clear her influence would not be enough to change this. I had to consider what else could be done for the children and possibly for me.

~

Finale

There are moments in life that have been markers for change. Over the years, through the different jobs and paths I've taken, the relationships I've been in, each one seems to mark a period of change for me. Change has been the only constant thing in my life thus far, and as Mama would say, it's the only thing you can count on. I was beginning to feel that this point in life was a new marker and change was on the horizon. In the family, there had already been changes; with Daddy's health, Mike was now considering coming home more often, and Annie was just a step away from making partner. Now that I am back home, I have changed my décor in an effort to revamp my surroundings and forget the past and focus on the future. I've been secure in my job for the last five years, but more and more, with the changes being made, I realize that I wanted to change my life to reflect what I believe in.

Perhaps, that's why I've always had so much change. For years I tried to fit into everyone's box, and it was uncomfortable. The dreams of my sisters and brothers were not mine, the dreams of Mama and Daddy for me weren't mine, the dreams of my boyfriend weren't mine, and now the dreams of this mayor are not mine either. It is time for me to change and embrace what is for me. I truly believe that working with the children has enriched my life, and I love the team I work with every day. However, I also understand that I am afraid to embark on something new because it involves stepping out on faith. I have done it before, but as I am getting older, I realize that I have less of a safety net than before. I don't want to have to move back in with my parents to get started again. I want to be able to stand on my own two feet and embrace the challenges that are ahead of me. I know my family will support me in whatever I do, probably with some teasing along the way, but this time I feel that I need to do what is best for me.

Mrs. Nether and I met again, and she told me that although she felt my ideas were great, Mr. Thomas was adamant about moving forward with his plan. There was a slight hint of, "you need to get in line with this" to the conversation and I immediately understood what that meant. "Although we value you and your work, do as the boss says, without question."

The ending of that conversation propelled me to think even more about what Annie said. Maybe it is time to think of starting something on my own. But with that I need a plan and more than just my brain. So, I reached out to Annie and asked her to begin looking into some of those companies that would be helpful in providing funding. I can't say that it will start tomorrow or even next year, but now I have a goal in mind for me.

I'm working on forming a proposal, and with Annie's help, I may have some legal assistance as well. Mama and Daddy supported the idea and even agreed to help me with start-up costs, if necessary. I hadn't called Dr. Jackson yet because I realized being back home that I need to learn what it means to be me before I enter into another relationship. I want love and to experience all it has to offer, but first I need to love myself. There have been a few lonely nights where I had to really consider how I even allowed myself to be connected to someone who took me so far from what I am. In truth, I am just discovering who I truly am, and I need to cultivate that seed before I can share it with anyone else.

In the end, I don't know that I would have asked for any of the events that have transpired over the past six months – Daddy's diagnosis, surgery, my break up, moving into my parents' house and back out, and trouble at work. But what I can say is that it has all helped me to put my life into perspective. There's only one person to thank for that – God. Even in the midst of total chaos at times, I never felt alone. I felt that God had been with me and my whole family through this experience and I am forever grateful.

These experiences taught me how to love myself. When you are forced to face yourself in the mirror, there's no hiding who you are and what you have become. But looking at myself has shown me places in my heart that needed to heal. And taking care of Daddy has given me the chance to learn myself and hear his story. I am overcome with joy at who I am becoming. This journey, at times painful, has taught me to cherish every moment and every memory; to thank God for my triumphs and trials, because both have shaped me. In the end, all things really do work together for good.

I Found My Joy

I found my joy.
It wasn't in a box or under a rock
It wasn't put away under lock and key
All this time, my joy lived inside of me
It just took me opening my eyes to see
What I was created to become
The narratives of the world are undone
Now that I am free
There's no one that can change what I see
My vision is magnifying my ancestral identity
Rooted in the depths of stolen soil
My joy surfaced between the toil
Of sleepless nights and unending days
I realized what was missing when I refused to conform to others'
ways
I found my joy but in fact it wasn't lost
And for eternity I vow to protect it at all costs.
"This joy I have, the world didn't give it, the world can't take it
away."

EPILOGUE

PHOENIX RISING

And one day she emerged. Unscathed, yet, once scarred; spotless, but once dirty; healed, but once broken; whole, yet, once shattered. Out of the ashes she stepped intentionally into a new era. No longer would she dwell in the stories of the past. Her truth was not erased, her tribulations not removed, but she refused to be defined by them. As she shook off the residue of life's disappointments, she emerged from the fire, through the smoke, and out of the ashes as a woman redefined. What fireman puts out a fire and reignites it? Like a fire that had been extinguished, she saw no need to rehash the hurts of yesteryear; she was ready to embrace the newness of self, purpose, and what was yet to come.

****

Stay tuned for more from Grace and Joy...

ACKNOWLEDGEMENTS

There were times in and along this book journey that I never thought I'd finish. But thanks to the plethora of support I had from others, and an overwhelming amount of time afforded to me during the global pandemic, it is done. To God be the glory!

This work of heart would not have been completed without my greatest supporters, my mom Cynthia and my daughter Raven. Thank you, Mom, for instilling the love of books in me and sometimes ignoring the light that was hidden under the covers many nights as I read. Although you had no idea what I was creating, when I shared the news, you welcomed it and even volunteered to be one of my beta readers. Thank you for being willing to read my story, without gawking at some parts, and for building up my confidence as a writer. You have always had my back in everything I do, and for that I am forever indebted to you. I hope to continue to display support to those who mean so much to me, as you have always done for your one and only child.

To my Raven, you are my inspiration for being better every day. Once you knew about the book, you never quit asking, "Mom when are you going to finish writing?" You were my unknown accountability partner, and nothing made me happier than to hear you say, "Mom I'm so proud of you!" I love you more than words can say.

To Rocky, my puggle "son" who has stayed faithfully by my side since day one, keeping me company all those nights while I was feverishly trying to finish. And thanks for keeping my feet warm at the foot of the bed when I was exhausted from the day.

To my best friends– Hadiya and Quincy, both of you keep me from the ledge in a different way! Hadiya, thank you for always being my cheerleader and my common-sense reminder of what's important. You are the epitome of BFF! Ride or die forever!

My be fri, Quincy, you are truly an inspiration. No matter what I've gone through, you have been tried and true, a patient ear, and a gentle influencer for me to examine my choices. And little do you know, the ideas you shared for your stories inspired me to finish mine. Thank you for being a friend!

To my girl Miriam, you read my book before anyone else did! Through some chapters we laughed and cried, and it amazed me how similar some of our journeys have been. Thank you for telling me I was dope, always encouraging me, and not letting me settle for less.

Special thanks to Adrienne Gibbs, my birthday twin and writer extraordinaire. Your life inspires me to keep pushing. When you agreed to write the foreword, I was incredibly honored to have your name associated with this work. Mustang Divas for Life!

Thanks to Lori, Nancy, Torian, LaDonna, and my S.I.S.T.E.R.S. for your continued inspiration and support. There may have only been a few conversations, but your words inspired me more than you know.

Who would have thought my sorority sister and sands, Shanika P. Carter, would be my editor? I truly believe in the master plan! Thank you, Shanika, for your guidance, expertise, your patience, and candid feedback. I am so grateful to you, and it is because of you that this book is a reality. This is just the beginning!

Thanks to my beta readers – Mom and Libby, who were instrumental in building my confidence as a writer and made me believe that someone besides me would love this story.

To my coworkers and friends, Elizabeth and Paula – plus Ronell – thank you all for your encouragement, your laughter, prayers, and consulting. Your faith in me helped propel this book forward.

Thanks to Safwat, my Egyptian hairdresser for over 10 years. Thank you for sharing your insight into the uprisings in Egypt and the stories of how the inequalities in Egypt affected your family and yourself. Listening to you while you slayed my hair made me research the culture even more and appreciate the diversity in our world.

Special thanks to my extremely talented cover designer Ahmad Lee. You captured my vision better than I ever could on any website!

Many don't know, but I have been writing since I was a child. I've always heard words in my head, and they are replayed like a broken record in my spirit until I write them down. I had heard the prologue to my book and the title many times in my head before putting it on paper. The person who inspired me to write it down was my Pastor Emeritus, Charles Jenkins. Every Sunday for 15 years, I listened to your sermons. Little did you know that God was using you to speak to me, and on many occasions you preached my book's title. It was because of your obedience that I was able to overcome my fears of the unknown and write the first words to my story in 2008. For years after that, many days I began writing because of the inspiration you dropped in my spirit at Fellowship Chicago.

Finally, to Adonius Johnson, who joined me on my journey to understanding who I AM. You transformed my life and helped me to step into who God has always wanted me to be. Thank you for getting me ready for my bigger, better, and greater. For all of your advice, for connecting me to Ahmad, for your wisdom, I am truly grateful for our connection. I am grounded because of your teaching and your generous contributions to my life.

To the numerous people who believed in me, because of you all, this book is! I love you all forever!

This is a work of fiction. Any resemblance to actual events or people is purely coincidental. Thank you!

Don't Smell Like Smoke

Self-Reflection Journal

In writing this book, I wanted readers to first read for enjoyment of course, but also to read for purpose and self-examination. In each of the chapters, there are moments that can trigger a situation or circumstance that invoked similar feelings that the character had. In writing these stories and even in rereading, I was led to examine how I processed the events in my life that were similar to the stories, and to reflect on the emotions, trauma, and resilience that have surfaced in my life.

Now that you have encountered the stories of Grace, Faith, Hope and Joy, I invite you into a journey into yourself, to examine these four elements, relating them to self and helping you to become aware of some of your steps through the fire, and to help you emerge not smelling like smoke.

On each page you will find a question to consider and an affirmation to speak over yourself as often as you wish.

REFLECTIONS
ON GRACE

Grace is defined as God's unmerited favor. It is freely given, and given out of God's love, not because of anything we have done to warrant it.

In 2 Corinthians 12:9, Paul writes about when he was given a thorn in his flesh. He writes that this thorn was given to him so that he would not think too highly of himself or become arrogant. This thorn can be seen as anything that comes into your life to remind you that you are but a human who must work within human limitations. He says that he begged God to take it from him three times, but God answered, "My grace is sufficient for thee, my strength is made perfect in your weakness." Afterwards, Paul goes on to say how he learned to appreciate the affliction that he had because he knew that God would show himself strong through his flesh being weak.

In Grace's story, she is afflicted through her experiences with her father being absent, overcoming family expectations, the stress of navigating college, understanding true friendship and love. Grace shows us what it looks like to try and replace what was missing from life with people. But in the end, God's grace is what helped her through every situation and helped her to see that God is the only one who can fill the void.

What is missing in your life that you are trying to replace with people?

I am whole as I am. My worth is found in myself not people or things.

Where is God telling you there is more? (Think of areas in your life – family, career, relationships, dreams, etc.)

I will not limit myself, my abilities, or my dreams. There is more for me!

What trivial circumstances have you allowed to overtake your thoughts?

I am in control of my thoughts, feelings, and emotions.
I can manifest what I want.

Are there relationships that need to be released in order for you to have more?

I am allowed to remove that which is unhealthy for my life.
I determine who and what will surround me.

What area of your life do you need to depend on God's grace to fill a void?

I am leaning on God's grace to guide me. God is gracious to me.

REFLECTIONS
ON FAITH

T hroughout this chapter, the main character is often spoken to by her mother in these words, "Now, Faith." If you have read the Bible, this may remind you of a familiar passage – Hebrews 11:1: "Now faith is the substance of things hoped for, the evidence of things not seen."

Faith is about what or who you put your confidence in. When someone remarks that they have faith, it is assumed that they have a belief that something will happen, regardless of whether it seems likely.

Some people try to define faith in tangibles or things you can see and experience. It is the logical human mind which reverts to factory settings and believes that things should be able to be explained. However, faith challenges the human mind because it is the opposite of probability. Probability gives you a mathematical equation that says this is the likelihood that something will occur. After so many attempts, within certain parameters, you are bound to get that outcome. What can be disturbing to those who lack understanding of faith is that there are no parameters. Faith (in the spiritual sense) hinges on believing in something where the outcome is tangibly unknown, yet the spirit seeks to rely on God's faithfulness to man to fulfill that which is unseen.

In this chapter, Faith is found in a situation that gives her very little hope for an unseen positive outcome. Yet, it leaves one to ask is she lacking faith or is her faith overcome by her fears? In what seems to be a fairly emotionally and sometimes physically abusive marriage, Faith finds herself stuck, placing her hopes of something different on the back burner as she attempts to operate out of fear of Lucas' wrath. It is not until she "steps out on faith" to attempt to accomplish her dream of being a journalist, that she has some confidence rebooted and she is now able to use it as a catapult to more faith.

Where was her confidence lacking? That is an interesting thought. Was she lacking confidence in herself, Lucas, her situation, her abilities? Each one could be argued to a point. However, it is not until she regains some self confidence that she begins to realize that she can actually change her story. Even once she did, she was still scared. Does that mean she lacked faith? Or does that mean that faith and fear can co-exist, and the winner is what determines your path.

As you reflect on this chapter, there may be many points that mirror your life. Use Faith's story as a self-reflection tool for where you need to increase your self-confidence and self-worth in order to step out into faith and become the person you were meant to be.

How do you define faith? (Take a moment to answer this in your own words).

My faith is fueled by my belief and not my circumstances.

How do you exercise faith in your daily life?

I am a faith filled person. I walk in faith every day.

In what areas are you confident? In what areas is your faith weak?

I am committed to building my faith up. I am stronger than I think.

What fears may be holding you back from having faith?

*I am driven by faith and my belief in what is to
come not my fear of what could be.*

Where do you need to "step out on faith" and do it afraid?

I am launching out into new territory, by faith!

REFLECTIONS
ON HOPE

Hope hinges on desired expectations. When you hope for something, it can give you the strength to fight another day; to look forward to something better and expect that it will come.

Hope has no promise, yet the thought of hope can inspire a nation. President Obama ran on hope and was successful twice in inspiring others to expect something better, to believe that their desired outcomes would arise. Some hopes happen. Some don't.

Hope in this chapter dealt with many issues that were not deeply explored but are underlying. Failure was an underlying theme in her story. Failed marriage, failed relationship, failed at keeping a house. For some, just one of these things would cause you to lose hope. Perhaps, before we go further, the question is what has caused you to lose hope? What didn't go the way you expected? Think about that before we venture into what we put hope into.

Hope put her hope into herself, at the beginning. Then she met Ant and her hope transferred to him. How often do we put our hope into people, only to be disappointed? It isn't that people intend to disappoint us; they are human. When we put our hopes onto others, we set ourselves up for failure. Not that we shouldn't hope, but our hopes must be beyond a person or a job or something that can disappoint. What is that, you ask? Well what is the one thing you can put expectations on that you have control over? Yourself.

Although Hope wasn't wrong in loving Ant, she probably had many let downs that she should have dealt with within herself first. But what I love about Hope is that even through all her pain, she found a way to continue to have hope in her possibilities by returning to school, getting a promotion, valuing friendships, and even hoping for love again. What can we learn from Hope? The value of true friends and support. Even though Hope, Dan, Joan, and Ant had different friendships, they all lasted throughout a course of years, through understanding one another, through some tumultuous times, and they were able to pick up and remain friends. And when they lost someone they all loved, they came together to get through it.

Another lesson we can learn from Hope is about love. We hear of her divorce, her relationship with Anthony, and the ups and downs that came with it. The Bible says in 1 Corinthians 13:4-8, "Love is patient, love is kind. It does not envy, it does not boast, it is not proud. It does not dishonor others, it is not self-seeking, it is not easily angered, it keeps no record of wrongs. Love does not delight in evil but rejoices with the truth. It always protects, always trusts, always hopes, and always perseveres. Love never fails…" There were moments of love in Hope's story; some were what love is and some were what love is not. Beyond the words, love is an action. We should examine our stories in order to learn the true display of love as it was intended by God.

Finally, I believe Hope teaches us about overcoming obstacles and hurt. If you live long enough you will experience both. Regardless of whose fault it is or what transpired, the goal is to be able to get beyond it and to live a healthy prosperous life. Hurt comes in many forms. We can feel hurt from our own actions or those of others. But it is important to examine each situation and realize what role we played in it. We also have to examine the decisions we make. Some things cause us more hurt. Even in an attempt to cope with hurt, we can hurt ourselves more. Take some time to examine where you have been hurt and how to heal. Healing begins with admitting there is an issue, addressing it, asking God to come in and show you how to get through it, and yes, sometimes healing involves therapy. Seeing a therapist has such a stigma to it. We don't want to be judged by others or looked at as not being able to handle our problems. However, if we want to continue to hope and have a healthy mental well-being, we must first be willing to do whatever it takes to heal.

Take some time to reflect on the many lessons we learned through Hope.

In your life, what has caused you to lose hope? What didn't go the way you expected?

I am letting go of disappointments.

Who are your true friends? Who can you count on through any phase of life?

I am surrounded by a circle of friends who I can depend on.

Think of people you "love". What actions do you put with that love?

I am a giver of love.

Do you display more of what love is or what love is not in your relationships (romantic or not)?

I am the picture of love through my actions, words, and deeds.

How do you show love to yourself?

I can love because I love myself first.

What do you need to heal from?

I am healthy, healed, whole, and well.

What steps will you take to begin your healing process?

I am willing to work towards my healing daily.

What do you want to come away from the healing process with?

I am completely restored.

REFLECTIONS ON JOY

Oftentimes in life when people consider joy, they are really thinking of happiness. Happiness comes from things – material or situational – that you may acquire.

People say, I will be happy when I get a house, a car, finish school, lose weight, find a boo, etc. But in actuality, all of those things are fleeting at best. Houses can be sold or foreclosed on, cars will depreciate, weight will fluctuate, and love comes and goes.

For many years, I made the mistake of putting happiness in the place of joy. What I have learned from my many life experiences is that joy is unwavering because joy comes from God. Joy is the ability to stand firm in the belief that it will all work out, even if it gets rough. It doesn't come from having things, but from having inner peace and a connection with the spirit that allows one to understand that all things do work together for their good.

In the chapter Joy, she was intent on doing so many things to please others. In some instances, she was trying to live up to their standards or she never had any standards of her own. Unfortunately, she was defined and redefined for many years by the words and thoughts of others, sometimes those closest to her.

The first glimpse of Joy finding her joy was in her finding her purpose with the children. Yet, this was still defined by the parameters of those around her. The beauty of her story is that she was able to pause, even though it was due to a turbulent health situation and examine what she really wanted for herself. Even when approached with opportunities for a possible relationship, she realized that she needed to define her own life before sharing it with anyone else. When we truly embrace joy, we embrace maturity and self-awareness through God's love. God wants us to have joy, but not at the expense of compromising who He created us to be.

Where in your life have you mistaken happiness for joy?

I am grounded because of my joy.

What have you been doing out of 'obligation' to others?

I am obligated to value myself first.

If you were to take a look in the mirror at your life, is there any area where you need to better define what it looks like to you and not based on what others say or think?

I set my own standards.

What will your life look like when you have joy?

I am embracing the fullness of joy.